The Hammer Of The Gods

So You Want To Be A Star

The Hammer Of The Gods

So You Want To Be A Star

Book One of The Druid Trilogy
by Andrew Marc Rowe

SOPHIC PRESS

For Reid, Mike, and Zack.
All of that filthy shit you've had to put up with over the
years? Turns out I was just working out my material.

Foreword

The Hammer Of The Gods: *So You Want To Be A Star* (Book One of The Druid Trilogy) is the first novel in The Avalon Cycle.

That said, I can say that I have never been prouder of my writing, which is perhaps a reason to call up the loony bin and look into having me committed. I do love making people laugh and I feel like this is probably the best shot I'll ever have at doing it.

Joseph Campbell once said that a tragedy is just an unfinished comedy. Sitting here, writing this foreword during the COVID-19 pandemic, I know that there is plenty of tragedy at the forefront of the world. Who knows when we'll get to the point of comedy? But escaping to a fantasy realm where jests and japes are number one on the list might help give you, my dear reader, a little break from the barrage of sadness that seems to be gushing in at the seams.

If not, well, at least I'll have inserted depraved notions about sexuality and divinity into your mind, which, for me, will have been enough.

Much love,
Andrew

The Avalon Cycle

Like all of my cycles, there are eight books total set within the world of The Avalon Cycle. You can start with the prequel novella (always free), the first main book in the series (you are reading it), or the first book of short stories. After that, you'll probably want to read them in order.

The Druid Trilogy (Main Arc)	Tales of Courtly Valour (associated short story collections)
Top Man *The Epic Wager* (A Prequel to The Druid Trilogy)	**Emerald Helm** Tales of Courtly Valour I
The Hammer Of The Gods *So You Want To Be A Star* (Book One of The Druid Trilogy)	**Ruby Helm** Tales of Courtly Valour II
All Knotted Up *The Price Of Fame* (Book Two of The Druid Trilogy)	**Sapphire Helm** Tales of Courtly Valour III
The Flower Of Creation *Every Show Needs A Finale* (Book Three of The Druid Trilogy)	**Topaz Helm** Tales of Courtly Valour IV

Warning

This is a bawdy tale – think an epic limerick joke. In the pages that follow, you will find all manner of unexpected utterances, cursing, swearing, vulgarity, depravity, shagging, onanism, lewd acts, questionable table etiquette, and many of the other kinds of things that some human beings tend to find funny. If you do not count yourself a part of such sophisticated company, perhaps this is not your book. But if your funny bone be tickled by such material, have I got a tale for you...

Someone call the talking doctor
Somebody get a SWAT team
There he sits getting away with murder
How dare him live out his dreams

But Peter Pan would understand
His schemes and dreams and ploys
Best keep an eye on his sleight hand
He's such an altered boy

Altered Boy, Jimmy Buffett

Perhaps there is a reason that there is no fool piece on the chessboard. What action, a fool? What strategy, a fool? What use, a fool? Ah, but a fool resides in a deck of cards, a joker, sometimes two. Of no worth, of course. No real purpose. The appearance of a trump, but none of the power: Simply an instrument of chance. Only a dealer may give value to the joker.

Fool, Christopher Moore

El Goblerino

The halls of the Goblin King's 'castle' looked as though they had been erected with mud and twine, which was not far off the mark. Barely larger than the hovels of the goblin shantytown that surrounded the castle itself, all of the dirty little corridors eventually brought one to the main room of the squat edifice. During the day, goblin petitioners could make direct requests of their regent as he sat farting atop his throne, which was appropriately constructed of the bones of his enemies (mostly squirrels and rats and pigeons, though a human - a farmhand who had lost a pretty serious bet to the Goblin King - found his final resting place under his gobliny arse). The King enjoyed denying the petitions - not for any particular reason, but because of his nature, he reveled in suffering. Not serious suffering, mind you, because goblins are not total villains. More on the inconveniencing side of things.

For example, in one of his prouder moments, the King was asked by a pair of goblin women who both lay claim to a goblin baby to solve the problem for him. Rather than some elaborate scheme to get the true mother to reveal herself, he told the women they would split custody of the child for now. They would have to draw straws (to be provided by the King himself) for the baby. He said that he would host the drawing of straws later on that week. When they returned, he was nowhere to be found (on a Royal Fishing Trip, as it turned out). The goblin women were told by one of the courtiers to return the following month, and again,when the King was unavailable, the next year. All the while, the babe was growing in a split custody arrangement. Eventually the kid got older (it doesn't take long for goblinkind), told his mothers that he thought they were both 'right cuntish' and that he was done with them (goblins are not known for their manners), then made his way down to the local tavern, where he was hired on as a brewer's assistant.

The King called the evasion of the straw drawing a demonstration of his wisdom as King. The hangers-on at court agreed and fawned over him. His detractors secretly whispered to one another that he was just a yellow bastard who didn't have the stones to actually deal with confrontation. Which was definitely closer to the mark.

By night, the main hall was cleared of the throne, which was pretty light thanks to the bird bones. It became the place where the Goblin King, his Queen, and the Royal Goblin Brats (a title chosen by the King himself) could all get together to eat their dinner. The food invariably consisted of haunches of roasted pig meat eaten directly from the bone without a vegetable in sight, as well as copious tankards of ale for the King. There was also the unending chaos from the countless children that were always coming up from his regular coupling with the Goblin Queen, which had become a passionless and perfunctory affair. There were so many Goblin Princes and Princesses by the time the stranger came by the castle that snowy November day that he had trouble making his presence known.

"My lord King," said the newcomer, who was brushing the snow from his cloak and looking down at the Royal Goblin Brats zooming around his feet.

There was no response.

"My lord King!" shouted the man over the din of the children's shouts.

Still nothing. This new person pulled his hood back, revealing a green face framed with long black hair. The goblin's nose was long and hooked, he had about five hairy moles scattered across his face, his ears were enormous and stuck out to the side, one eye was lazy and didn't follow the other, and one of the tusks jutting up from his lower jaw was broken and blackened with rot. The goblin approached the table where the King was dining and casting glances down his wife's corset as the grease from the pig flesh sprayed out onto his grey beard. Unlike the goblin who had approached him, the Goblin King's face looked more in line with human standards of beauty - smaller nose, ears flat against his head, no moles, both eyes tracking the heaving of his wife's breast in parallel. In fact, if you took away the tusks and green skin, he might have looked rather dashing to another human.

To the Goblin Queen, however, the King was as ugly as sin.

"My lord King!" tried the newcomer once more. "I come with news from Albion."

"We're on Albion, ain't we?" asked the King, turning from his wife's tits. "And what're you doing here, then, eh? Petitioning hours are over. Quality time with the Queen and the Brats, you know?"

"Ha," said the Queen, looking up from her plate. She had been pushing around bits of pig meat with an extended green finger (only lower class goblins debased themselves by using

3

cutlery). "Oh, hello, sir," said the Queen, batting her eyelashes at the fine specimen before her. "Welcome to Pustule Hall! Please, have a seat, have some pig! I think we have a few of the sweetmeats left..." The Queen rooted around in the mass of half-eaten pig before her. "Yes, here we go, the spear, just for you!"

"Nawp," said the King, tearing the morsel from his wife's hand. "That's mine, it's always mine, you know that, woman." The King looked at his wife. "What are you doing calling it the 'spear?' You been hanging around with those Tuskless down at the Drenched Rat again? It's roast pig's cock. I suppose you'll be wanting to take up the knife and fork like a fucking human, now too, will you?" With that, the King put the pig's spear in his mouth in one go, smacking his lips as he chewed. "Pure fucking delectation, eh?"

The newcomer did a bad job of disguising his revulsion.

"What's the matter?" inquired the King. "You a Tuskless, too? Been spending so much time around the humans that you can't stand to watch a goblin eat a pig's cock, is that it? For the love of Gluttor, some days I wish we never left the Slit."

The Slithering Depths, the Otherworld whence the goblins escaped some years before, was generally regarded by the goblins as far worse than anything they had encountered in the human realms. In reality, it was more in keeping with the character of a human version of paradise - verdant jungles, fertile fields, warm temperatures, little illness, docile herbivorous animals (which tasted awful to the goblins), a goddess who did not interfere with the affairs of creation... though that was putting aside Gluttor, Lord of Pain, and Gamblor, Lord of... Gambling, both of the goblins' patron deities.

4

"Ah, you do, do you?" said the Queen, laughing a derisive laugh. "If we went back to the Slit, there'd be no end to the sunshine and fresh fruit and veg. Do you want that? Albion might have its faults, but look at that!" She pointed at the window, through which flakes of snow could be seen falling against a backdrop of grey. "Snow in November - this place is fucking amazing! And this!" said the Queen, picking up the roasted pig meat and taking a massive chomp. "Better than eating shite, that's for sure!"

"Whose shite?" asked the King. "Cause let me tell you: one time, in the Slit, I came across this delicious steaming pile that some rats got into-"

The newcomer cleared his throat.

"Alright, pretty boy," said the King, sighing and taking a long draw from his mug. "What's your news?"

The Goblin King put his arms up above his head, yawned, and relaxed further into the chair. The fire before him, crackling on the small hearth of his chamber, cast shadows among the ratty draperies and curtains that ran along the edges of his bed. The sound of the fire could do nothing to drown out the loud snores of the Goblin Queen, a noise that kind of put one in mind of a lumberjack pounding away at a tree with an ax. Disgusting and annoying as it would have been to a human, it put the green-skinned regent into a lull of comfort. Like most things that humans found sickening and ugly, goblins generally found beauty in the nauseating. The Queen, with her bulging eyes, hooked nose, big ears, and general asymmetry, was well-regarded as a beauty throughout the realm, a beauty which grew with each passing day. Unlike with humans, the older, the sexier with goblins.

The King, though, he would never be beautiful to other goblins. He had been keenly aware of this throughout his life. Which is why he made the deadly bet to become King in the first place - he would have been happy enough to be killed if he did not become the leader of all goblinkind in the result of the wager... at least, all of the goblinkind who left the Slit behind. No longer fueled by a death wish, the King felt a responsibility to his people. He could not simply abandon them to their fate as target practice for the humans. After what had happened when they were on the Isle of Cambria when he was away, when King Arthur and his men had come and put every last one of his people to the sword...

The King picked up his mug and took another draught. The ale had become as warm as the room itself, which made it taste even better to the King. Fermented too long, utterly flat, sour in a vomit-like way, most humans would turn up their noses at goblin ale (except a section of the populace with long mustaches and beards who poo-pooed much that was popular and imagined themselves connoisseurs). The King smiled at the vessel before placing it on the little table next to him. Then he frowned as he returned to his ruminations.

Trucking with gods like Gluttor and Gamblor was one thing, but these ones from the Blessed Isles were something else. The King felt that he could not trust anything that grew on Albion, be it human, god, or otherwise (pigs for their flesh was a notable exception). This god, though... it seemed as though its desires aligned with those of the Goblin Horde, as the King's people had taken to calling themselves. It was actually quite accurate, given their numbers and the way that they liked to array themselves as one big mass during their doomed attempts at combat.

That was the hook, the King knew. The goblins were absolutely terrible at fighting. The King himself had become

6

a passably average fighter with a mace only because he had trained for years and made frequent pleas to Gluttor for some aid in inflicting pain, rather than receiving it (Gluttor was a masochist deity). That meant that the King's reputation preceded him wherever he went - he was rumoured to be a fighter without compare. And, as it happened, whenever he clashed with human fighters, he was only matched up with the most utterly bad squires and men-at-arms who knew better how to wield chicken legs than swords or axes. So it was that the King's reputation had grown, but it was a house of cards - an illusion that could be blown down by a gust of wind in the form of a competent human fighter or two.

What the King had not known until his conversation with that unknown goblin earlier was who exactly it was the goblins had to blame for their ineptitude with arms. Because the goblins did bear them, and with great panache. They put swords on their belts, axes on their backs, bows in their hands. But these were more akin to decoration than anything of practical value. Goblins thought they could scare off humans with a mere fierce appearance. Which worked only some of the time. The other times, the green humanoids were slaughtered where they stood. All for the delight of Gluttor, Lord of Pain.

Their beloved god: the very reason why they could not master their weapons. It was Gluttor who had been undermining the goblins in their efforts to defend themselves from the humans of Albion. He loved to see his flock suffer (which, truth be told, most of the goblins rather enjoyed as well). But after what had happened with King Arthur and his knights on Cambria, it had become clear to the Goblin King that the very survival of the Horde depended on something fundamental changing. Which meant adoption of one of these human gods.

But they were all so focused on human ideals of beauty and love... which was absolutely anathema to the green-skinned bunch. There was no god of gambling, no god of suffering. All of the things the goblins held dear were not represented among these humans of the Blessed Isles. The monks who worshiped this One True God, the ones who self-flagellated and screeched doom and burned down buildings seemed an alright sort at first, until the King realized that their agenda included pushing every living thing towards a life of celibacy, whereas the goblins reveled in their sexuality. Cernunnos, the Horned One, seemed like he might be a good candidate to align themselves with, or perhaps The Morrigan, goddess of war. But Cernunnos cared for little else aside from sex and The Morrigan, also a beauty deity, could not abide the ugliness of the goblins. The King had almost struck a deal with Clapperleg, god of death, until the pale-skinned monstrosity told him exactly what the cost of his blessing was.

This new god, the one who had sent that goblin to the castle earlier that day, perhaps this god was the one. It was not of these lands, this deity. It had come from somewhere far to the south, an arid desert where nothing grew. According to the envoy, this god was the enemy to all things fair, a patron of the ugly, the monstrous, the sinful. It could give the Horde power over magic, make them warriors, turn them into a self-sufficient force of nature which would no longer be pushed around by these humans. By swearing the blood oath to Dagon, the Goblin King could finally get his revenge against Arthur of Camelot.

The King picked up the knife for the umpteenth time that night. The scratchings on the metal of the black blade were unfamiliar, but there was a sensation that accompanied putting it into his hand that simply sung to the goblin regent.

He felt intimately familiar with the implement, as if he had been using it to cut his morning pork since he was a boy. He opened his palm to regard the wrapping of the handle. Grey and fraying, the cloth looked as if it had been around since the dawn of time. On the pommel, a piece of bone had been carved into the image of some strange tentacled amorphous thing. Jelly-like and without hard edges, it looked as though it were some kind of gelatinous creature that washed up on the beaches of Albion from time to time.

The King made a grimace of determination, closed his hand, stood, and swayed for a moment. Then he looked down at the mug, picked it up, and downed the dregs. He was in uncharted territory now, the King mused to himself as he set the mug down. He was about to go where no goblin had gone before. Aside for, perhaps, the goblin who had given him the dagger in the first place, though he might not have actually been a goblin. He disappeared into a puff of orange smoke after he gave his speech and delivered the thing. The Queen had made him promise that he would not use the dagger before she went to sleep, that, no matter the danger to the Horde from the humans, he would stay true to the traditions of goblinkind.

The King had gripped the blade and the lie had come to him so easily. He promised he would throw the thing into the lake in the morning. He might yet, the King acknowledged to himself. But not before he completed the ritual.

The Goblin King looked on the snoring form of his wife once more. What was it the envoy had said to him, some title in a foreign language that slipped off the tongue like rendered pig fat? He was the Goblin King, but with Dagon, he could become... El Goblerino. The King liked that.

The King liked that very much.

9

Dาy of thε Dาau6า

Sigbjorn Gulbrandsson was dead, to begin with. His corpse, which looked like nothing more than an ancient husk of a mummy, was soaking up the afternoon sunshine from the dirt of the burial grounds near the temple at the top of the hill in Ygglheim. A few such corpses littered the dirt roads and paths of the sleepy little village, from the temple all the way down to the half-dozen quays and docks that extended into the small bay that led in from the ocean. But it was from the area around Sigbjorn's corpse where one might find the evidence of what had occurred.

The burial mounds - about seventy or so - had been disturbed. Normally kept in good repair by Seer Jogrim, the holy man who shepherded the souls of the people of the village, all of the humps of earth had been turned up, exposing black dirt and toppling the little pyramidal collections of smooth stones that were used as the graves' markers. In short, the burial grounds were a complete mess. It looked very much like some insane grave robber had had his fill of corpse exhumation - and more. Given that the Norsemen never buried anyone deemed important (those special were cremated on a small boat kicked out into the bay

11

and set alight), and given that they were not in the habit of burying people with anything of value, this hypothetical resurrectionist would have been doing it purely for the joy of handling bones and rotting flesh.

But that is definitely not what had happened.

Down in the village, smoke rose from a handful of chimneys near the water. The majority, though, remained cold, in spite of the growing spring chill that was deepening as the day wore on. If you were familiar with the regular habits and routines of the village, you would have noted that there were far too many ships missing from the docks. It was not yet warm enough that the longboats employed in the summer raids would have been sitting in port ready for launch, but the fisherpeople would have been finished with their morning hauls by noon. By this point, they would be gutting and cleaning their catches, before putting them up on the racks to be dried in the last snatches of sunlight for the day. Instead, not a single boat was in sight. Nor were any human beings. At least not until the door to one of the long houses with a smoking chimney was thrown open and a man was tossed bodily onto the ground.

"You're lucky I do not slay you where you lie," said the man standing at the threshold to the supine one in the dirt. "But there has been enough death today. You will gather up the corpses - all of the corpses - and we will burn them. We are never going to bury another body in Ygglheim, not while I am the Jarl." The standing man, who was dressed in a dark tunic, with a silver-white chain around his neck and full bearskin over his shoulders (with the bear's head peeking out atop his brow), put one hand on the bright pommel of his sword to accentuate his point. "Don't you fucking come back here until all of the bodies are gathered, you cunting Loki-touched bastard." With that, the Jarl spat on the ground next to the lying man. Then he turned back into the long house and said, "Porsi, get your fucking arse out there and help him."

A very young man, one who looked around the same age as the one lying on the ground, slipped by the Jarl with his hands up. Out of the long house, Porsi breathed a sigh of relief when he heard the doors slam behind him, then he extended an arm to the figure on the ground.

"Well," he said as the lying man took his proffered help and stood up, "that could have gone better." Porsi paused. "Thank you, Gudleik. You won't hear it from him, but thank you for what you did. Without your intervention... well, I'm not sure if any of us would still be breathing."

Gudleik nodded at Porsi. "Jarl Heinrich is just looking for someone to blame... I'm used to it, brother. Ever since that blasted Seer told the village I was cursed by that fucking dickhead of a god, I have been blamed for every crop failure, every miscarriage, every fishing boat lost to the waves." Gudleik paused. "You're more likely the one who caused this by digging up the corpseweed near the graves."

"Ha," replied Porsi, motioning to one of the husks near the long house and making to grab its feet. "You get her shoulders." Before Gudleik could comply, Porsi pulled on the foot with one hand. "Wait," he added. "They barely weigh more than a loaf of bread. Let's pile them up here."

The men worked in silence for a while on the bodies that had been left near the docks. When they were forced to move away from the area near the Jarl's long house, Porsi began to speak again.

"You know, your immunity suggests that you might indeed have something to do with this," reflected the young Norseman. "I mean, you were able to look at them without them draining you. Do you think perhaps Loki-"

"Ah, piss, Porsi," said Gudleik, warning in his tone. "You want the truth? I don't know why they rose. I know that you did for a while - saying that Hel had raised them up, babbling about Ragnarok and a Valkyrie and a plot to bring about the end of the world. But then, you simply shut up like a clam and I had to coax from you an admission that you couldn't remember what had happened this morning."

Porsi opened his mouth, tried to form words, then closed his mouth again.

"But I do know this," Gudleik said. "I believe now. I believe I was cursed by Loki when I was a kid. I was transformed by the trickster bastard into a fuck-up of epic proportions. It's why everything I touched - every single thing I tried - why it has always turned to shite. After this morning, though, I'm wondering whether it was a curse or not. If I had not been able to face them..."

"We'd likely *all* be dead, instead of just most of Ygglheim" finished Porsi. "I know. And I thank you again. I might not be able to remember what happened when that draugr tried to drain the life from me, but I do remember its face. Old Ornir, back from the dead... I cannot believe this is real, brother."

"I know the feeling," replied Gudleik, grabbing the dried husk before him. It had belonged to a little girl who had not seen more than six summers. "Whatever is going on, the gods are involved. If I ever get my hands on Hel..."

"She's dead," blurted Porsi.

"What did you say?" Gudleik turned to his friend with an eyebrow cocked.

"What?" asked Porsi, genuine inquiry evident on his face.

"Just now - you said that Hel is dead."

"Did I?" said Porsi. "I... I don't remember. All I remember saying was about Ornir, who we watched go into the earth last autumn, coming back from the dead. When I saw that hand come up through the burial mound-"

"Yes," replied Gudleik, shaking his head. "Nevermind. I believe you, though. Hel is dead. What are we going to do without the Queen of Death? Does this mean that Ragnarok has started?"

"Well, she's not the queen of *all* death, just the shite and boring kind," Porsi offered, grabbing the shell of a man with one hand. "You know, there's still Valhalla and Folkvangr, Odin and Freya's realms, not just Helheim. Still plenty of afterlife."

"Yeah, Valhalla for those of us who die noble deaths as warriors or Folkvangr for skalds or craftspeople!" said Gudleik. "I was never destined for Valhalla or Folkvangr - I knew from the day I sunk Rikard's fishing boat just by existing that I was going to Helheim."

"I thought you didn't believe that you caused that," asked Porsi. "You know - didn't the boat just spring a leak because the old bastard never caulked the joints with pitch right?"

"It's hard to maintain skepticism when the whole fucking village thinks that you're an agent of chaos!" Gudleik fumed. "Plus - risen dead? Purple magic? Look, let's just get these fucking corpses piled up before Jarl Heinrich has me killed for bringing a plague of draugr down on Ygglheim."

Silence reigned once more as they finished up with the bodies in the village proper. It wasn't until the men began their trek up the path to the temple that they spoke again.

"You know," said Porsi. "You don't have to go up to the burial grounds. I can take care of it. Why don't you go to the temple and get Jogrim... I'll do what needs to be done with your father."

Gudleik remained mute for some time, studying the dirt of the path before him. Sigbjorn had been the first one to die.

Gudleik had to watch the draugr, with purple-hued magic pouring from its eyes, suck the very life from his father's body while Gudleik stood by helplessly. He had tried to cut the draugr's head off with his father's sword, a method of attack that was about as useless as trying to cut off the creature's toe. The blade got wedged in the flesh and soon became too frosty to hold on to. A few moments later and the draugr had become as a young man again, whereas Sigbjorn lost every bit of his life to the thing. The look of his father's dessicated face as he fell to the ground...

"Yes," Gudleik said quietly, adjusting the sword on his waist. It felt strange to be carrying his father's sword on his hip, but without it, he would not have been able to fight the draugrs off into the boats. "Alright. I am going to see if Jogrim has woken up yet. You take care of father. Don't wait for me. I will meet you back down at the Jarl's long house."

"Gudleik," said Porsi, putting a hand on his friend's arm. "I am here, brother. Do not forget that."

Gudleik smiled thinly at his friend. "I know. Thank you. But I need to see about some guidance from the beings who got us into this mess."

The temple at Ygglheim, like all of the temples scattered across Midgard, was a building in miniature of the temple at Upsalla, where the Seers trained to do their work of providing soul sustenance to the people. It was made of wood, had a tall peaked roof that cut down on sharp angles towards the well-maintained gardens that surrounded it, and it never ceased to conjure up some sense of authority in a Norseman who came upon it. Well, most Norsemen - Gudleik had long since stopped trusting anything to do with the temple for its association with the local Seer, Jogrim. Jogrim was not a bad man, but he was the one who had told everyone in Ygglheim that Gudleik was cursed by Loki soon after he reached thirteen summers. Which meant that everyone, aside from Gudleik's immediate family and Porsi, who was the son of a shunned and lowly bondsman to the Jarl himself, simply gave the boy a wide berth. For Gudleik's part, before his social exile, he had publicly embarrassed Jogrim for his incessant drinking (for which there was a story of woe that no one in Ygglheim had even the slightest inkling).

In the result, there was a lot of bad blood between Jogrim and Gudleik,

But those thoughts had gone by the wayside in the wake of what had happened in the burial grounds. It had started with a vision of Porsi's, the sighting of a Valkyrie flying above the fishing boats in the bay. Except that Porsi insisted that it was not a vision. An atheist like Gudleik, Porsi had been shaken by what he saw. Insisting that Gudleik come with him to see what Jogrim thought, the blind old man who had lost his balls to dogs owned by the Jarl (again, some more history that won't be gotten into here), Jogrim told the boys to go and dig up corpseweed so that communication with Odin could be established. Corpseweed, it turned out, was the vegetation that grew on the burial mounds.

When the draugr rose, which happened soon after Porsi and Gudleik were at their labours of harvesting the stuff, the undead monster that had once been Ornir, a recently-buried man, had caught Porsi in a death gaze, paralyzing the young man and draining his vitality. Gudleik's father, too, was affected by the draugr when he tried to intervene and looked upon it. Sigbjorn found himself ensorcelled by whatever magic, which manifested as purple fire, had animated the body. He dropped his sword. Strangely, though, Gudleik proved to be immune to whatever power was flowing

17

through the draugr's corpse. Picking up his father's sword, Gudleik rushed the thing, tripped, and... cut the draugr's cock off. Which proved to be a fatal blow.

Unfortunately, Gudleik did not learn from the first fight. When more of the undead things rose from the mounds, including a rotted creature that soon had his father, Sigbjorn, in the same sort of thrall as Porsi, Gudleik tried to attack the draugr by cutting off its head (the higher one). The sword got lodged in the creature's neck and the magic of the draugr soon froze the blade so badly that Gudleik had to drop it. Moments later, Sigbjorn fell away, a husk like the ones that the young men had cleaned up later in Ygglheim. The draugr muttered something to Gudleik in an ancient version of the Norseman's tongue, which concluded with 'Loki,' and then... well, the thing, which now looked like a young man with amethyst eyes, turned and began walking down to the heart of the village. The rest of the draugr coming out of the earth simply ignored Gudleik.

Owing to Porsi's salvation and Sigbjorn's death, Gudleik learned two things: one, no one but Gudleik could look at these things, so the Loki-cursed man would have to act as eyes for the whole village. Two, always, always - always - go for the dick. As for Porsi, well...

After he had come out of the trance, which included something of the visionary, Porsi was raving about the goddess Hel, Queen of Death (who, it was not lost on Gudleik, was daughter to Loki). He said that she was draining the souls of the living to exchange with her own dead worshipers, and that she planned on taking Ygglheim. He kept on this way until he passed out, leaving Gudleik to carry him past a number of shambling corpses who were making their way down to the long houses of Ygglheim that fateful morning. As Gudleik passed the temple, he saw that Jogrim was being drained by a draugr just outside the front doors - this one a woman who looked like barely more than a skeleton. Though, Gudleik smiled to himself, she was filling out quite nicely as she drained the soul from the blind old Seer.

It must be understood, the depths of Gudleik's hatred for Jogrim. As an atheist, Gudleik was certain that the reason that Jogrim told everyone that Gudleik was cursed by Loki was out of spite for Gudleik embarrassing the Seer in front of the village for his constant drinking. He refused to entertain the idea that there was anything of substance to Gudleik's claim, no matter how terribly all of his attempts at jobs and tasks turned out for him. And they did, at that. Gudleik refused to see his failures as anything more than a string of bad luck, though those around him were not so enamoured with hatred for the Seer that they could not see the truth of the Seer's words.

Still, after the morning's events, Gudleik had to question everything he ever thought he knew about reality. Draugr were real, magic was real - the truth of the gods was not much of a further leap from there. So, perhaps the Seer was right. That did not mean that Gudleik should help him... did it? Sighing, Gudleik cast off his loathing (as well as Porsi, who he made sure to lay face down in the muck, in case a draugr tried to get 'a look' at him), and approached the pair. Then he realized a fatal flaw in his plan to save Jogrim - the woman didn't have a cock! So, improvising, Gudleik figured that secondary sexual organs were just as 'good' as the primary kind, and tried slicing off the draugr's breasts with an overhead slice from Sigbjorn's sword.

It worked a fucking charm, it did. She went down the way the first had.

Jogrim, however, did not get up immediately, as Porsi had. So, Gudleik turned around, scooped up his friend, and proceeded down to the village, where he... was already too late. Entranced by the draugr, men, women and children were drained of their life force, leaving dessicated husks and revitalized things that spoke ancient Norse and looked as if they were in the prime of their lives. These formerly dead creatures, wearing nothing but tattered scraps of cloth, seemed unperturbed by the chilly spring weather as they hopped on the boats in port and sailed out to meet a cluster of fishing boats that had gathered in the bay. Then they simply sailed off into the horizon, leaving Gudleik scratching his head. When the Jarl opened the door to his long house and saw Gudleik standing there, the young man needed to think fast. The Jarl was one of the few people who had been kind to Gudleik during his teenage years, even going so far as to give him a job in the stables, tending horse for more mithril than Gudleik's labours were worth. But the survivors would want a scapegoat.

So Gudleik lied. Just a little. More of a massaging of the truth. He told everyone that he had scared off the draugr because he had been immune to their magic and cut a cock and a pair of tits off. The Jarl had been beyond skeptical, but when Porsi came to and backed him up (about how he de-penised the draugr and saved Porsi, anyway), the Jarl satisfied himself with theatrical ire directed at Gudleik... which had mostly been a show for the others. Gudleik was grateful for that, and reminded himself that he owed the Jarl fealty that went beyond the formal kind dictated by the whole Jarl-subject relationship.

"Ah, Gudleik," said Jogrim, coughing, "that is what you look like."

Gudleik, pulled from his ruminations, looked up to see Jogrim's eyes staring at him. For his entire life, the Seer had used a stick to get around, owing to the milky cast that surrounded the blue irises of his useless eyes. Now though, the cloudiness had dissipated, leaving very clear and sapphire-hued orbs that were framed by a grinning face.

"My boy," said Jogrim, turning on his heel and beckoning Gudleik into the temple. "How happy am I to see you. Thank you. I know that you saved my life in spite of your hatred for me. I also know that the gods have plans for you - big plans!"

"Jogrim, erm, your eyes - you can see?!"

"Really, Gudleik," said Jogrim, turning and laughing, "after all you have seen today, my working eyes are the biggest shock to you?" He pulled a flask from his belt, took a swig, then proffered it to Gudleik. The young man took it and drank deep of the mead. It burned, Gudleik coughed, and Jogrim chortled once more. "Come, come, I have plenty more where that came from."

"You are addressing me directly, instead of using those fucking statues. Does this... does this mean that the Loki curse is over?" asked Gudleik.

"Not in the slightest," replied Jogrim. "But you have an ally now, my child. One who will help you to succeed. Oh, yes, I know he will."

"Umm, are you alright, Jogrim? You seem different... not so... morose. You do know that three quarters of the village just had their souls sucked out by draugr, don't you? Including my father." Gudleik slumped. "It's not exactly a happy day."

Jogrim frowned. "No, you are right. You indeed are right. It is not a happy day... but I saw her, Gudleik. In my vision, I saw my Helga!"

"Who?" asked Gudleik. He had never known that Jogrim even had any family.

"Nevermind, Gud... do you mind if I call you that? Gud?" Jogrim swept up the flask from Gudleik and took a swig.

"Maybe you should sit down, erm, my friend," said Gudleik. "I fear that this morning's events might be... a bit... much. For you."

"Ah, Freya's spectacular tits, boy, I'm old, I'm not a fucking invalid," said Jogrim. "Besides, there's no time to waste. Ragnarok is not going to stave itself off!"

"Ummm, what?"

the fucking faery

Enyd the faery was getting ploughed in the ring of toadstools that grew in the little clearing behind Rosmerta O'Ceallaigh's cottage. The spring rut was on, and Enyd's lover had wanted to take her somewhere special. Donk was this male faery's name, and 'lover' might have been too generous a term. Like many of the animals in the forest, faeries went into heat, did a little mating ritual, fucked their brains out, then returned to a life of celibacy for the rest of the year. The babies were typically raised by both parents in a partnership role (though there were a few separations and blended families in Avalon), but faeries did not experience the same love that humans did.

At least, that was the story that Enyd had been feeding Rosmerta for the three years she had known her.

Faeries looked like humans would, were they no more than a foot tall. Also distinguishing the magical creatures were the pastel shades of hair and the big multi-coloured butterfly wings on their back, wings that let the creatures zip around wherever they damn well pleased. Finally, the faeries were in command of magic, a power that had been given to them by their Queen, Brighid. Brighid was formerly a goddess of the Blessed Isles, a daughter of the All-mother, Danu, who had broken off from her brothers and sisters in the pantheon known as Danu's Children and created Avalon. Avalon, well...

Not much was known about Avalon, except by those few who had made blood contracts with the fae. Magicians like Merlyn and Morgan le Fay were indeed such people, but there were many more would-be druids who had decided to cast their lots with the apostate goddess. Stories of death and misfortune followed those who had sworn themselves to Queen Brighid (or one of the faeries, which meant the same thing), and the popular wisdom was this: don't fuck with faeries. They might promise you magic without fetter, but they were dangerous and their ways were inscrutable.

The problem with the popular wisdom is that it came invariably from one place: druids. Druids were those venerable priests and priestesses of the old ways, the ones who swore their oaths to the children of Danu who were still loyal to their mother. The gods of the Blessed Isles hated their sister Brighid for what she represented: heresy, a total break with tradition. She wanted to give magic to anyone willing to make the blood oath, and for any reason. Whereas each of the other gods had specialties and restrictions on their abilities, and the druids who served them were equally empowered and fettered. On the isle of Valentia, where Rosmerta lived with her druid father Keandre, that meant Cernunnos.

On paper, Cernunnos was a god of fertility and growth. In practice, well, Cernunnos was a fuck god, through and through. The randy old bastard lived for the old in and out, no matter with whom, between whom, and for what reason. The only thing he had a problem with was rape - other than that, he loved the clam and sausage dance. Or a pair of clams scissoring away, or a round of tummy sticks between male lovers, or several fishes and several sticks, on the tummy or in the bum or the mouth. Equal opportunity coupler, was Cernunnos. Equal opportunity multipler, even. In fact, like any good fertility god, orgies were Cernunnos' favourite thing in the world. Which is exactly what was going on in the faery circle near Rosmerta's house.

It wasn't just Enyd and Donk. There was Bella, Irenicus, Oompa, Paulie, Denise, Xavier, Wilma, Frederique... even the sprightly young Koko was desperately trying to get his weiner into the bun of a beautiful faery of equal inexperience named Uma. There was much 'oohing' and 'aahing' and groaning and sharp intakes of air. Except, given their diminutive statures, it sounded to the untrained ear like the time-traveling wizard Merlyn had fed a bunch of children that strange gas he called Heel-Ium and they were shouting.

"Cernunnos damn it all, Enyd, you and your friends gotta do that here? I'm trying to concentrate."

Rosmerta, long red tresses spilling over her shoulders and freckles evident on a softly-featured and beautiful face, stood shaking her head near the back door of her cottage. She was wearing her mother's old faded yellow apron over a spring dress made of dyed green wool. Bits of coarsely ground flour were evident on the front of her apron. Her hands were coated in the stuff and a sheen of sweat was glistening on her forehead.

"Come on now, Rosie, lass, you've made enough of those bread dildos that you could whip a dozen up in your sleep," Enyd said, putting a hand on Donk's chest and shushing the others. "It's the spring rut and all - you know, call o' nature an' dat."

"You can fuck down by the lake," fumed Rosmerta. "Hell, you can fuck in Avalon, can't you? Why do you have to come here and disturb us mortals?"

"Rosie, you know we're mortal, too," said Enyd, smiling faintly. "But... we can't. In Avalon. It's gotta be here in your world. And it has to be in a mushie circle. Dis is da only one fer miles around, dontcha know."

"So, find another one!" shouted the young woman. "Fuck! Fuckin' faeries!" She turned around, entered the cottage, and slammed the door.

"Guess I'll just put this back in," said Donk, trying to line himself up.

"Ah, fuck off, ye knob," replied Enyd. She tittered. "Aye, fuck of *with* yer knob. We ain't goin' back at it. Learn to read da fuckin' room, eh?"

"Umm, we're in a forest, Enyd," said Koko, grinning at the fact that he had finally managed to get it in. "This ain't a room."

"You know what I mean." Enyd pulled on the leotard and tights that was the current fashion in Avalon. Then she put one hand to Donk's chest. "Don't ye go too far now, ye frog-cocked bastard." This was a standard faery compliment for girthiness. "I've got to go speak ta me Rosie." With that, Enyd flapped her enormous bright cerulean wings, ones that looked as though they had been plucked from a blue morpho butterfly, and took to the air. She made the short flight from the circle to the open window around the other side of the cottage, managing to slide in before Rosmerta saw what was happening and could slam it shut.

"What are you doing here, Enyd?" said Rosmerta, shaking her head. She put the dough back on her work table and took a seat in a chair nearby. "You must have guessed that I'm not in the mood to talk."

"Oh, aye," said Enyd, putting her bum down on the side of the counter and tucking her wings back in. "I've noticed. But that's when it's most important to talk, I find." Enyd attempted a smile. "What's got ye down, Rosie, lass? Yer young, ye've got a good head on yer shoulders, yer tits is pert, yer sellin' those bread dildos for an ounce of mithril apiece and dem dat buys 'em comes back every week or two, owin' to their lack of... stayin' power."

"You mean how they fall apart from use? Or how Cernunnos has cursed the women who buy them with his fiend?"

The thrice-baked bread olisbos was indeed one of Cernunnos' specialties. With his enchantment on the things, the pleasure that they offered was without compare on the Blessed Isles. Hell, perhaps in all of the human worlds, but Cernunnos' wouldn't know. Like all gods, his sphere of influence was limited to where his believers resided. And in his case, that meant for the most part, the Isle of Valentia, one of the many islands that neighboured the big one, which was divided into Albion (and the Kingdom of Camelot) and Caledonia (where many warring clans vied for power). Unlike the big island, Valentia was a (mostly) peaceful place, home to many a sleepy hamlet like Erybos, the town in which Rosmerta and her father Keandre dwelled.

Nonetheless, what Cernunnos did with his druids and bread dildos did not sit right with Rosmerta. She knew that the women who bought the things became addicted to them, nearly instantly. After one of the townswoman had shown up at her cottage one morning when the girl was twelve, bearing an unhinged look in her eye and sharp words for Keandre when he told her that she would have to wait a few more hours for her replacement for the one that had fallen apart on her, Rosmerta decided that she would never *ever* use a bread

27

dildo. For Cernunnos' part, he thought he was doing his druids a favour, keeping their services in demand in spite of the fire and brimstone promised by the encroaching holy men who had sailed in from southern lands.

Given half a chance, the monks, these Brothers of Christ, would put every druid in the Blessed Isles to the pyre.

They had done it, too. On Albion. After striking a deal with Arthur, whose loyalties were torn between this Christian god and the call of Avalon through the friendship of his enchanter, Merlyn, the Brothers of Christ had swept through the land, killing druids, destroying the cairns, and clubbing to death everyone who got in their way. Rumour had it that they had even killed The Dagda, one of the most ancient and powerful of Danu's Children. If she did not have it on good authority, Rosmerta would not have believed that it was even possible to kill a god.

And this is the life her father wanted for her? To become a druid like him, to swear the oath to Cernunnos and go down with the ship? Arthur wasn't going anywhere, nor was Camelot. Which meant that the threat of the Christians would be nipping forever at her heels. She was already shunned by the people of Erybos, owing to the presence of Christians and the way they had wormed their way into a position of influence among the townsfolk. No, they would not kill Keandre and Rosmerta, not yet anyway. They had the power of the bread dildo and the poultices that helped to heal wounds and make the cocks of the elderly men of the village work again. But how long would that last? How long before those bloodthirsty monks worked the towsnsfolk into a killing frenzy?

This is not even getting into the fact that the thought of swearing the blood oath to Cernunnos come Beltane disgusted Rosmerta. Rosmerta had no interest in becoming a druid. Her dream lay with the lute collecting dust in the corner of her room in the cottage. She wanted to learn the bard's trade, but she could not get her voice to cooperate with her playing. She could sing passably well - in fact, she sang all kinds of different songs as a result of her work as a druid. The poultices usually required a song to activate the magic, as did the potions. And, of course, the bread olisbos. But sing as she might, her skill on the lute would not and (it seemed) could not get better. And to actually keep the rhythm of her playing in her mind as she sang? It was impossible.

All Rosmerta wanted to do was to become a bard and play for the court in Camelot. She had no interest in the strange mix of Christianity and faery magic that ruled the place - as far as Rosmerta was concerned, that was all politics. The girl wanted to write songs about the brave knights and their exploits. She had heard the stories - about the Questing Beast, about the Holy Grails, about Sir Gawain and the Green Knight, about Launcelot and Guinevere. In her more serious moments, Rosmerta knew that it went beyond Camelot - she wanted to write songs for the Caledonian Lairds and maybe even travel to the lands beyond the Blessed Isles. Rosmerta's heart's desire was to become a bard of great renown.

But, as it stood now, that would never happen.

It was enough to make a girl despair. Despair that Enyd kept trying to capitalize upon, every time she offered Rosmerta the magic of Avalon. If Enyd was to be trusted, the faery could help Rosmerta could become a bard of untold skill. She would simply have to auction off her soul to the faery queen Brighid as a... condition precedent. Yes, contractual language was appropriate, because the terms of the blood contract were non-negotiable. No blood, no skill. No skill, no becoming a bard. No becoming a bard, and, well... Rosmerta O'Ceallaigh could look forward to a life of bread dildos and existential threats from Christian zealots. But every single person she had spoken to about it, from her father to the master lutenist widow Brigantia, had told her the same thing: do not be fooled by the faeries. Becoming a druid was the smart, safe bet.

So why did it feel so wrong?

"Hey, Rosie," said Enyd. She had taken to the air and flown up to wave her arms in Rosmerta's face. "Come back to me, girl." Enyd put a hand through her powder blue hair, which was cut short like a man's. Or to be fair, perhaps men cut theirs like faeries. "Thinking about me offer?" she added, hopefully.

"Which one? The blood contract? Or the one where you asked me to help out Macha with the randiness treatments?"

Macha, a goddess of war, one of Danu's Children and one third of the triple goddess of fate and war known as The Morrigan, was apparently experiencing a loss of sexual desire. Enyd had asked Rosmerta to come help. Although Rosmerta was not yet a full blood-sworn druid of Cernunnos, she had sufficient knowledge and power to give the goddess the enchantment she sought. Enyd told Rosmerta that Macha was a proud goddess, one who would not debase herself by actually approaching her brother Cernunnos, the perverted old goat of a god, for his help. And if a blood-sworn druid helped her, Cernunnos would know by nature of the implicit communication that comes with a blood contract. So it was only her, a druid-in-training, who could deliver the magic that Macha needed. Rosmerta had not told anyone about it, no one except for the widow Brigantia, whom Rosmerta had visited on a mission to deliver a bread dildo the day before. Brigantia had told her to cease in her folly, that she was being duped by Enyd, that this was some ploy for her soul. And, truth be told, Rosmerta knew she was right.

Still, the young woman took up a lock of hair with her finger and began twirling it and staring off into the spring morning sunshine. Enyd was about to speak again when the door to the cottage slammed open.

"Rosmerta O'Ceallaigh, how many times have I told you about having that faery in my home?!" Keandre's form filled the portal, one finger extended out towards Enyd's shocked form. He was wearing the green tunic and silver awen pendant that showed he was one of Cernunnos' blood-sworn. Under his arm, he was clutching a massive tome, which was bound in leather the same shade of forest green as the clothing he was wearing. "Get out!"

Enyd looked to Rosie, patted her cheek, then zipped back out the open window to rejoin the others, who were still going at it in the circle outside.

"I swear to Cernunnos," said Keandre, slamming the book down on the small table near the workbench. "We have enough problems in this village without me having to worry about a fucking faery mucking things up worse!" Seeing something in the cowed expression on his daughter's face, the man softened. "I'm sorry to yell, dear. But I have had a day."

"It's alright, Father," said Rosmerta, dropping her tresses and absently grasping her own awen pendant, which was carved from the tooth of a bear. It had belonged to Rosmerta's mother, a bright light of a woman who had been snuffed out in a wintertime wolf attack a couple of years prior. Keandre saw what she was doing and his face fell even further.

"Beatha's pendant," he murmured. "You look like her, you know. Just as she did, when she was your age. It was around then that we met, you know. At the Samhain Festival in Caledonia. I took one look at her and said to myself, 'she will be mine or my name isn't Keandre O'Ceallaigh!'" Keandre paused. "How many times have I told you this story?"

31

"At least a few dozen." Rosmerta laughed, but there was no mirth in it. The wound of her mother's death was still fresh, even though two years had passed since the woman had died her horrific death. Rosmerta let go of the necklace and looked up at her father. "Where have you been, Father? You said you would be home last night. What happened? Did you find the hexstone that was interfering with the poultice?"

Rosmerta was referring to the plight of Erybos' ealdorman, Aiden. He was an aging man, one who was having trouble pleasuring his wife... at least, that was what he had told the O'Ceallaighs. Nearly everyone in town knew that Romana the tailoress, wife to huntsman Calder, had been cheating on her husband with the ealdorman. Aiden, for his part, was quite proud of the fact that he had made Calder a cuckold. In fairness, the man left his wife alone for months at a time when he went into the woods for stags, though Aiden did not have so easy an explanation for his philandering. His own wife, a kindly woman named Boadica, never said a word against her husband, preferring to simply ignore the very obvious insult. As it was, Boadica found herself beloved as a hard-done woman betrayed, whereas her husband was whispered about as a devil.

Still, the O'Ceallaighs did not judge. Nor did Cernunnos, god of fertility and growth. He had no interest in the marital contracts between the people living on the Isle of Valentia. All he cared about was fucking and pregnancy and reproduction of the human race. Which is why Keandre had consulted with his patron god after he found the source of the anti-poultice magic. He had assumed at first that it was a hexstone, manufactured in the port town of Landerneau on the southern tip of heavily-forested Valentia, a place known for this kind of magic. Instead, when he used an enchanted dowsing rod to find the magical rock, it turned out to be a human skull, inscribed with strange and unfamiliar writing that glowed red. Keandre knew that this meant the intercession of another god - one who was not one of Danu's Children. This was from something foreign to the Blessed Isles. The druid then summoned his deity and they proceeded to... question Calder about the provenance of the skull.

Calder found himself much worse for the wear after his encounter with Cernunnos. And the goatish god had gotten a name for the unknown interloper deity - Loki. After intimating to Keandre that he knew of the alien god, Cernunnos passed judgment on Calder. A judgment that made Keandre squeamish as he reflected back on his time at Calder's home.

"It wasn't a hexstone, and it wasn't good," Keandre finally told his daughter. "I am staying here for the night, and then I must be off. Cernunnos needs me to take a trip with him."

"A trip?" asked Rosmerta. "To where? Caledonia - Danu's land? Is it for the Samhain Procession? Are you going to consult the All-mother? It's still March - Samhain is not for months. We still have Beltane and the summer to go yet!"

"Easy," Keandre said, slumping down into a chair lined with cushions. "Easy, girl. You know what I told you about assuming things. This has nothing to do with Danu - at least, not yet. Cernunnos wants me to accompany him to... well, to someplace I have never heard of. Midgard, he called it." Keandre rubbed his chin. White and grey stubble had started to sprout - he would have to shave again, and soon. "It will be a long trip. I will be gone for months."

"What?!" asked Rosmerta, taking a seat in another chair nearby. "Why? What happened?"

"Some other god from this Midgard is encroaching on Cernunnos' territory," said Keandre. "I have to go to Midgard, perform the rites to allow him to travel to this other land, and act as his hook in the material world as he… negotiates with this Loki. You remember what I taught you about the gods, don't you?"

"They cannot exist without us," nodded Rosie. "We are as much a source of power to them as they are to us. They need our worship to survive."

"Quite right," said Keandre. "Just look at The Dagda. He didn't die to that Christian angel because he was strong. He died because all of his druids were slaughtered. As long as we keep the old ways, we will not lose the patronage of our gods. But if we do give them up, we must live with the consequences of our actions." Keandre paused to look at his daughter. "You do understand what I'm saying to you, don't you girl?"

"I must become a druid to keep the old ways alive," said Rosmerta, nodding gravely. Then her face changed. "But why me? Why can't it be someone else? I don't want to be a druid!"

"Ah, for the love of - Rosie, we've been over this a million times! Do you want the Christian angels lording over Valentia? Do you want to submit to their brand of life? Look at the Brothers of Christ! All those monks want to do is flagellate themselves for having 'impure' thoughts and make sure no one else has sex. They want to kill us for what we represent and would, too, if they had the support of the people of Erybos, as they have done in other places on the Blessed Isles. Their entire reason for being is to put a shield up between the natural cycle of life and human beings! Mark my words, girl - if Christian shame becomes our god, we will be paying for this disconnection from nature for centuries."

"Father, don't you think you might be being a bit overly-dramatic?" Rosmerta attempted. "If I don't become a druid, there are dozens all over Valentia. The old ways will not find themselves abandoned. And besides, it's not just anti-sex.

This Christ of theirs taught unconditional love and forgiveness. Certainly, that is not an evil-"

"I will not debate theology with my own daughter, in my own home!" roared Keandre. "Look at what you're wearing around your neck, girl! Do you think your mother would have wanted you uttering these kinds of blasphemies?" Keandre dropped his tone to the disciplinary one he had been using with Rosmerta since she was a child, whenever he wanted to make himself understood. "You're going to swear the blood oath to Cernunnos on Beltane, with or without me here. Do you understand?" Rosmerta did not immediately respond. "Do you understand?!"

"Yes, Father, yes. Please, just stop." A tear rolled down Rosmerta's cheek. Outbursts as had just been demonstrated by her father were rare. So rare, Rosmerta could not remember the last time it had happened. *If* it had happened.

"I'm sorry for yelling, Rosie," said Keandre, noticing his daughter's expression. "I am... it's just, all of this has been a bit much. I had to watch him castrate Calder- oh, never mind, Rosie, I shouldn't have said that, either." He softened entirely then. "I *am* sorry, Rosmerta. For all of it. If I had any choice in the matter, I would stay here with you. But as it stands, Cernunnos commands me go and I must do it."

Rosmerta nodded. "What about me? What will I do?"

"You're a woman now, Rosie," said Keandre patiently. "You will abide here. The people of Erybos still need us. You need to prepare for the Beltane Ceremony."

"Will you teach me what to do, before you go? I never expected I would have had to go through this without you."

"Neither did I, child," said Keandre, shaking his head with a melancholy expression on his face. "Neither did I."

Merlyn the Magnificent

"I... I need your help, my Queen," said Merlyn, shaking his head in shame. "We have a problem. A serious one."

"Oh?" replied the shadowy figure, hidden behind the velvet folds of the Avalonian portal the old magician had conjured up in the top room of his tower. Merlyn would have stepped into his mistress' realm, but he did not want to leave his father behind. At least, not yet – his father owed him some further explanation. And Danu's Children, aside from Queen Brighid herself, were not permitted to enter Avalon.

Merlyn's father, as it were, was a magical creature known as an incubus. Straddling the line between something like a faery and a god himself, Balor the Tumescent, as he was known, spent his days traveling the Blessed Isles, fornicating with women and generally causing havoc with what he wrought. Children born of the union between woman and incubus turned out to be very sensitive to magic and the invisible realms. Because of this, some of these children were shunned as insane (mostly in the towns where Christianity had taken root). Most others were inducted into the druidic traditions of the Blessed Isles, which varied depending on which island one found oneself (each island had its own patron god). A small few, the disorderly types who did not want to become slaves to the children of Danu, decided to bind their fate to Queen Brighid, patron goddess of the heretic and ruler of the enigmatic Avalon. There was no geographical limitation to Avalon's influence.

Still, as had been pointed out to Merlyn more than once, you're hardly a successful rebel, answering only to yourself, when you are still bending the knee to a Queen. To that, Merlyn had simply scoffed and told such critics that they did not quite understand what Queen Brighid actually did.

"What is it, Merlyn the Magnificent?" came a sultry feminine voice through the portal. The Avalonian portal was a conjured doorway that could bring a magician through to the land of the faeries, or it could simply connect a person from one point in the known world (and it did have to be a known place to the traveler) to another. It looked a bit like an oval that hung in the air, with long red drapes that fell loosely into the human world and bunched at the bottom. It always reminded Merlyn of the way that show curtains looked in auditoriums when he visited the future and took in the technology and social change that would be coming down the line. For that was another power of the magic of Avalon - time travel. At present, though, the portal was doing what it was supposed to be doing - connecting the magician to the throne room in Avalon.

"You know I don't like that title, Your Highness," said Merlyn, adjusting the horrifically tailored and poorly fitted robe that was his regular style of dress. "Every bloody bard, minstrel and skald from here to Asgard uses it – *the Magnificent*," he scoffed. "It is my father, Your Highness,"

37

continued Merlyn. "He has cursed me. Or rather, he has delivered a curse. It was cast by the Goblin King."

"And?" said the voice, expectantly. "And what is this curse? What must you do? Or what must you abstain from doing?"

"It's... well, it's magic I had never heard of before. It seems very strange and ancient. At first, I thought it was magic from the Slithering Depths."

"Ha!" laughed Brighid. "The goblin gods are completely useless - Gamblor and Gluttor. All those two care about is gambling and pain. But Gluttor cannot help his goblins to inflict it - he wants them to suffer, not any other race. That's why they're such terrible fighters, so that their monstrously useless deity can get off on the stuff."

"Aye, a masochist pervert of the highest order," said Merlyn. "So, here is what the curse does-"

"It'll rot his fingers and shrivel his cock off if he doesn't comply and kill Arthur!" said Balor, who had been listening and got tired of waiting. "Like a mummy's cock, it'll be. I saw it happen, I did, at the Goblin King's court."

"Merlyn, would you please ask that fucking incubus to leave the room?" asked the Queen. "I simply cannot abide his presence."

"Ah, you're just cross that I bairned up your beauty of a faery Margreet and now she's bound to the Isles," retorted Balor. "It's not my fault - she used her feminine wiles to lure me into a coupling during the spring rut." Balor ran a hand through this shiny black hair.

The incubus was dressed in the style popular with the highwaymen of the forests of Albion. Leather jerkin, green cloak, folded felt hat - he simply exuded the 'bad boy' mystique of the era. And he appeared young - not too young, mind you, but in that midpoint between youth and middle age that suggested some level of competence and wisdom but guaranteed that his cock worked. He looked in precisely the way that a woman would find him desirable. With good reason, for the incubus' nature was to fornicate. Balor could charm the pants off of all but the most dedicated of maidens and loyal goodwives, and he knew it. As he was having the conversation through the portal, the incubus even had the audacity to think that he would be able to seduce Queen Brighid herself. If she could see him. And if she wasn't safely protected by her precious Avalon from the oversexed creature's magic.

"You fucking clod!" shouted the Queen. "She's living in Glastonbury. Aengus Og, my brother, is protecting them for now. But he is nearly spent and weakening! Look at what happened to The Dagda in Londinium! What do you think the Christians will do to a faery and a half-breed incubus/faery when they discover her?"

"Offer her some of their wine?" attempted Balor.

"They'll burn her on the fucking pyre!" Brighid shouted. Merlyn and Balor could hear some heavy breathing, which began to recede after a moment. "I suppose I shouldn't be angry with you, Balor. You are an incubus - a walking cock and balls. It would be like getting mad at a scorpion for stinging."

"You know," said Balor, "that reminds me of a story, about a scorpion and a frog..."

"Everyone's heard that fucking story, knave!" said Brighid. "You'll not charm me with your tales."

"Getting back to the issue at hand," said Merlyn, pushing up the mound of terribly-made hat that had fallen over his face, "the Goblin King has some kind of magic that will kill me if I do not comply with his order to kill Arthur."

"No," said Balor, "It won't kill you. It's just do the whole fingernails turning black and shriveling your tackle up into a useless mummy cock. You'd survive. Hell, I think you could live a full life-"

"For the last time," said Merlyn, "living that mummy cock life is not going to happen! I'd sooner die!" Merlyn punched his father in the arm. Hard. "How would you like it, you fucking greasy lothario? If you couldn't gallivant around the place, seducing and knocking up human women and magical creatures?"

"Well, *I* actually wouldn't be able survive," replied Balor gravely. "I mean, I'm like a horse - the cock is all I've got, ken?"

"No, I do not fucking 'ken,'" Merlyn said. "Horses are, among other things, beast of burden and their balls are taken from them regularly - for the love of Brighid, there's even a word in the lexicon for such a creature - a gelding!"

"Heh, 'lexicon,'" said Balor, pointing at his son with his thumb and addressing the portal, in spite of the fact that he and the Queen could not actually see each other. "Check out the nerd what I sired, Brighid."

"If you had spent any time with me as a child or a young man," Merlyn continued, undeterred, "if you had given any mithril to mother to help support us when we were barely scraping by in Londinium, maybe then you'd know that I am quite attached to my cock. And I would prefer if I didn't lose it!"

"Oh, I understand," said Balor, deftly reaching into one of the poorly-sewed pockets of the magician's robe and plucking out a small black rectangular device. "I understand very well that you know of more uses for a horse and you're an onanist *par excellence.* And that your tastes are depraved, my young jacker! Show us how to use it! Bring up the moving picture where the lady is getting ploughed by the horse! Don't mind us, you can go to - hell, I'll join in! How's whacking it to bestiality for a bit of father-son bonding?"

Merlyn, who had grown accustomed to traveling between timelines in the portal, reached out to grab back the artifact from the future that Balor had stolen from him. The incubus tittered and stepped back. The device lit up his face in the poorly-lit tower room as he pressed and tweaked it.

Merlyn's tower, erected in the no-man's-land that separated the lands of Albion to the south and the wilds of Caledonia to the north, was a monument to strangeness and sagacity. Each level seemed to be its own ecosystem, with strange creatures and mystical delights that the wizard had brought in from around the world and different time periods. One level was dedicated to Roman antiquity, one was a testament to prehistoric cave art, one was filled with dangerous fauna from a distant jungle land, another housed a full city of kobolds, another was a black abyss that into which the magician could thrust his enemies, where they would find themselves falling forever... at least, until they died from dehydration or a heart attack. The tower did not obey any of the laws of time and space - it was complete and utter unbridled chaos made manifest. And it seemed that the thing had gained sentience at some point and had started to reproduce. Merlyn decided, after a while, that the tower was not a benevolent being. He had noted with some trepidation that there were new rooms in the tower, places that housed shambling corpses and dark and bloody torture chambers and...

Nope, Merlyn mused, can't think about that now. The magician told himself that he had bigger fish to fry as he conjured a long lasso made of what looked to be lightning and snapped it forward and around his father. It landed around his neck and he pulled.

"Urk," said Balor, dropping the device with a clatter and grasping at the thing sending pulses of painful energy shooting down through his feet. "I... was... just... playing... around..."

"I know," said Merlyn. "But we don't have time for this shite."

"Merlyn," called the Queen. "How much longer are you going to waste my time? You cannot kill Arthur, I forbid it. Deal with the rotten fingernails and the mummy cock, if it occurs."

"I thought you might say that," said Merlyn, tying up his father's hands with electrified bonds. "But you have every reason to get involved in this, Brighid. The Goblin King and this new master of his is not going to just go away." Merlyn paused. "He tried to fix this, you know. My father used magic to turn himself into a little version of the Goblin Princess, to try to persuade her father to cease with his campaign against Arthur."

"And I would have gotten away with it, too," said Balor, who could speak a bit now that the electric lasso was not pressing so tightly around his neck. "Except there are about two dozen Goblin Princesses, and that dirty old fuck on the throne doesn't give a morsel of a shite about any of them. He cares about being cuckolded, though. He nearly killed me with dark magic when I tried to seduce the Goblin Queen. Turned myself into a right sexy Goblin man and applied my best techniques, like the introductory booby honk before I said a word to her. She might have pretended that she didn't like it, called the guards and her husband and called me a disgusting pig of a goblin who needed to be slain for his impertinence, but let me tell you, the Goblin Queen is gantin' on what Balor the Tumescent is packin'.'" Balor smiled lasciviously, gripped his crotch, then stooped so that he could pick up the device again. Merlyn hauled on the lasso, which elicited a shriek from his father.

"You know," said Merlyn, turning back to the velvet folds of the portal, "your dream of liberating this place from the gods is never going to get off the ground if we don't cut off new, foreign ones before they have a chance to sprout. If the Goblin King teaches his subjects about this new god of his - if more of them swear blood oaths - Camelot would be in danger. Everything we've built would come crashing down around us. Certainly, that is not your wish."

Silence reigned for a moment. Well, it tried to reign before it was interrupted by a wail from Balor. Merlyn, shook his head, conjured something out of the ether, and approached his father.

"What's that?" said Balor. "Is that a gag? It looks like a little orange ball! No, don't no! Ummph!"

Merlyn guided his father to a chair, where he forced the man to sit down, before turning back to the portal.

"You make a good point, Merlyn," said Brighid. "This new god represents a problem to our vision. Do you think that you can deal with it?"

"I... I honestly don't know if I can do it alone," said the magician. "I did some research. This god the Goblin King serves, this Dagon... it has allies. One of them already tried to make an incursion into Albion. Do you remember Arthur and his Holy Grails? How he had nearly destroyed the world by conjuring these ancient beings back into reality?"

"Arthur is a moron," said Brighid. "A well-meaning moron - a moron who has done a great deal of good for this country - but a moron nonetheless."

"A moron that we raised up to his current position," Merlyn agreed. "Well, the god who duped him with the Grails was of the same pantheon as this Dagon," said Merlyn. "I am concerned. I am very concerned - beyond the mummy cock thing." Merlyn stroked his prodigious white beard. "You know, I have been terrified of the Goblin King, and not just since the slaughter of those fops on the Isle of Brittany. What worries me more..."

Well, though Merlyn, this is it. Doing what Merlyn had done, the completely heedless use of magic... he knew that the day of reckoning would come eventually. With luck, all Brighid would do would be to chastise him verbally. Without luck, well... maybe the mummy cock thing would not be such a bad fate.

"I think you need to come through, my Queen," said Merlyn. "You need to see what's going on with the tower."

Bragi's Favour

Jogrim's temple looked... different to Gudleik. The place originally appeared as an in-miniature version of the big long steep-roofed monstrosity that existed in Upsalla, the spiritual center of Midgard that Gudleik had only ever heard whispered about. Aside from the intricate red painting of a runic prayer to Odin on the side, it did not look significantly different to the long houses which made up the community near the water below. It had always just seemed like a place that was trumped up as more than it was in reality, especially after Gudleik suffered the curse and had started to hate Jogrim. Now though, as he stepped through the grand double doors and into the nave, things felt different. It was almost as if there was a lightness to his being, one that he had never felt before.

"That'll be Bragi's influence," said Jogrim, who was walking ahead of Gudleik. He did not turn to face Gudleik as he spoke.

"What?" asked Gudleik. "How did you-"

"I'm a Seer, Gud my boy," said Jogrim. "I know you do not believe in the gods - that you never thought you were cursed

45

by Loki and I was just making it up to torture you. But you were. Oh yes, you were."

"So what's changed?"

"You now have an ally," said Jogrim. "One who will not let you down. One who will help you to fight against Loki and the coming Ragnarok." Jogrim came to a stop in the apse, near the carved statues of Odin, Freyr, and Freya, the three patron gods of the temple. The statues were about two feet tall and were staring out at the pair from their place in the walls. In the middle of the semi-circular chamber that opened up onto the rest of the pews in the temple, there stood an altar. The altar was made of ash logs criss-crossed one onto the other beneath a large metal bowl in which Jogrim lit fires and various herbs and offerings to the gods.

"Is it one of them?" asked Gudleik, pointing at the different figures on the wall. Outside, when it was just the draugr, still the young man doubted. But now... he was not sure what to believe.

"No," said Jogrim, smiling. He took another swig of mead, then crouched down beneath the statue of Freyja. He pulled open the little wooden cupboard and liberated a massive jug and what looked to be a chalice made of battered gold. Jogrim handed the chalice to Gudleik, pulled the thick wooden cork from the green-hued glass of the jug's neck, and poured up what appeared to be a dark red fluid.

"It's mead," said Jogrim. "I know it looks like blood, but that's only because it's been sitting on a few bushels of macerated rose petals for the past few years." Jogrim finished pouring, then fetched out a little carved bit of triangular wood that served as a funnel from the cupboard. "Put that cup down on the altar and help me fill my flask, if you wouldn't mind, Gud."

Gudleik complied, aiming the device above the funnel as Jogrim poured. The smell was unlike anything Gudleik had ever sensed before. "Are we just getting drunk, Jogrim? I don't know if Jarl Heinrich would appreciate that, given the circumstances. I mean, we have just been decimated by draugr! They took our boats! Who knows where they are headed! They might be sailing for Baldr's Land or Thor's Land as we speak!"

"Patience, my friend," said Jogrim patiently. "We need to draw your benefactor out. His love of rose mead is legendary. A few swigs of this, a little sacrifice on the altar, and you will be ready to swear the oath."

"Swear the oath?" asked Gudleik. "You mean a blood oath?!"

The power of blood was one of the few things that bound the worlds of men together. Across the land and sea, humans of all creeds worshiped different gods and paid homage to different rituals, but there was one with which no one could interfere. The blood oath was a ceremony of immense value to the acolyte of a given god, but it also meant something irrevocable. Once you swore allegiance to a god, there was no breaking the contract. There was nothing to do except what your god willed. Nobody could disobey. One might discover great power, but one paid for it with one's very soul.

"Have you done it?" asked Gudleik, his voice a whisper.

"Ha? Swore an oath to *one* god? Look around, Gud, I could not do that," said Jogrim, pointing to the three statues. "Us Seers, as a rule, serve a triumvirate. We cannot swear the oaths to a single deity, because we would be shutting out two of the three. Freya was my first – blood-sworn – and I had to pay with two other sacrifices for Odin and Freyr." said the Seer, rubbing his eyes.

"Do you all give up your sight? All of you Seers?"

Jogrim nodded. "Yes. Although I would say we give up our eyes to gain our sight. Gods need sacrifice in order to give power. It cannot work any other way. I'm sure that some of them, gods like the Valkyrie Eir or Thor - I'm sure that they would prefer if we did not harm ourselves in order to curry their favour. But... I think, like most people, you are under a false impression of what a god actually is."

"So, tell me," said Gudleik. "What is a god?"

"I..." Jogrim attempted, then fell silent. "I will not say. You must understand that it cannot be told. You need to see it for yourself. Anything I said to you would simply be misinterpreted. A perversion of the truth. Just know that they need us as much as we need them. And a blood oath, properly considered, does not mean giving up one's ability to self-determine. It merely seems that way. If a good man binds himself to a god of goodness, like Baldr or Freyr, where is the lie? If an evil man binds himself to Angrboda or to Fenrir, does that mean that he has lost his will? You might question how people might redeem themselves, but the gods do not have the same ideas of good and evil as we do. There is only a tension between creation and chaos." Jogrim sipped at his flask. "Mmm, definitely worth the wait."

"Who is the god? Who is the one who has smiled on me?"

"Not yet," said Jogrim. "You will find that this god is exactly the one that you've always wanted to find... it's a question of destiny."

"Destiny?"

"Yes, destiny. You have been destined to find him since the moment you first stepped foot onto this world, just as I was destined to become a Seer. We scream and kick and make mistakes and drag our toes throughout our lives, but our reticence turns out to be a necessary thing in order for us to appreciate what we find."

"How do you explain the Loki curse?" asked Gudleik. "How do you explain the fact that I spent seven years cursed by the trickster god? Totally shunned, completely left out of everything except for friendship with Porsi?"

"The curse isn't over, Gudleik," said Jogrim quietly. "Still Loki sits upon your shoulder, conducting you. But you have an ally now." Jogrim sipped the flask again. "Please, drink, Gudleik. You need to drink in order to see."

Gudleik picked up the cup. The metal of the bowl was battered, as if it had been dropped several times over the course of its life. The metal around the lip seemed a little sharp. He recognized that it might cut him if he pressed it too hard against his mouth. He took a sniff of the fluid inside. Roses, alright. But the sharp alcoholic note of the mead sliced through the scent as well. And something... different, yet familiar.

"Are... are there mushrooms in this brew?"

"They are a sacrament, Gudleik," said Jogrim. "An offering to the gods."

"I... I can't have the mushrooms now," said Gudleik. "Getting drunk and mushroom entranced - don't you feel any responsibility to Ygglheim? To the people of the village? My father is dead, Jogrim." As the words turned over on his tongue, the full weight of what had occurred on the burial grounds hit the boy. "Father... he..."

"What can we do, hmm? How will we follow the draugr? Do you know what they plan? Do you have any idea what to do? Would you prefer to simply go to Jarl Heinrich's long house and stand around uselessly while the rest of the village seethes and blames you for this?" Jogrim's eyes narrowed. "And they will blame you, Gudleik - you and Porsi. Mark my words - your time in Ygglheim is at an end. That is, unless you want to have your head separated from your body by an angry Norseman's ax, while you stand or while you sleep."

It was a thought that had graced Gudleik's mind more than once. The Jarl might have forgiven him for his association with the plague of draugr, but the people of Gudleik's village had lost mothers, fathers, brothers, sisters, children. Gudleik was not so young so as to be ignorant of the way that human beings tended to... rally around ideas of revenge when they were in pain.

"So getting drunk and hallucinating - that is the way forward?"

"You need the grace of the gods - one god in particular, actually. But this is how they communicate with us - one of the ways. Certainly your way, right now. You need to open the channel between Midgard and Asgard. One day, you will not need the sacraments to speak with the gods. But as it stands right now, you have twenty years of blindness – your youth – to deal with. Me, I've got eyes *and* sight now." Jogrim upended the flask and drank the rest of the contents. "Hurry up," he said. "Destiny awaits!"

Gudleik put the cup to his lips, closed his eyes, and drank.

"Good, good," said Jogrim. He picked up the jug and refilled Gudleik's vessel. "Come on, now, you didn't think it would just be the one cup, did you? Again."

Gudleik complied. The fluid burned as it went down, putting the young man in mind of an experience drinking with Porsi the previous summer. The two of them had drunk far too much mead, betting each other who would fall down from drunkenness first. It was fun... for the moment. The next morning, Gudleik had woken up in wracks of pain he would not wish on anyone. He could not move from his bed until nightfall, and even then it was simply to attempt to drink some water before vomiting up bile.

"Three times, Gudleik," said Jogrim. He cleared his throat.

Odin's mouth, Odin's arse
Highly sought, utterly fraught
Seek ye out the one, not the other
Suttungr's price
Father's blood spilled
The prize might be bought
Not with mithril nor gold
But with a heart extra bold
For the god of the poet
Will not quail nor show it
Unless his man know
The true cost of love

The recitation complete, the formerly blind Seer bent to fill Gudleik's cup again.

"What's that?" asked Gudleik. "God of the poet? Bragi?"

"Yes, Bragi, he is the other. The one who, even now, guides your fate, Gud, my friend."

Bragi! The god of the skalds! Gudleik had hardly given any thought to his dream of becoming a skald since the morning's events. He had wanted to become one, to gain the Seer's blessing, so that he wouldn't have to go on his summer raids and die due to his cursed lack of skill. To this end, he had bought a crappy old lyre from a drunk jester months before. Jesters, as musicians without the support of Bragi were known, were looked down upon by Norseman society. They were without the protections offered the skalds, who were the chosen of Bragi. Skalds were given an untold level of leeway by the people of Midgard. Deemed sacred, they could not be interfered with, not even if they enticed the daughter of the Jarl into a public blowjob in the Jarl's long house. Which is what Gudleik witnessed the first time he saw a skald. Skalds were 'top men,' seemingly much more interesting than the warriors who participated in the summer raids every second year.

Gudleik had tried to learn how to play, trying over and over again in his father's long house every night. He had proven to himself two things with his efforts: one, he would never become a skald, as he was not getting any better. Two, he had better come up with a new plan to avoid getting into combat with foreigners in the summer raids, as he was worse with the sword and ax than he was with the lyre, and he was fucking abysmal with the instrument. Still, though, the young man was as hard-headed as his father and brothers. He did not stop playing the lyre, in spite of his utter lack of ability.

"Bragi... Bragi is my god?" asked Gudleik. "But I am no musician. I was thinking of casting my lyre into the bay: that's how bad I am, Jogrim. And what will playing music do? I need to learn how to fight! Perhaps Odin - yes, perhaps I could swear an oath to Tyr or Odin! I could avenge my father!"

"The third cup, Gud," said the Seer, motioning to the cup, which he had filled while Gudleik was lost in thought. "Tell me - without the draugr around, what would you want to be doing? I know you have been practicing, every night, Gudleik. You think because I was blind I didn't see? I saw how much you were trying to change your fate. So did the gods, it seems. But the way that we expect things to occur is rarely how they do occur - do you understand what I'm saying to you?"

"Are you saying that I caused this?" asked Gudleik. "The draugr - it was my fault? That is what the people in the Jarl's long house were saying..."

"You are still thinking in terms of cause and effect," said Jogrim. "Where you are going, into Bragi's world - those ideas have no weight. There is only music. Poetry." Jogrim put his hand on Gudleik's forearm. "I will not lie to you, Gudleik. You skirt and tempt madness as a skald. But madness is a necessary part of the life of a poet. Your madness will show others the value of it, and they will follow you into the storm. Where they too shall know freedom."

"You still haven't answered me, Jogrim," said Gudleik, shaking free of the old man's grasp. "How is me becoming a skald going to do anything against the draugr?"

"What?" said Jogrim, laughing mirthfully. "You think your sword arm is going to stop Hel from sending her draugr to wherever it is they go? You think that you, soldier of destiny, are going to singlehandedly stop Ragnarok from occurring? You are part of the world, Gudleik. You have to give to the world, that is all. That is all any of us can be expected to do. Give to the world, and you will be taken care of. I can't tell you how things will happen in the future, or even if Ragnarok can be stopped, but I do know that if you do not take that final drink of mead, all hope for Midgard is lost. It really is that simple. Become who you are or fail us all."

Gudleik raised the cup to his lips, pausing before allowing the drink to pass into his mouth. "And what of Loki - you said I was still cursed. If I drink the mead and swear the oath to Bragi, what of Loki - will he be shut out?"

"Ha," said Jogrim. "Ha! You think that you can escape the reach of chaos? Do you really think that there is some point in your life when you are going to be free of Loki? Just look at the story of Thor, brother to Loki. Thor is patron of those in need and lost causes. Loki is the one behind most of the misfortune in our world. Loki brings about that which Thor must help clean up. And Thor loves his sibling, not in spite of his nature, but because of it." Jogrim paused to wave his hands at Gudleik, willing him to hurry up. "Remember - a skald must skirt madness in order to become what he wishes to be. Madness is not Bragi's domain, it is Loki's. There is a lesson there, Gudleik." Jogrim paused. "And besides, they made a bet on you."

"What?" asked Gudleik, but Jogrim had placed his palm underneath the cup and upended it into Gudleik's mouth. The young man considered spitting it out, but then decided that, whatever this new life opening had in store for him, no matter how mad skaldhood drove him, he would almost certainly prefer it to the half-life he had been living in Ygglheim up until that point.

The mead burned as it went down.

Out of the Fog

King Arthur of Camelot was getting old, no two ways about it. He rubbed the white stubble on his face. Lines which had been shallow dips in his skin had become deep valleys as the years had passed. He was still quite handsome, but he was most definitely on the cusp of the change that took a man from the last vestiges of youthful beauty and into the fullness of his age. What had happened to the years? Along with these ruminations came thoughts of Guinevere, his once-wife, escaped from the gallows, taken by Launcelot off into the northern forest, where they had disappeared... perhaps to Caledonia? How Arthur had regretted his reaction to his discovery of their love. Still, the King's life had been long - over sixty summers. Plenty of time to make decisions to regret.

Arthur glanced up from the polished metal of his looking glass to stare out his bedchamber window. Far below his perch in the white-stone castle, which was nestled in the center of the city of Camelot, he could see the people running their morning messages, bouncing between this market stall and that one, leading horses and donkeys through the well-rutted and muddy roads, moistened with the spring rain that had been falling all morning. There was a smell on the air, a petrichor much more welcome than the usual rank stench of piss and shite that seemed to permeate the whole of Camelot. Merlyn had advised him about this thing he had discovered in some future land, a sue-wer? Whatever it was, it kept the human waste below ground and prevented the spread of disease, which was fairly common within the cities and towns of Albion. Arthur had laughed him off, telling him that he did not trust his Avalonian magic. Now though, with the stink wafting up over the smell of the rain once more, the King regretted the hastiness of his decision against the sue-wer. And was reminded of his own need.

"Emilia," called Arthur, standing from his seat before the mirror, "I am off to the market. If Ramses comes looking for me, tell him I have gone to see about that thing that we spoke of at court a few days ago."

Arthur's bedchamber consisted of a massive four-poster bed, a few chairs, a small book case carved in the Argosian style (Argosia being a small town dedicated mostly to craftsmen in the heart of Albion), and the little coiffing station that the King had just been using to examine his own countenance. On the bed, the form of a woman several decades the King's junior was laying languidly in the nude, separated from the cool air entering the window by just a thin linen sheet. She was beautiful, a thick brown mane spilling over the big fluffy pillows of the bed. Her eyes were blue, her nose was perfectly formed, her ears had that quality that made you want to run your hand around them and gently press on the lobe. When she smiled, it was to reveal straight white teeth, a fairly uncommon thing in the Kingdom of

Camelot. And Emilia Deschain, daughter of one of Arthur's dukes, was anything but common.

"Tell him yourself," she said, putting the pillow over her head. "I'm sleeping."

"I just told you, I'm not going..." Arthur willed his blood down. He could not go a bout of rage right now. Not when he had such an important mission awaiting him. "Look, just tell him I'm out and I will be back in a few hours. You can do that, can't you?"

Emilia threw the pillow off her head and looked straight up at the canopy of the bed above her. "I said I'm sleeping!" she shouted, then huffed and pulled the pillow back down.

"Christ, woman, you are some pain in my hole," said the King. "Still a fucking child."

"Aye," said Emilia, sitting up and looking at Arthur. She grabbed the underside of her enormous and pert breasts. "But I'm that, aren't I? A *fucking* child?"

"A filthy strumpet girl who needs a good rodgering," agreed Arthur crossing to the bed, grabbing her by the neck, and kissing her savagely. "But I've not the time right now. I'll stop by Brindel's shop and get us a poultice or two so that we might have a bit of fun later."

"You're lucky that druid can make your cock work, Arthur, my liege," said Emilia, falling back into the bed. "Without that fellow greybeard's magic, ye'd both be thinking back wistfully on the days when you could get your soldiers to stand at attention. I'd be gone, of course," added the young woman. "Into the bed of some young buck who can satisfy me. You'd be left here, all alone, cold bed and dreaming of a woman... oh, I'm sorry, Arthur. I am. I didn't mean to-"

Arthur brushed the single tear from his cheek. It had been an emotional morning, and thoughts of Guinevere's flight had never quite left the King's mind. The girl was a fine distraction, but Arthur would abandon her with an unmatched celerity if it meant another chance to see the woman of his dreams once more. Guinevere was his queen and she was long gone, escaped after Arthur tried to have her killed in a jealous rage. In her stead, he satisfied himself with the company of Emilia, whose lack of maturity made for a fairly one-dimensional relationship. It was a great dimension - fucking an attractive specimen of desire definitely has its perks - but it did not satisfy the King's soul. With luck, the item he was going to fetch in the market just now would do the trick in this pinch.

"Don't mention it," said the King. He walked to the door of his chamber. "Seriously," he added, "if I hear a rumour floating out of the kitchens that you made me cry, I will have you flogged in open court."

"Fifteen fucking knights, all disappeared."

"It would appear that way," said Ramses. The man was dressed like most of the nobles in Arthur's court: gaudily, with vibrant dyes applied to every visible bit of cloth. His jerkin was a beautiful canary yellow, although none of the people of Camelot had ever heard of a canary, it being an undiscovered tropical bird, and all. Nor could you call it a banana yellow, what with how bananas start their lives off as green, then move into yellow, before shifting into a brown spotted appearance, before finally turning black. Where would you peg such a shade? Also, you know, undiscovered tropical fruit. Whatever colour it was, it was bright, definitely yellow, and it was set off by a silver chain of office that told everyone around that he was advisor to the King of Camelot, Arthur Pendragon. Suspended from the chain was a small shield, a version of the kite shields used by the Knights of the

Round Table. It bore Arthur's crest: a Christian Cross, a dragon, and Excalibur, arranged neatly on a white field.

"Were they the good knights?"

"What's that?" asked Ramses. "What do you mean, good ones?"

"You know, competent," said Arthur. "I swear, that debacle with those three twits, the painter, and the sex portrait of the Goblin Queen..."

"Oh, you mean the Stuege brothers? Morris, Lawrence, and Ringlets?"

"Erm, we's right here, Your Highness," said Morris, looking around at his brothers, who were also seated at his long table in the King's dining hall.

The dining hall was the place where most Camelot business of serious import was conducted. It usually consisted of Arthur, his Knights of the Round Table, and the odd courtier, commoner, or courtesan filling the rest of the long tables that made up the enormous room. It meant that commoners and nobles could mingle, enjoy some meat and ale, and witness Arthur's wisdom in matters politic, though he did not usually come to decisions on his own. Aside from Ramses and Merlyn, his main trusted advisors, the knights debated Arthur and helped set a course for the Kingdom's policies. So, why not at the Round Table itself?

The knights were called the Knights of the Round Table, but they were soldiers. And if there is one immutable truth about soldiers, it is this: they're always hungry. The King tried bringing in food to the Round Table in the early days of Camelot, but the knights were men. Many of them men like the troglodyte trio currently giving the King a look that reminded him of chastised puppies always seemed to make a mess of the place. Though Arthur loved the round table as a symbol of equality between him and these noblemen, in reality he hated being elbowed by swinish types trying to voraciously shove bits of pork and bread into their mouths as quickly as humanly possible. The long tables were much more civilized, in that he could sit at the head and stroke one of his hounds behind the ear without worrying about errant bits of meat flying off neighbouring meals and into his chalice of ale.

"Right," said Arthur to the Stueges. "Yes, well, what do you expect? I send you off on a top-secret mission to bring back the Goblin Princess' portrait from that deviant painter Calyxus, and you come back with a jizz-stained mess of paint on canvas. You're lucky you never killed Calyxus - he's proving to be quite the asset in our Propaganda Office. But that was only by blind luck that he was knocked unconscious and not killed! You're nincompoops - utter fucking nincompoops."

"Yes, well," said Morris. "That's just like, your opinion, man."

"'My opinion?' 'Man?!' I am your King, knave!"

"Oh, right," said Morris. "Um, sorry, Your Highness."

"Christ on a cracker," sighed the King, scratching his dog behind the ears with some intensity, "I am surrounded by fools."

Truth be told, Arthur was a bit of a fool himself, and what he saw in men like the Stuege brothers reminded him a bit too much of his own lack of mental steam. Which is why he railed against them in open court the way he did. Unlike the Stuege brothers, however, Arthur was somewhat self-aware. He knew that he had a mind like a bag of rocks. That is why he usually leaned on Ramses and Merlyn in matters of strategy. Courage and valour - King Arthur had these in spades. Sense, both common and rare - of that he was in short supply. So again he asked Ramses about the fifteen disappeared knights.

"They were after the Questing Beast again, sire," said Ramses, sloshing his chalice absently. Appropriate for a fop of his magnitude, he was drinking wine imported from the Isle of Britanny. "It was sighted in Duke Eredin's land."

Albion used to be composed of several kingdoms, though they were now united under Camelot's flag. They had been conquered by Arthur in a series of bloody campaigns when the King was in his youth. As part of the end of hostilities, the kings of these other kingdoms - Mercia, Wessex, Northumbria, East Anglia - they all bent the knee to the King in Camelot as Dukes. Merlyn had warned him against letting these kingdoms continue as dukedoms... the men who had lost their crowns would not forget what was taken from them. By the time the treaty was signed, though, Arthur had grown tired of the killing. So, he took the children of the former Kings as hostages (including the beautiful Emilia) and told the newly-minted dukes to mind their Ps and Qs if they wanted their kids to survive.

"Northumbria?" asked Arthur. "There's nothing but frozen soil and goats in Northumbria. Why did they think the Questing Beast had moved its lair to such a land?"

"That's a bit uncharitable," said Ramses, laughing. "But not untrue. The place is like most of the open country outside of Camelot - not very fucking interesting at all. Not like here," added the advisor with a very obviously forced wink to a courtesan. "We are not certain why the Questing Beast moved, sire, nor how it still manages to elude our brave knights. One day, they will prevail and bring its head back to you, my liege, so that you can mount it on one of the many beautiful walls of this, your castle."

Arthur loved it when Ramses stroked his ego and sense of importance, which is part of why he kept him in the position that he did. The main reason, though was for information and counsel.

"Yes, yes," said Arthur. "Enough about the Questing Beast. All I've been hearing for the past year is about this God-damned Questing Beast. What are we going to do about the missing knights."

"Send a search party?" asked Ramses. "It would seem prudent." And obvious, mused Ramses, though he would never say such a thing to his King, no matter how much he thought it. "Perhaps," Ramses added, "Your Highness might like to lead the search party? Your recent... discovery would certainly help in circumstances such as these."

"Oh, you mean what Brindel sold me? The-"

"Perhaps my liege might want some more ale," called Ramses to the serving girl near the back of the hall. Then, he dropped his voice to a whisper. "Please, my King, do not speak of it in open court. The Brothers have spies everywhere."

The Brothers of Christ was the monastic order arrived from the south with a new One True God, the one to whom Arthur had sworn blood fealty. They were dour and violent and hated sex, but they also preached unconditional love and the redemptive power of their God. Arthur had had a very near brush with death in his youth and he felt he had been saved by the God peddled by these men, so Arthur's meteoric rise to power was accompanied by a similar advancement by the Brothers of Christ. Now, though, the situation had changed. Arthur had come to know their leader, Black Patrick, for a duplicitous snake. It was rumoured that he had the backing of an angel, a vicious one who bore a flaming sword and got off on smiting. It was a precarious situation, and any words breathed about Arthur's continued association with Merlyn and druids of the old ways meant more danger for Camelot.

"Erm, yes, Ramses," said the King. "Perhaps we can discuss further in my study after this meeting."

Ramses smiled, nodded, and thanked his own god that Arthur was still listening to him. The one time he wouldn't, when he was ensorceled by that venomous creature Alhazred, Ramses came to sense his own mortality (because Arthur had threatened to execute his entire court), and it scared him.

"Good, my King," said Ramses, fingering his pendant. "Very good."

"Please, tell me Arthur," said Ramses, "what is this hexstone?"

Ramses had cast off his jerkin on the side of the couch in Arthur's study. In his linen shirt, which better agreed with him, given the level of heat preferred by the King, the blonde-haired man was rubbing his sweaty forehead as he examined the rock in his hand. It had been worn down by the waves on a beach, though which beach that might be was not clear (nor was that detail of any particular interest to the pair discussing it at present). What really got the querying mind going was the runes that had been carved into the side of the reddish rock. They were very clearly not the work of the druids of the Blessed Isles. Too few spirals, which was a hallmark of Danu's Children, the local gods (even though the country of Albion was supposed to be exclusively Christian at this point). Instead, all of the symbols were composed of harsh lines.

"It's not from Landerneau," said Arthur, swirling his snifter. Brandy from the Isle of Britanny was a particular weakness of the King's. "Brindel said he got it from exactly who you'd expect to drop a strange magical artifact off - shifty, unpleasant to look at, obsessed with payment."

"It wasn't that creep Gareus, was it? The one who ensorceled you with that monstrous Alhazred?" Ramses put the stone back down on the low table between the chairs. "Perhaps it would be better if we just got rid of it."

"I trust Brindel," said Arthur. "But I know that I am too trusting by nature, so I will tell you what he told me. If you think we ought to destroy it, so we shall." Arthur sipped, grimacing as the fluid passed into his throat. "I no longer seek eternal life, Ramses. After what happened with the Grails... what happened to Sir Ector... I have no children, my friend. Mordred is dead. Guinevere left. I could probably bairn up some young thing yet, but to what end? My legacy is what? Getting into a bunch of wars, destroying a few druids' lives? The Dagda died because of me, Ramses. Sure, Black Patrick was the one who burned his followers to death, but it was only because I supported him."

"What are you saying?" Ramses looked at the stone once more. Then his eyes widened as he looked up at his King. "This... this is... you mean to summon a foreign god here? Another one?"

"The Brothers of Christ must be stopped. They have turned our once proud people into a fearful lot. They hate fornication and they would have every human being in Albion flagellate themselves for simply being alive. Black Patrick is a monster. His monks are monsters. That angel of his, that Cassiel, he is chief monster."

"Arthur, please," said Ramses, placing the stone on the table. "I am your advisor, and I must advise you against whatever you have plotted with Brindel." Ramses paused. "What about your blood pact, with Queen Brighid? You swore an oath to the faeries, Arthur. That is something that cannot be broken!"

64

"Under normal circumstances, you would be correct," said Arthur. "No living man can swear an oath to more than one god." Arthur stood, crossed to the bookshelf which was set into the wall next to the roaring fire, and pulled out a volume. The same strange script that had been carved into the hexstone was written on the spine of the book. He seated himself, opened up the book, and began tracing his words with a finger as he read.

"Let me tell you a little story, about a place called Helheim and a goddess named Hel."

Ramses shivered as he considered the placard above the small tavern in the heart of the city of Camelot. There was the image of what looked to be a humanoid face, except that this creature had a thick brow, a single vicious horn set into the forehead above its eyes, a wide jaw, and more tusks coming out of the bottom corners of its mouth. Ogres looked somewhat similar to goblins, but they had been a present threat for millennia before the little green things came through to Albion from their Slit. What made the man shiver was not the ogre's face, which was admittedly ugly. No, more troubling was the fact that it was being struck over the head with a mallet. It reminded the man a little too much of what had occurred with the King that afternoon.

The King had lost touch with reality again, Ramses mused. Merlyn would have to be consulted, things would have to be righted. Ramses had supported Arthur in many things, but the last misadventure, the time when that foreign wizard Alhazred had bewitched the King and nearly got him to choke the life from Ramses - that had been a wakeup call. He was labouring for an incompetent. A very charismatic and lovable incompetent, but an incompetent nonetheless. And this incompetent was possessed of the power of the throne of Albion. And now, potentially, a foreign god?

Why couldn't people just be happy with their gods? Or better yet, reality itself? Ramses had never sworn an oath to anyone - not Brighid, not this new Yahweh, not any of his angels, not Aengus Og, not The Dagda. He had plenty of opportunity, of course. Plenty of zealots who had tried to teach him why his or her god was *the way*. Ramses had spent plenty of time breathing and his conclusion had been this: there was no way, aside from the road that one walked. People could wax philosophical and eloquent about the reason to follow this deity or that one, but the truth of the matter was that all were headed to the same place.

And now Arthur wanted to transcend death - not for eternal youth, but so that he could swear fealty to a new god! Not satisfied with having the power of the Faery Queen behind him, he now wanted this new other god. The one bearing...

Ramses regarded the sign and studied the mallet. Then he sighed and murmured, "Better Arthur serve you, the Battered fucking Ogre. At least the lord of the drink repays his faithful with an immediate reward of drunkenness."

"What a pleasant notion," called a voice from behind Ramses. "Your god is my god." A thick fog had descended on the city - when had it happened? It was a clear night just a moment ago.

"Erm, aye," called Ramses to the voice. The speaker could not have been more than twoscore feet from him. There was something about the way that he had spoken to Ramses, some unctuous oily quality to his words that gave the man pause. And set his spine creeping with terror. "Perhaps we could go in and pay homage to our god. First ale is on me."

Silence reigned for a while. "Why would you buy a drink for me, a total stranger to you? You have yet to even see my face, Ramses."

"Erm, how do you know my name?"

"I know many things," called the voice. It was closer now. "I do like that name, Ramses. It reminds me of an old friend from down south. He served me well, though he was a bit of a clod. History had a bit of a different take on him, though. Ha! That's what you get for trusting humans to record things. They always throw in a bit too much poetic license for my taste."

Ramses had backed into the door to the Battered Ogre. Not turning his eyes away from the thick soup of fog before him, he used his hands to feel around for the door handle. If he could get inside, to where there were people, perhaps then he could... got it! The nobleman pushed open the door and slammed it behind him. He was about to sigh relief when he noticed how dark it was inside. It was a Saturday night - it should have been lit up like a Candlemas celebration. Instead, an impenetrable gloom hung before him.

How Ramses hated magic. And now, it seemed, magic was to end him. Was this what destiny meant? The thing that we fear most comes to end us in the night? He had never believed in such things, but now, teetering on the precipice of some unknown abyss, Ramses was finding himself reconsidering a great number of suppositions about reality that he had taken for granted. Magic was real, certainly - everyone knew that. But the whole gods, free will, fate - the debate about those things was as live in Ramses' world as it had been in any self-reflecting human being's over the ages.

"You are wondering what is to happen to you, Ramses," called the voice, which was now ahead of him, in the shadows beyond the threshold of the tavern. "You wish to ask, 'why me?' Why is it that Ramses, eldest son of a rich velvet merchant, why is it that you are being called into service by Clapperleg?"

Clapperleg. The god of death and pestilence. The god about whom mothers and fathers throughout the Blessed Isles would whisper to their children in an effort to get them to go to bed on time. If a little boy or girl was up too late, Clapperleg would come for them. The story had always terrified Ramses. More so than any other story. One of his earliest memories involved running from his bedroom into his parents' bed, after his mother told him a tale of Clapperleg and his great... monstrous... teeth.

"You were always my chosen," hissed the voice, which seemed like it could be no more than a foot from Ramses. "You were always meant to come here for our meeting, from the moment you were born. When you shite your keks as a bairn, this was your destiny. When you took over your father's business, this was your destiny. When you became King Arthur of Camelot's most trusted advisor, this was your destiny. This has always been your destiny, Ramses. Come, I have so much to show you."

It was true. The god did have much to show. And the first thing Ramses saw was the flash of bright white fangs and pain of an unimaginable magnitude blossom out from the space between his neck and shoulder.

ðanu

"I won't be around forever, Robbie. You'll need to learn what it means to be a Laird sooner rather than later. The way things are going with the other clans, with Albion, with Brighid and her damned Avalon..." Laird Fearghas turned from his son to look out the window of his castle, down at the measured and orderly way the people of the town below went about their business. In the distance, he could see the stables and the garrison barracks. Beyond that, farms stretched out further than the eye could see.

The Albians thought that he and his people were wild barbarians, without laws and always killing one another. It was a stupid rumour, started by dumb people and kept alive by idiots beyond measure. There was no shortage of those types in Albion, but he knew that there were clever types, too. Clever types like that Merlyn. He had the ear of that moron Arthur, which mean immense power. The wizard could not be trusted, enthralled as he was by Queen Brighid of Avalon. Merlyn had sworn blood pact to a heretic daughter of Laird Fearghas' deity, Danu, the All-mother. Danu wished only for unity among her children, and she had been betrayed by Brighid, an upstart bitch who thought that she could...

Laird Fearghas felt his blood boil. It was Danu's presence, he knew. That was the price of the blood oath that he himself had sworn to Danu - she would forever be in his body, his mind, his spirit. But neither could betray the other. That was a subtlety of god worship that eluded most atheists and ignorants. He might have given up a measure of his own self in the pact, but he had gained so much from Danu. Those who thought her cold and unfeeling simply did not know her as Laird Fearghas did. She loved, and cared, and raged against what was happening on the Blessed Isles. Oh yes, the Laird could feel his goddess' rage. He let his hand relax - it had clenched into a fist as he gathered his thoughts.

"We are going to start with something simple, eh lad?" Simple like you, the Laird did not add. He loved his son, but he had witnessed ample evidence of the boy's lack of intelligence over the years. "Let's look at the relationship between gods and humans." Laird Fearghas poured himself a dram of peaty *uisge* and sat down on the chair next to the fireplace. Robbie was lying on the settee across from him, his eyes half shut, despite the morning light. "Wake up, Robbie! I'm not doing this for my own entertainment. Sit your arse up and open your eyes, *now*!"

Robbie might have been a dullard, but he was an obedient dullard. The boy sat up at attention, hands on knees and eyes pulled open.

"No, you don't need to... look, just keep your eyes open, alright. You don't need to stretch your face out like that." Laird Fearghas eyed the *uisge* once more. He still had half a bottle left. Hopefully that would be enough to get through this lesson.

"So, here it is: humans worship gods and gods play with the fates of humans. That is the way it is here in Caledonia, the way it is in Albion, the way it is in the rest of the Blessed Isles - it's the way that it is throughout the entire world, beyond even our borders. Everybody has gods, even if they think they don't. Atheists are the worst of the lot, I think, because they do not really understand what gods are. Think of gods as... well, gods are what keep us pointed in the direction in which we go. We might think ourselves rational creatures but the truth is that it's the irrational that makes us do what we do. Our emotions lead us by the nose, and gods are our emotions. Kind of."

A bottle fly, lit up by the sun streaming in from the window to the Laird's little respite room, landed on Robbie's shoulder.

"Flick that off, will you? That! The fly! A fly has landed on your shoulder! Move your arm - OK, good. Thank you. No, please don't cry. Yes, I'm sorry for yelling son. No, I won't do it again."

Laird Fearghas sighed before continuing. He might as well have been reciting a text written in a foreign language to the boy, but at least he would feel better for at least attempting an education.

"So, gods are kind of like ideas made flesh and bone, but they do not live and die as we do. They can interfere in our lives as surely as we can with one another. But they need us humans in order to survive. We need food and drink." Sometimes a lot of drink, mused Fearghas. "Gods need belief. They need it or they die. And we need gods. Without them, we lose our direction. Some men worship their own minds as their gods, and swear a pact with them. But man cannot live on mind alone - the heart is the province of deities." Laird Fearghas drained his tumbler, stood, and poured another *uisge.* "Do you have any idea of what I am saying to you, Robbie?"

The boy scratched his head. Limp mousy brown hair cut into the shape of a bowl shed dandruff as the lad rubbed it. "Erm, like, gods is good to have and all?"

"I told you, boy," said the Laird. "All men have gods. You cannot be alive and not cling to ideas - it's part of the human condition. And it's a moot fucking point if you cannot focus your mind on reflecting on the damn thing in the first place." The Laird drank deeply once more. "Look, Robbie. Here's what you need to know: magic exists because of gods. We humans can do magic because we have gods. Only that magic is shaped by the gods, just as our will is shaped by the gods. We find the gods that are for us and those gods find us. That is unity. That's what Danu wishes to see - she has absolutely no interest in our lives beyond that. Her interference only comes as is necessary to keep things in order. That's what we men of Clan Fearghas - that is what we must defend."

Silence reigned for a while. Robbie lay over on one side again. "So, what are we defending? I'm not sure I understands, Faither."

"For the love of Danu... we defend order! Control - conscious shaping of the world. Order itself, that's what Danu is! That is why she is the All-mother! We follow order, wherever it leads us, boy. Brighid is her counter-point. She is chaos manifest. She thinks that human beings should be free to worship their own minds! Do you know what human beings think?"

"Ummm," said Robbie. "They think about like... fucking, and stuff?"

"Fucking, eating, sleeping, shiteing - yes, all *that* stuff. Also hoarding, deceit, treachery, dishonour - and love and beauty and poetry, too. Yes. Godless, they are led by the nose by instinct, instead of by fealty to something greater - that is the world that Brighid wishes to see come to the Blessed Isles."

"And... dat's... bad?"

"Yes, that's bad, boy!" Laird Fearghas drained his vessel, poured another *uisge*, then drained that one again. "The irony is, all these fucking idiots in the south who think themselves serving order along with their Queen Brighid - they are the harbingers of chaos. They bring disorder to the land and they will see the Blessed Isles fall to that monstrous Yahweh and his Brothers of Christ." Laird Fearghas paused. "They already killed The Dagda, boy. The Dagda was the greatest among Danu's Children, and they roasted him alive in Londinium. If you do not see how the alliance between Queen Brighid and the Brothers of Christ that exists within the King of Camelot will see the end of all of our ways, then you are blind, boy."

"Erm, I ain't blind, Faither," said Robbie. "I can see ya drinkin' *uisge*. Not deaf, neit'er. I hear ya talkin' nonsense."

Laird Fearghas launched his empty glass at the wall above the hearth. "Nonsense? Nonsense?! I am trying to save our way of life, Robbie! And I expect you to do the same! But I think that's too much to ask, you touched clod!" The sound of sobbing echoed through the chamber. "Oh, no, I'm sorry, son. That was much too far. Danu's rage... I have such a hard time separating myself from it these days. Yes, I'm sorry. Yes, I'll give you a hug. No, we don't have to talk about the gods anymore. Well, actually, just one more thing son, then it's done, I swear."

"The Otherworlds," said Laird Fearghas, putting his arm around his son and breathing *uisge*-laced breath upon the boy. "These are the realms between ours and the worlds of the gods. Magic lives there. Magic that can spill into the world of men only because the Otherworlds exist. The Otherworlds are the bridges between our ideas of gods and the manifestation of those ideas in our world. Danu made our line Lairds of the Clan by giving our ancestors strength with the shield and mace, boy. It was by magic that we were chosen, magic made us strong, magic made us victors. But magic has no power unless we believe in it. We cannot pass into the Sidhe, the Otherworld created by Danu, unless we believe. Nor can the blessings of Danu pass into us. We must believe - you must believe, son."

"I believes," said Robbie, tears continuing to stream from his face. The Laird used the back of his hand to brush it from his face. "I believes that we's blessed by Danu, I does, Faither."

"I know," said Laird Fearghas. "I know, son."

The Laird, feeling the effects of the whiskey swell in his chest, looked at the fruit of his loins with no small measure of wistfulness.

"That, Danu-willing, should be enough."

cuccing ceech

Brother Winfridus was the shepherd of the souls in the little forest town of Erybos. Well, that was what he aimed for, anyway. As it stood, he had converted the majority of the people of the town, and his Brothers were well on their ways at other villages on the Isle of Valentia. The problem, as he saw it, was a certain aging druid and his daughter, the latter of which had thick red hair, a thin nose, full lips, rosy cheeks-

The scourge snapped as it smashed against the bare flesh of the monk's back. Such impure thoughts were anathema to worship of the One True God. When Brother Winfridus pulled the cat-o-nine into the ambit of his vision once more, he could see blood dripping from the ends onto his monk's habit. The brown cloth darkened where the drops spattered and were absorbed by the woolen cloth. He would have to take it to the launderess' cottage once more. Nola, the launderess, had pupped a half-dozen bairns, and yet her body still filled her simple dress in all the right ways, with curves around her chest and rump that-

"Aie," whispered Brother Winfridus as the scourge struck him again. So many impure thoughts, and so little time for his work in striking away the devil's influence on him. His back was becoming raw and he had spent nearly a half hour striking himself. Any more and he was in danger of falling ill as Brother Darrin had done, needing care from the sole medically-trained individual in Erybos. The fucking druid, Keandre. Still it would mean getting a closer look at that Rosmerta-

"Last one, Brother," called a voice deep within Brother Winfridus' soul as the scourge struck home. "We have work to do."

The monk had learned the price of defying his angel a long time ago. He placed the whip on the ground next to him, pulled his habit back over his exposed back, stood, and nearly fainted from the speed with which he raised himself.

"We have no time for weakness, Brother," called the voice. "Get a hold of your senses - now!"

"Yes, Lord."

"I am not your Lord," it replied. "Your Lord God is One. I am but one of his messengers."

"Yes, Lo- erm, Cassiel."

Cassiel was one of the angels who accompanied the Brothers of Christ on their mission to the Blessed Isles. It was the monks' job to convert the heathens from their ignorant pagan ways and into the lap of the one true God. By hook or by crook, the people of Valentia, as well as Albion, Vectis, Cardigan, Gilhool - all of the Blessed Isles would come under Christian rule or Brother Winfridus and his fellow monks would die trying.

That is what separated the monks from the people they sought to convert. They loved their gods, sure, but zealotry was something new. Only the adherents of the warlike gods within the pantheon of Danu's Children knew how to fight. And their way of fighting involved the tactics necessary to fight an enemy horde on the open battlefield. The Brothers of Christ had no qualms using deceit and treachery to get what they wanted. They were the chosen of the One True God, Yahweh, after all, which meant that whatever they did to win was justified by the result: total and utter assimilation of all the worlds of men.

They wanted to save their souls, of course. At least, that was what their angels told them. Without the One True God, all of these people would be subject to eternal damnation in a hellfire of their own creation. If that meant killing a few so that some might see the urgency of their conversion to the worship of the One True God, then this was an acceptable price to pay. Yeshua, the man who had brought the word of God to the people, he had sacrificed himself on the cross so that all would see the power of the One True God. The least the monks could do in repayment was to self-flagellate, kill heretics, and teach others about the value of denying one's own sexual appetites.

Yes, there it was. One of the chief reasons why Keandre the druid and his daughter Rosmerta needed to be purged from the land. Their god, this Cernunnos, the lusty impish thing with a cock the size of an elder oak tree - he was an abomination! Thick brow, black skin, massive ram's horns coming out of its head - if ever they needed a personification of what was evil about the world, this Cernunnos was a perfect image. Perhaps, though, it would be better if his skin was red, to inflame the idea of hellfire.

"I like it," said Cassiel in Brother Winfridus' mind. "When you get back from your task, see if you can get some red pigment from the general store.'

77

Brother Winfridus looked to the easel standing at the far end of his room. On it, a half-finished portrait of Cernunnos stood, facing out towards the front of the monk's small room in the rectory. He had used charcoal to get the outline of the monstrous creature right, his eyes slanted and without an iris (the god's actual eyes were green, but that made him too human, Cassiel said), his face curved into a wicked grin. A tail with a sharp spade at its tip, something that Cernunnos lacked, was another suggestion from Cassiel, something to give the god an alien quality. There was no trouble interpreting what was on that canvas as an evil being.

"Once it is complete, we shall have to have reproductions. These shall be spread throughout the Isle of Valentia, to your brothers who are even now working to break the spell of this devil on the innocent souls of the people."

"Reproductions, Lo- erm, Cassiel?"

"Yes, reproductions."

With that, the angel materialized in the man's room. Dressed head to toe in shining metal armour, he bore a scowl, a longsword on his hip, and a shield on his back. His helm was visored and the visor was thrown up, revealing a face that suggested two things to Brother Winfridus: one, that his eyes were too far apart and his teeth were fucked up, making him a fairly physically ugly angel. Two, that it was extremely strange to see his benefactor spirit as a man who looked like he had barely lived through eighteen summers.

"You can stop staring, Winfridus," muttered the angel. "This is what happens to all deities when they are killed. They come back young again. Cernunnos might have won the battle, but I will take the war."

Winfridus scratched his head. "All deities? I thought you were an angel and there was only One True God?"

78

"Yes!" said the angel, sidestepping the question and ploughing on with his follow-up. "As I said, Winfridus, you shall be required to make reproductions of your painting. I am thinking that twelve copies will be necessary, for starters."

"Twelve copies?!" asked the monk. "That will take me months!"

"That would take a normal man months, Winfridus," said the angel, taking a seat in the monk's small bedroom chair and spreading his legs. "You, on the other hand, have the blessing of the One True God. You shall complete the work in less than two weeks."

"Ha! Perhaps if I don't sleep."

"For the love of- do I really need to spell it out for you? I will give you-"

"Oh, we'll use magic?"

"No, you fool!" roared the angel. "*We* do not use 'magic' - do you think us the same as these heathens? The One True God uses miracles to demonstrate his power!"

"M-m-miracles?" asked Brother Winfridus, trembling at the angel's yell and threatening body language. "That's... different than magic?"

"Yes! They are wholly different! Magic is the province of devilry, miracles are what Yeshua used to demonstrate God's power."

"Right," said Brother Winfridus. "Well, they're both 'M' words so maybe they're not totally different-"

"Do I have to make you get out the whip again, Winfridus? You know what happens when you question me. They're different - just rest assured that they are different!"

Winfridus couldn't help himself. He was always an inquisitive sort. "How?"

"'How' what?"

"How are they different? I mean, magic seems like it's a bending of reality into folds that go beyond the rational mind. When these heathens use magic, they call on their gods or their faeries to give them the strength to create all kinds of different impossible things. With miracles, we call on the One True God and he does those things for us. They seem like the same thing, only we's got a special name for 'em."

"They are different, Brother Winfridus," said the angel, his words dripping with poison, "because I say they are different. Now, do we need another lesson in the frailty of the flesh? Or are you ready to set out on your task?"

Brother Winfridus was silent once more. "Do you think I could wake her up first? You know before I torch the place? It just seems like... you know, murder."

"Murder?!" said Cassiel, standing up and drawing his blade. He pointed it at Brother Winfridus. "Murder?! This bitch's precious Cernunnos killed me in front of the entire village and he turned the place into a fuck fest the like of which would have been right at home in Babylon. Do you want that again? More orgies? More spitting in the face of celibate Yeshua and the One True God? You owe the people of Erybos more than your yellow-bellied lack of stomach."

"Wasn't Yeshua balling a prostitute named Mary?" Brother Winfridus caught the angel's glare. "I'm sorry about asking..." said the monk. "But Rosmerta – she's not a full druid yet, though. She hasn't sworn the blood oath. She might still be saved, brought into the fold. Rumour has it that her father is gone for a long time. She is unprotected. I could just pluck her, take her back here, keep her penned and fed until she realizes the error of her ways."

The angel sheathed his sword and rubbed his chin, which was shorn clean and bore no lines of maturity and age. "Hmm, perhaps that might be - wait, I know your mind you filthy pig-dog! You would think of shagging her while she was here! You already fantasize about this Rosmerta. Do you think I will permit you to bring her into your home, where you might give in to your fleshly desires? Get out the scourge, we are not done this morning's preparations." The angel picked up an object from the low table next to the monk's bed. He held it up to the candlelight.

"You still have hours before dawn breaks," said Cassiel, turning the hourglass over. "One half-hour of further purification of your body and mind should not interfere with the plan." The angel placed the hourglass on the table, crossed to Brother Winfridus, pulled his habit down over his back, placed the cat-o-nine back in his hand, and said,

"Kill the bitch. Kill this Rosmerta O'Ceallaigh before she has a chance to blossom into an enemy of Christ. Nip this fucking flower in the bud."

Ironically, it was fucking that saved Rosmerta. Not that she was engaged in it - the girl slept through the initial moments of excitement. No, it was Enyd, who was still in faery heat. She had convinced Donk to come out to the circle once more, just the two of them this time. She was riding the male faery, silently mouthing delight to him (she did not want to wake Rosie), when she saw the hunched over old man with a torch creep up to the window of the cottage. Using some strange device (which was undoubtedly magical), the monk jimmied open the window to the main part of the cottage, dumped a small bucket of what smelled to Enyd's sharp nose like liquor, then threw the torch in. It took no more than a moment.

The place went up. Keandre kept all kinds of dried herbs hanging from his rafters in the main part of the cottage, where the work bench and the kitchen were located. Dry and brittle, they caught and wildfire spread throughout the cottage. Orange flame exploded out of the open window before a moment passed.

"Rosie!" shouted the faery, hopping off Donk and not bothering to put any of her clothing back on. That was when Enyd noticed the hulking angel creeping in from the woods behind the monk. The faery slapped a hand over her mouth to prevent any more noise from escaping. Hopefully, the angel had not heard her. Enyd had heard too many stories of angels throttling the life from faeries throughout the Blessed Isles.

"Huh, wuzzat-" began Donk. Enyd put a hand to Donk's mouth, motioned to the angel, who had not noticed them yet, and turned away.

"We need ta get ta Rosie's room," she whispered.

As it was, between them and the window to Rosmerta's bedchamber stood the two figures. The angel put a hand to the monk's shoulder and pointed away. From her vantage, Enyd thought she heard 'it will look like an accident,' but she could not quite be sure. Nonetheless, after a moment, the pair disappeared back into the cover of the forest. Enyd and Donk zipped towards the window. Inside, Enyd noticed that Rosmerta had kept her door closed, though grey smoke was still filtering in through the cracks around the door. The faery breathed a sigh of relief as she hammered on the window.

"Rosie, get up!" whispered Enyd frantically, hoping that the monk and the angel were far enough away that they wouldn't hear the escape attempt. "Let me in!"

At first, it seemed like the girl would not stir. Enyd was preparing to get Donk to help her force the window when finally the girl inside woke and looked up at the small window cut into the side of the cottage.

"Enyd?" she said, confused. Then she visibly sniffed the air. She turned to the door and saw the smoke entering the room. "Enyd!"

"Let us in, girl!"

Rosmerta, her eyes wild, climbed from her bed and opened the window. It was barely big enough that the faeries could fit through with their wings flapping. Still, they manage to get in with the girl.

"Yer naked," observed Donk, whose simple handle was no ironic nickname for a faery with a plethora of sense. It was as fitting as fitting could be.

"'Course she's fucking naked ya touched git," said Enyd. "And so are we. Look, we need ta get ye out of here, Rosie. That way is death," said the faery, pointing at the smoking door. "We're going to have to improvise." With that, Enyd said a few words in a tongue that sounded kind of like the one of the Blessed Isles, though it had a strange lyrical quality to it. Whatever it was, the language of Avalon always sounded beautiful to Rosmerta. The faery finished the spell and waved her hands. A great oval materialized from the ether in front of the trio, right in front of the door, which was starting to give off a rather unsettling amount of heat.

As soon as Rosie laid eyes on the velvet folds of the curtain hanging within the portal, she recoiled in fear. "That- that'll take us to Avalon!"

"Aye," said Enyd. "And ye'd best come through if ye wants ta live." The faery squinted her eyes, smacked herself in the head with an open palm. "For the love of Brighid, I almost forgot." She turned to Rosmerta. "Quick, yer lute - where is it, Rosie?"

"What? My lute?"

The instrument, which had been gathering dust under the girl's bed after months and years of personal torture, was not exactly at the top of the list of things that Rosmerta thought were important at the moment.

"Yes, yer lute! Without it, I can't guarantee your safety in there, girl."

"I don't understand!" said Rosmerta, dropping to her knees and pulling the instrument out from underneath the bed.

"Ye will! Now let's go, before yer reduced to a roast, Rosie, girl," shouted Enyd, pointing at the velvet folds. In the other room, the sound of a beam splintering under the pressure of the inferno spurred the girl into action.

Lute in hand and naked as a jay bird, Rosmerta O'Ceallaigh took her first step into Avalon.

ᛗᛁᛟᛚᚾᛁᚱ

"Thor, god of fucking thunder himself!" Loki punctuated his words with a hip thrust. "Or maybe fucking, pause, thunder. How would thunder fuck? I expected it would be loud and quick." Loki exposed his trademark shite-devouring grin. "How goes the battle? Keeping chaos at bay as Ragnarok slowly creeps in around you?"

Thor was seated at the long table at Valhalla, next to Odin's throne in the portion of the feasting hall reserved for the gods. Odin had passed his son the *bragarful*, the enormous and ornate drinking horn named ironically for Bragi, god of poetry. Odin loved Thor (and to a lesser extent, Loki), but he had little time for Bragi. In truth, his youngest had disappointed him in a very significant way. He had gone on his own path, which is exactly what gods are supposed to do, but still it stung the All-father's pride that Bragi was no great warrior. Thor, on the other hand, was exactly that.

"Hello, Loki," said Thor, after drinking from the bragarful and passing it to his brother. "I expect this latest fucking debacle is your doing."

"What? Me?" said Loki, feigning innocence. He took a sip. "And what 'fucking debacle' might that be? I haven't scheduled an orgy in a fornight!"

Thor waved his hand in the air and a little portal, barely bigger than a large dinner plate, manifested in the air before the three assembled gods. The din of Valhalla, the shouts and laughter and screeches of delight, became muted. "That fucking debacle," Thor said, pointing at the conjured image.

Within the portal, several small fishing vessels were cresting waves which could only have been found on the open sea. The swells were enormous and the skies were dark. Rain was spattering down upon the vessels. The sound of thunder cracked in the distance and flashes of light brightened up the surroundings every few moments.

"I don't see the problem," said Loki. "Looks like a few idiots from Midgard decided to go on their summer raids early." Loki put two hands on the side of his face in mock surprise. "Why did you cause a storm for those poor innocent fishermen?"

Thor shook his head, put his hand out into the air, and made a pulling gesture. The image zoomed in on the boats. Standing dully around the decks were creatures in tatters of worm-eaten and dirty clothing. Their rags looked like they had just emerged from the grave because, well, they had. They were youngish and looked healthy, having recently feasted on the souls of the living. Their eyes were half-open, but through the slits, the gods could see the colour purple peeking out into the rain-swept air.

"Hel's thralls," said Thor. "Draugr. Yet another of your attempts to bring Ragnarok about early, brother. Don't you ever get tired of being caught trying to pull this shite off?" With that, Thor clenched a fist. Lightning struck the bow of one of the ships, splintering the hull as the crackling energy slammed through into the water beneath. The vessel began to take on water. In a moment, it sunk, submerging the draugr into their second, albeit much more watery, grave. Thor turned back to his brother. "You know that me, father, Tyr, and all the rest of us Aesir are simply going to put an end to it."

"Do I now?" said Loki, who broke into a dazzling grin once more. Big perfectly square teeth caught the light of the many burning torches of Valhalla. He reminded Thor of the humans who took up the traveling merchant's cart and sold used goods from the side of the path around the towns of Midgard. Or perhaps, more accurately, the type of merchant who would go door to door in a village attempting to sell objects used for sexual gratification to the adult of the house. "Why, look at that," added Loki, "the storm is clearing up."

Sure enough, through the portal, which was beginning to flicker strangely, it was evident that the dark skies had fled. Sunshine painted the slats of the boats with its bright and cheerful affect. The draugr remained immobile as the seas flattened out and became calm. Thor made gestures in the air, but the image below remained undisturbed. Eventually the portal winked out of existence and the raucous sounds of the feasting hall became audible once more.

"You've taken them out of our sphere of influence," said Thor, laughing mirthfully. He did that a lot – he didn't take much seriously. "What does that matter to us? Midgard is the land we rule - if you and Hel wish to go and conquer new lands without worshipers, I would very much like to see you take your best shot."

The influence of a god is tied to the presence of worshipers on a land. Midgard was full of people who loved and hated the Aesir, Vanir, giants, trolls, dwarves, and all the rest of the creatures which made up the pantheon of gods and mythical

87

creatures of their land. As a result, the power of the gods was strong on the various lands, islands, and territories of the Norsemen. The gods could come and go as they please between Midgard and Asgard (and Helheim, Niflheim, Alfheim, Vanaheim, and the rest of the nine worlds), provided that Heimdall was around and the bifrost was available. But Midgard had its limits - gods could only go where people who believed in them were to be found. They were barred from the other lands of the world of men.

Loki laughed right back at his brother. "Yes, brother, what does it matter? Please do sit on your hands and do nothing - I would so love that. To reshape the world as Loki-"

"If you're not going to drink from that," said Odin, pointing to the bragarful in Loki's hand, which had remained there after his initial sip, "pass it down the line. You know the rules, son."

"'The rules,'" said Loki, distaste crunching his smile into something ugly. "Yes, I know the rules." With that, Loki took a massive swig of the mead and threw it down the line to one of the dead warriors making merry. It sailed through the air, perfectly upright, directly into the hand of the warrior, who caught it and drank. Then he passed it to the man to his left, roaring with delight as he did so.

"I expect Hel is recovering from her death, is she?"

Hel, daughter of Loki and giantess in charge of the underworld called Helheim, had been aboard one of the boats while it was still in a bay near the fishing village of Ygglheim. She had been slain by a Valkyrie, a lesser warrior goddess known as Aslaug. Hel had goaded the Valkyrie into doing it, threatening her with the notion of taking the soul of her one true love, a human man created to be her consort, down to Helheim with her. Helheim was the place where those who died dishonourably or of old age were taken (there was seen to be little difference in Norseman culture). It was well-known that if Hel were killed in Midgard, Ragnarok would not be far behind, yet still the Valkyrie could not stop herself from slaying the goddess - she loved the man, Gulbrand, too much to let the daughter of Loki have him.

"She looks like she's a teenager again," said Loki, smirking. "I told her that she might consider dying to be a cheaper option for revivifying her beauty than going to one of the Seeresses in Asgard for one of their... remedies."

Loki was referring to the blood magic cast by the less scrupulous of the residents of Asgard. As it stood, dead humans who evaded Helheim by either being killed in battle or mastering their craft in life were taken to either Valhalla or Folkvangr, respectively. Sometimes, those humans wished to leave what amounted to heaven within their world (usually because it did not match up with what it was billed as - heaven, like all parts of creation, had its dark side). Dead, they could not return to Midgard. So they were forced to wander the streets of Asgard, the city of the immortals. The craftspeople usually were hired on to do what they did in life, whereas the warriors were forced into... less conventional roles. There had not been a war in Asgard since the Aesir and Vanir signed their peace treaty untold millennia before.

"Yes, well," said Thor. "Maybe were your daughter not such a cunt, fair Idunn would hook her up with one of her youth-bestowing apples. In this pinch, I'm sure that dying to a Valkyrie's blade is not as fun as sacrificing an elf and stealing its youth."

"What?" asked Loki, doing his best mock innocence impression once more. "I would never condone my little girl engaging in such horrific and unjust behaviour. It is, after all, against 'the rules.'"

"Which means you probably do condone it," said Odin, who had been rather content to sit and listen to his sons trade conversation. "I love you as I love all of my children, Loki-"

"Hopefully not the way you 'love' Bragi," sniggered Loki.

"As I said, all of my children," repeated Odin, unperturbed. "I assume that you and Bragi did work out your differences? He came to me, seeking redress against you for cursing his chosen. He raised the issue of a young man... Gudbeik, I think?"

"Gudleik," corrected Loki. "Yes, yes I think that we sorted him out. A twin blessing for the boy. Mine and Bragi's."

"Let me guess," said Thor. "You wagered his soul against Ragnarok? That if Bragi wins, Ragnarok is delayed? If you win, the world ends? Cast the runes to see what his powers and weaknesses are?"

"However did you guess, brother?" said Loki, one hand against his mouth, mock aghast.

"Because you've done it with half the pantheon, you clod," said Thor. "And still, our champions defeat you. You must love to lose bets, brother, for you simply cannot help yourself from placing foolish ones."

"You sound like him," said Loki, shaking his head. "Like our dear brother. He too loves to talk about destiny and triumph always beating ruin. Mark my words, Thor - ruin can and does happen to people. There are those who are completely destroyed by their destiny."

"Yes," said Thor. "Only it's gods like you who like to pretend like the stakes are higher than they truly are. Without you, even the concept of ruin could not exist. Your entire reason for being is to sow fear and discord within the hearts of men." Thor pulled Mjolnir from his belt and placed it on the table between them. "My job is to see that, when the chips are down, the spark of courage might be found. And we both know how that fight goes - we've fought it over and over and over."

"So?" replied Loki. "Sometimes I think you really spend too much time with the mortals, brother. You speak as if these lives that they live are journeys, battles to be won, missions with end points. Even Ragnarok - this whole thing is a complete far-"

"Loki," said Odin warningly. "Do not tempt fate. Ragnarok is very real and very deadly to all of us. I know that it is your nature to seek its arrival, but do not pretend like it is some small matter that might be ignored. If it's ignored, then it will indeed arrive. What you've done with Hel is very clever - I expect that I will be hearing from a revivified Aslaug soon, once Heimdall permits her to pass through here to Valhalla. But take this matter seriously." Odin paused, then smiled. "I forgot who I was talking to for a moment - go ahead, be unserious about the whole thing. It is your nature, after all."

"Thank you, father," replied Loki. "Preaching radical self-acceptance - that is very forward thinking of you."

"If we do not accept our own natures, how will we ever show others that it's prudent to do the same?" Thor asked.

"Now," said Odin, beaming. "Isn't this nice? How I love it when my boys wax philosophical in my hall. It's almost as if that is the very reason we Asgardians exist." The god paused and looked down the table at the dead humans. Men were using their teeth to tear meat from bone and were downing their horns with great relish. Most were very obviously merry. A pair of them, though, were yelling at each other. They stood from the table and the men around them made space. The dead warriors proceeded to smash each other with their drinking horns, before raining blows with their fists. Eventually they fell to the ground, a battle which Odin could no longer see. After a moment, one of the men stood, nose streaming blood and face puffy with fresh bruises. He took a drinking horn from a passing shieldmaiden and downed the contents before goosing her rump. The shieldmaiden, disgusted, cocked a fist back and smashed him in his bloody nose. He collapsed once more.

"Well, to offer philosophical nuggets and to go to war with one another over trifles." Odin shrugged and took a bite of his own meal, which consisted of a massive roasted leg of an avian of the type that lived in the roosts around Asgard. "Speaking of which: tell me, Loki. You have managed to export worship to another land beyond Midgard. I would be very pleased if you told me where it is you are now permitted to go and who your worshipers are. Perhaps we might bring more of us Asgardians to the place." Odin cracked his knuckles. "It is about time we have another clash with a foreign pantheon."

Thor sighed and picked up Mjolnir, replacing it on his belt. "You know that when we fight other gods, humans die?"

Loki laughed. "Death is part of the deal, brother. You say it as if it's a bad thing."

"I am no fan of senseless death, Loki," said Thor. "You might think I love these humans too much, but I would say that I am perfect according to my own nature. Whatever you plan to do in this new world with Hel's thralls, know that I am already making my way there."

"I know brother," replied Loki. "Wherever I go, there you are."

"And vice versa," said Thor, patting the head of his hammer. "And vice fucking versa."

The Tower of Butthole

"We can't let all of this serious plot development and philosophical stuff go on without a few jokes about split anuses. It simply will not do."

Merlyn stood at the threshold of his tower, before the great doors set into the rough-hewn stone that made up his domicile in Albion. The door itself had spoken, great big fleshy lips having sprouted out of the side of the ornately-carved oak planks. Beside the wizard, a woman wearing a thick red hooded cloak, which was pulled down over her features, stood nearly a head taller than the lanky Merlyn. She was an enormous woman, though she was as rail-thin as Merlyn himself. Beneath the cloak, she was much better dressed (though that was no great feat, given Merlyn's tailor), wearing a delicately embroidered black dress which sang loudly with an iridescence of coloured threads. Her face remained obscured, though, even when the magician opened his mouth to speak.

"It seems that the tower is perverting all of my powers, creating a fell shadow of my light," said Merlyn. "Just now, it broke the fourth wall, whereas I am a master of the fourth dimension."

"You could probably teach us about split anuses and perversions," continued the tower, whose voice was high-pitched and nasally, even more so than Merlyn's prototypically nerdy patois. "That device you brought back from the future, the one you watch horse porn with Arthur on - that's only the start of your kink. Oh yes, wizard, I've been watching you."

"As I said," Merlyn muttered, his eyes darting from the door to the woman in a too-quick manner, "this evil thing likes to lie."

"No one believes you, Merlyn," taunted the tower. "But let's get back to our chat about split anuses. A magician, a monk, and a dryad walk into a bar. The magician says, "I'll take a pint of Cornelius' Finest." (I modeled his character after you, Merlyn). The monk says, "I don't drink, but I'll have some of your peanuts." The dryad says, "one time I got taken in the arse by Cernunnos."" A noise that reminded Merlyn of the rimshot he had heard in the comedy clubs of the 20th century resounded through the meadow.

"That's not funny, tower," observed Merlyn. "You're like every automaton - you don't understand humour."

"Ah, everyone's a critic. And I have a name, you know."

"And that is?" said the woman.

"Gary." The tower responded before adding, "Don't pretend you don't know my name, wizard!"

"Gary, then," said Merlyn. "Perhaps you'd like to tell us why you're summoning demons into the first level of the tower? And perhaps, while you're at it, you can explain that?"

Merlyn pointed at a tiny facsimile of the tower, rooted in the ground at its side and no taller than Merlyn's waist.

"Why, that's my little boy, Hubert!" boasted the tower. "A chip off the old cobble, this one. I tell you, he's only out of diapers and he's already summoned his first monstrosity from the black depths of a hidden realm.

"Squeee," said Hubert, bouncing around as it shrieked. It looked to Merlyn as if it were made of rubber, the way that it moved.

"Look of 'im go!" said Gary. "The little buggers are bouncy at his age. Once you get to be a crank like me, it's like you can't even take one direct hit by lightning without losing a half dozen bricks in the mix."

"That's not how towers are built!" shouted Merlyn. "You weren't built like that! You were stacked up out of stone, with masons and mortar and the whole works. You were-"

"Conjured out of thin air into this realm," interrupted Gary. "Yes, yes, you took Arthur's mithril - the mithril which was supposed to pay good Albion labourers for their efforts - and squandered it on Cornelius' Finest after you stole me away from my home realm."

"Oh," said the woman, cocking her head to one side. "And where's that?"

All of a sudden, Hubert's door burst open and a tiny oranged-skinned imp wielding a pitchfork walked out into the meadow, roaring and brandishing his weapon at Merlyn. The wizard crushed it beneath the soft sole of his crudely-sewn shoes. A shrieking noise began emitting from Hubert.

"Aww, what'd you have to go and do that for?" asked Gary. "That was his first demon, and you went and killed it for no reason! It was just trying to make its way, same as you and me. Who are you to play Judge Judy and executioner?"

"Judge Judy?" asked the woman, looking to Merlyn.

95

"I knew you were watching *The Simpsons* on my phone when I was asleep!" roared Merlyn at the door. "Brighid damn it Gary, we talked about this!"

"I'm standing right here, I'll damn what I want," the woman said, pulling her hood back. Black curls spilled out across her shoulders, framing a face that dazzled in its perfection. Her skin was alabaster, her nose was aquiline, her brows were... thick and bushy and connected in the middle, and suddenly covered by a pair of horn-rimmed glasses attached to a plastic nose and fake mustache.

"Umm, my Queen," said Merlyn. "I think that Gary has woven a spell upon thee." Merlyn flicked his wrist and when it snapped out, it was holding a white-painted oval hand mirror. "Look!"

Queen Brighid looked shocked at first. Then a smile cracked her face, followed by a grin, and ending with a laugh of epic proportions.

Merlyn was aghast. "He shows you no respect, my Queen! I mean, those are a facsimile of the face belonging to Groucho of Clan Marx, a serious man detested for his slow-wittedness centuries in the future."

"Now who doesn't understand humour?" remarked Gary.

"Shut it, you!" said Merlyn, whirling on the door before turning back to Queen Brighid. "Please, my Queen, we must purge the evil from this land."

"Oh, come now, Merlyn," said the Faery Queen, "it's not all bad. I mean, he is clearly a family man. Erm, tower."

Merlyn shook his head in disbelief, getting even more flustered as his limp sock-esque hat fell into his face. Pushing it back onto his head, he retorted, "Family tower? Where is Mrs. Gary, I might ask? No doubt he is a deadbeat!"

"His son is literally right there," said Brighid, pointing to a whimpering Hubert. "And who knows, maybe Mrs. Gary isn't in the picture. Maybe he isn't married, you prejudiced slob! And I don't see her around - maybe little Hubert here has a deadbeat Mom! Or *maybe*, for a wizard who spends so much time in the future, you really are stuck in the past, Merlyn. Or, the present. Or, you know, given how terrible conditions are, a little bit in the future. But not as far into the future as you've been, Merlyn - the age of... what do you call it? The horse porn thing. A smurtpone?"

"Um, a smartphone, my Queen."

"The age of smartphones," repeated Queen Brighid, before resuming her furious affect. "You've no bloody excuse at all for being a clod! Apologize at once!"

"Actually," said Gary, "there is no such thing as tower marriage. Nor do we really have anything you might call a gender. We reproduce asexually, though they gestate inside of us like mammals. Out through the shitter, though." Gary became mock conspiratorial. "You know, I said there'd be more split anus jests, but crapping out a solid loaf of rock is no joke. I won't be able to shite right for at least a month."

"You don't shite!" Merlyn fumed. "You're a fucking tower!"

"As if!" said Gary. "I *wish* I didn't shite. Awfully inconvenient, it is, to find a time to sit down when no humans are watching and squat out a deuce."

"Oh," said Merlyn, folding his arms. "If you do shite, where is the evidence? Aside from Hubert here, of course."

Hubert made a pleasant sound at his continued acknowledgment in the conversation.

"You know gravel?" asked Gary. "Where do you think it comes from? Just plops down out of the sky? That's building feces, brother."

"Gravel is just crushed stone," muttered Merlyn, wiping the side of his face in frustration. "It's rock that's been bashed up a bit. Buildings do not poop!" Merlyn turned to Brighid. "Do you see? Now do you see why this evil needs to be purged from the land?"

"All I see is a high-strung wizard wearing the best of a touched girl's fall collection having an argument with a tower about whether gravel is secretly defecated by buildings when there are no human eyes to see it happening." Brighid turned to Gary. "I'm sorry about this, Gary. I truly am - he normally is quite well-behaved. I mean, if he wasn't, I wouldn't have allowed him to swear a blood oath to me."

"A crock of shite," roared Merlyn. "A crock of fucking shite, that, my Queen. You are a worship strumpet, taking it from any magic-enamoured young neophyte looking to master the heavens and stick the big one to Danu's Children and this Yahweh and his angels in the mix. I only came to you because The Dagda wouldn't have me. Cast me off for being weak-willed, I- oh."

It was at this point that Merlyn noticed that he had incensed his goddess to the point that she was incanting a spell and pointing her hands in his general direction.

"No, wait, my Queen, there is still the horde of demons that needs to be dealt wit-"

Merlyn did not get to finish his sentence, as the incantation finished and he suddenly discovered that the world was much bigger. Or he was much smaller. And he could no longer speak. Everything felt strange to the wizard, and when he opened his mouth all that came out was a loud croaking sound.

"Merlyn," seethed Brighid. "I have never been so insulted in my life. You brought me here, from Avalon, where I was attending to important matters, in order to interfere with the lives of a very funny and earnest tower, who simply seems happy to live and let live."

Merlyn tried to speak a further warning to his Queen about the demons, which were, even now, filing into the first level of the tower through a portal crackling with black lightning and fuming brimstone-laced smoke. He opened his mouth wide and said,

"Ribbit!"

SOLFÈGE

Randulf Randulfsson, father to Porsi Randulfsson, bondsman in service to Jarl Heinrich of Ygglheim, was one of the few men who were spared in the draugr plague that swept through the village after his boy Porsi and that fool Gudleik, the cursed son of Sigbjorn Gulbrandsson, cast some sort of spell upon the dead. At least, that was the story that was spreading throughout the remnants of the town like wildfire. All of the widows and children were looking for someone to blame, and all that was necessary was the right conditions and a thunderstorm would be created. Vengeance would be sought, and if it could not be gotten from the young men, then they would seek it from the sole remaining patriarch attached to them.

It was not a situation with which Randulf was unfamiliar. The reason he was a bondsman, which was the fancy name given to a slave who happened to be of Norse blood, was that he had accidentally trampled a nobleman's daughter when he was out riding in his youth. The girl had simply leaped from the bushes and neither the horse nor the rider had any time to react. In the result, the girl was killed and Randulf was enslaved by his Jarl. It had occurred at a village to the southwest of Ygglheim, at a place called Mimir's Rest. It was not anything like Ygglheim, which was a sleepy little fishing town set into a cove on the coast. No, this place was farther south, warmer, and much more... metropolitan. It was an out-sized village when Randulf left, which happened nearly two decades before. By now it would be a full city, a place to rival the great Upsalla to the north. Still, Mimir's Rest had been his home - a home which he left none too soon, enslaved or not.

Randulf shook his head as the memories of Jarl Danski saving him from a crowd bearing woodcutting axes and vicious expressions fluttered back into his consciousness. He had not thought on that in a long time, not since his wife Eyja left Randulf and Porsi to their devices with Jarl Heinrich, after the latter had bought Randulf's bond from Danski and brought them here, to Ygglheim. It was bad enough that Randulf had turned them into pariahs with his little accident, Eyja had told him. We don't need to go live in the sticks, too. Eyja had still been free to do as she wished, and what she wished had nothing to do with either Randulf nor Porsi. Unkind voices that surrounded Eyja throughout her life whispered that the woman looked like a donkey - all teeth and fucked up skin that seemed always to be inflamed with acne. But she sang well enough - beautifully, even - so she thought she would remain at Mimir's Rest and try her hand at training to become a skald in service to Jarl Danski.

Total and utter betrayal at the hands of a woman whom Randulf had loved. He was such a good man that he never once brought up the fact that he would not have been on the horse that night if Eyja had not insisted that her husband go and fetch her some mead from the meadery, miserably threatening his expulsion from their long house if he did not.

Porsi had been squalling in his crib while the woman got herself drunk night after night. The local Seer had told Randulf that he had seen it before with women who had recently given birth - it took its toll on some more than others. Randulf only ever lay eyes of compassion on his wife for her troubles, getting her all the mead she could drink and caring for their infant son as his mother descended into the depths of drunkenness nightly. Nights turned into weeks, turned into months, turned into seasons, into two years of dissolution.

Thoughts of abandonment never once crossed Randulf's mind - he would help her through this latest assault on her mental health, no matter how brutal it became. At least, that was his plan until that unfortunate little girl, a sweet thing name Ibrild, darted out in front of his horse. She had been playing a game of hide and seek in the dark with her friends. The sensation as the horse passed over her shadowy shape, the soft thumping below the animal's hooves, the sickening feeling as Randulf brought the horse to a stop, the discovery of the girl by lantern light, the blood exiting her nose, her wet gasps as her crushed body struggled to breathe, the way that the death rattle had suddenly stopped and her form went still in Randulf's arms.

Not for the first time, Randulf pounded his legs as he knelt in prayer to Thor, looking upon the little effigy of the thunder god on his altar, asking his patron 'why?' Why was life so cruel? What had he done? He had never tried to do anything but act appropriately - to be a good man for his wife and son. And he was totally destroyed in the process. He would never choose to be evil or to take a selfish path - that simply was not his way. No matter how unfair he was treated by fate, Randulf would never give in to a desire to help to make the world burn. And the temptation to do so had been strong.

Now, though, everything was in flux. Randulf did not know what his son had done - or even if he was involved in the raising of the draugr. All he knew was what the other survivors knew: that Gudleik and Porsi came wild-eyed and shouting down from the burial grounds after the draugr had swept through, drained dozens of their lives, and stolen the boats. The young men told the Jarl a story about collecting corpseweed for Jogrim, the Seer, because Porsi had had a vision of a Valkyrie flying among the fishing boats out at work that morning. It all sounded so damned far-fetched, but Porsi had been so insistent...

"Randulf," came a shout from the door. "You need to come - quickly. Seer Jogrim is alive!"

The voice belonged to Atla, one of Jarl Heinrich's servant girls. Atla had helped Randulf raise Porsi when the pair had arrived in Ygglheim, nearly naked and most definitely afraid for what was to come next. Atla and a few of the other women helped to soften the impact of the transition, and Randulf had always thanked her for it. Standing from his little bedroom shrine, the man grimaced and shook out his arthritic legs before pulling on his cloak and opening the door.

"There is something different about you, boy," said Jarl Heinrich, looking upon Gudleik. He had taken on a considerably softer affect now that they were away from the crowd that wanted Gudleik's head on a pike. "Jogrim is very much right about that." The Jarl rubbed his beard betwixt his fingers. "But I do not think it would be... appropriate for you to be leaving so soon after what happened this morning." The Jarl paused, then put a hand upon Gudleik's arm. "Your father is dead, Gudleik. Do you not wish to bury him? And your brothers? They will all be given a proper send-off. Even now, my slaves are cutting the bows for the boat pyre."

Gudleik opened his mouth, put a hand up, and then closed it. Gudleik was one of six brothers and, aside from his mother, he was the sole survivor of his family. It was a fact that the boy was hoping he would not have to process that reality until he was out on the road with Jogrim, going to wherever it was the Seer thought he could learn how to wield his... weapon, as Jogrim had called the old lyre they had fetched out from his room in his father's long house.

"Please, Gudleik," said the Jarl. "Stay for the funeral - you cannot simply up and leave right now. I forbid it!"

Jogrim cleared his throat and said, "Do you really think you can guarantee the boy's safety, Heinrich? Even now, the crowd gathers outside your long house. If Gudleik isn't killed in his sleep, he will certainly be slain in full view of the village. Honestly, how do you think your authority will be able to stop it? The price of vengeance is one that many of your subjects are willing to pay. We need to get out of here - tomorrow morning, we need to ride."

"Enough," said Gudleik, silencing both of the men. "I have lived nearly half my life as a shunned boy in this village, barely given half a glance by anyone, except one laced with scorn. Now, when Jogrim, the Seer who pronounced my curse, tells the people of Ygglheim that I had nothing to do with the deaths of their loved ones, they are not prepared to listen any more. Oh, but they listened when I was younger - how they listened." Gudleik spit on the hard-packed dirt of the chamber. "I will mourn my family in my own way. I say goodbye to my mother tonight and we ride in the morning." Gudleik looked at the Jarl and took his arm gently. "You have always been kind to me, Jarl Heinrich. Even when news of the curse was delivered, you gave me work and you never judged me for it. I would like to stay and mourn, but I would prefer to stay alive. There are things at work here - things that I am still coming to grips with myself."

"Gods and magic, is it?" asked the Jarl, shaking his head. "I'm sorry, Jogrim. I always thought the old stories were just stories. I agreed with the boy's assessment of the curse - I believed you simply said he was Loki-confounded only because of some jealous rage at a slight offered by a twelve-year-old child. I did not interfere because I know that you have the village's respect, but I did try to make Gudleik's life easier where I could." The Jarl took a seat in one of the chairs that Gudleik had put in the stables so that he might relax when his tasks were completed. "Now, it seems, the whole thing was true all along." Jarl Heinrich paused. "What does this boy playing a lyre have to do with anything, Jogrim? Aren't wars fought with weapons and ships and armies?"

Jogrim crossed to a horse, put a hand up to its face, and muttered a curse when the animal tried to bite his fingers off. "Some wars are indeed fought that way. And some wars need strength of ax arm and skill with a shield and cunning strategy and all the rest. Other wars - well, other wars do not. There is a storm brewing, a clash of gods the like of which Midgard - and the lands beyond Midgard - have never seen. Men like his father and brothers, fighters in the realms of men, they can only draw power from the gods. Gudleik and his ilk - the skalds and poets - their magic is of a different kind. They have the power to alter the fabric of creation, simply using words and images. They are completely useless in a fight for a body's survival, but as for the battleground of a man's soul - they are unmatched." Jogrim took a swig from his flask. "Nonetheless, their foe remains one of the most wily and destructive, worse for a man even than the simplicity of a battle of arms."

"Oh," said the Jarl. "And what foe is that?"

"My own self," said Gudleik. "He's still in here, with me, my Lord," he added, tapping the side of his head. "Loki, I mean. He still plots to move my hand, to sway me from my path. He wants me to fuck up, more than anything in the world he wants me to make a mess of it. And he fights dirty and unfair and dreams that his will is stronger than mine."

"Ha, that is right, Gudleik," said Jogrim. "Gods are immortal - the only battles that they can fight are battles of will. Align yourself with your true source of will, and you will move mountains."

"How about I just learn how to get decent with the lyre, first?"

"Yes, let's try doing that," Jogrim agreed. "And fortunately, I have just the teacher for you."

"Come with us, father," said Porsi. He was standing at the threshold of the small room that had been their home since arriving in Ygglheim. His father had taken one look at Jogrim, listened to what the formerly blind Seer had to say, then turned on his heel and came back to his room, where a mid-afternoon lunch was awaiting him. Porsi was not far behind. "Your contract is just about up - I'm sure the Jarl will allow it. I know you would like to see Mimir's Rest again. I'm sure that Mother would be-"

"Don't presume to know anything about your mother, boy," muttered Randulf. "She left you, remember? She left you with me so she could go off drinking and pretending at that Thor-cursed lyre of hers."

"So, what? You'll stay here, with Jarl Heinrich? As I said, your bondsman's contract is nearly up. Do you think he will continue to let you simply live here?"

"I thought we would make for Thor's Land. See about maybe getting some work at the Nyxheim Mines. Do you remember that drifter Vilky? The shifty one who was looking for work on Rikard's boats? Before they ran him out of Ygglheim, I got to speaking with him about it. It's unskilled labour-"

"You're out of your bloody mind, Father - that's troll country! You'd risk getting your limbs torn off for what? The chance at whatever scraps of mithril the Thurisaz Company is willing to give up in exchange for your black lungs? People escape that place to come to Freyr's Land, not the other way around."

"If you think a former bondsman is getting a job in a place where everyone knows who he is, you're the one who's out of his mind," said Randulf. He had been eating his lunch - a bit of chicken and a few roasted tubers. For some reason, the food stopped agreeing with him. He put the chicken leg down and shook his head. "It'll be worse in Mimir's Rest. Ibrild's family will not have forgotten my face. I'm as likely to get shivved by her brother as survive a night in the tavern."

Porsi made fists with his hands, stopped, then took a deep breath and opened them again. He crossed to his bed, which was right next to his father's chair, and took a seat. Then he lay back and put his feet up.

"Damn it, boy, look at those boots! Atla will have your head!"

Porsi looked down, saw the mud, saw the staining on the wool, then shook his head and dropped them back to the floor.

"Do you know where that mud came from, father?" asked Porsi. "The fucking burial grounds. After dead people got up and nearly killed me. They killed more than half the village. The remaining people want me dead. If I go and you stay, you will be a constant reminder to them of their dead loved ones. It does not take a great mind to understand the implications of that particular problem." Porsi stood once more. "Look, I would like for you to come. To guide us. To help us find mother and to see if you can talk her into helping Gudleik learn how to play the lyre. I don't pretend to understand why it needs to be done, but I do know that I saw a Valkyrie this morning, I was nearly killed by purple magic, most of the people of this village are burning in a pyre outside, and a once-blind Seer now has his sight. If I'm trusting anyone with how to deal with this, it's the damn Seer. If you want to go play 'let's pretend nothing happened' up in Thor's Land, you can fill your fucking boots."

"Hah," said Randulf. "Of course you would say that now."

"Say what?"

"'Fill your boots,'" replied Randulf. "It was your mother's favourite thing to say, I used to think. I told her I was going out to work, 'fill your boots.' I was going to drink ale with my friends, 'fill your boots.' I was going to make love to her-"

"Odin's spear, Father, you really have to tell me this?" Randulf asked before pausing. "Really, she'd say that to you before you had sex? That's not very romantic or loving. In fact, it sounds like she was just dismissing you all the time. You do know that it means: 'just do whatever you want,' right?"

"Eh, you wouldn't understand," said Randulf. "It was a term of endearment when she said it."

"The stories you've told me, Father, all point to an inescapable truth." remarked Porsi.

"And that is?"

"Mother was a miserable fucking alcoholic cunt."

"Yes, but she was *my* miserable fucking alcoholic cunt," Randulf replied. A sense of wistfulness had invaded his tone.

"Alright, let's go to the Jarl and see if he will let me end my contract a few weeks early."

The trip to Mimir's Rest normally would have taken a few days, sailing down the coast in one of the ferries which sometimes ran between the small fishing towns and the main hub city of Freyr's Land. Given that all of the boats of Ygglheim had been taken by the draugr, the party of four had to set out on a walking journey to Mimir's Rest.

It had been named after a dead Aesir god, the wise counselor to Odin who had helped the All-father as he blundered his way through Asgardian history. During the war between the Aesir and the Vanir, two factions of gods, Mimir had been slain, though his effect on the world had not come to an end. It was said that Mimir kept a well of his own blood hidden from the gods - at least, that was the case until Odin coaxed him into giving him a drink of the stuff (after sacrificing one of his eyes to the thing, of course).

It wasn't quite the Mead of Poetry, a drink made from the blood of some strange being constructed from the spit of the Aesir and Vanir called Kvasir. That stuff was said to be shepherded by Bragi now, and given only to his most deserving skalds. But Mimir's blood was celebrated in its own way. It was said to be pure wisdom, and anyone who drank of it would be forever changed.

To be fair, it hadn't worked much of a charm on Odin. The All-father remained just as dense as he had been before he cut his eye out and offered it to his advisor before drinking the blood from the well. Still, Odin's relative ineptitude in matters of the mind was a well-kept Asgardian secret. Most mortals believed that Odin was as brilliant as Mimir had been before his death at the hands of the Vanir. The Seers of Upsalla were not so disengaged from the truth of the matter, but there was disagreement between even these wise keepers of the knowledge of the gods. Some whispered that, even though it might seem that he made stupid choices, Odin's decisions were born of a wisdom that went beyond rationality. What looked like foolishness was actually sense, and for him to engage in the sensible would have been the height of folly.

Few believed that line of thinking, though. Nor did many really question the fact that the creatures in their stories went around drinking blood all the time. It seemed like no one really had a problem with cannibalism, as long as it was in liquid form. Take one little bite of flesh, and you were an anti-social psychotic deviant, deserving of death. Drink the blood, all was well.

This was the argument in which the party was engaged when they came upon the dwarf in the middle of the road.

"Oh, so you'd just have us eating a roast leg of human, since the gods are drinking the blood of each other, is that it?" Jogrim asked Randulf.

"Look, all's I'm saying is that it don't make any sense. If you're going to be drinking blood, might as well go the whole meal deal, am I right? And didn't you tell us one time about some ancient southern barbarian gods that spent their time eating their mothers and fathers?"

"What?" returned Jogrim. "The Greeks? That was once - and it was the father who ate all the kids! He was a villain! He was killed and his family was imprisoned!" Jogrim paused. "Besides, those are all lies. Ours is the one true faith."

Randulf rolled his eyes. "Oh, give me a break - didn't you tell us that humans create gods and gods sustain humans? Doesn't that mean that there is no one true faith except all of them? That is why religion is deserving of our respect - not because it needs to be protected as the truth, but a human being's right to believe is a necessary part of the protection of fundamental freedom?"

"Ha!" said Jogrim, rubbing a tear of laughter from his eye. "No trouble telling that you've been on the bottom of the food chain for most of your life. 'Fundamental freedom,' he says. You were just freed as a bondsman - you wouldn't know fundamental freedom if it came up and bit you in the-"

"Uh, Jogrim," said Gudleik, "I think this needs your attention."

"Hark, O merry band of travelers," said the dwarf. He was dressed in extremely shiny plate armour, onto which a landscape of incredible detail had been carved. The interlinking breast and shoulder plates formed a kind of triptych that depicted wildlife like bears and foxes running wild on a backdrop of forest and fjord. It was a true crafted marvel and caught the eyes of all four of the men. They barely took notice of the ax hanging from the diminutive creature's belt, which was similarly beautiful and which had an edge so keen the morning sun glinted off the polished surface. Next to him was a cart, one whose axle was broken. The leather straps which had been used to attach the cart to a missing beast of burden looked as though they had snapped as well. In fact, the extremely well-kept dwarf was a strange contrast to the wreck of a cart next to him, but a dissonance that none of the men took heed.

"My name is Ruvark the Magnificent, and I need your aid."

"Uhh," said Jogrim, at an uncharacteristic loss for words.

"You're a bit south for a dwarf," said Randulf, no man for niceties. "You've got your papers?"

"Erm," said Ruvark. "Well, that's quite an opener. Can't say I'm surprised, though. You're humans who don't seem to have seen the shiny side of a chunk of mithril in an elf's age. Hel's breath, you look like slaves, the lot of you. Except you, holy man. Only, not quite a holy man with those peepers looking like that. Not even proper blind: did you flunk out of Upsalla?"

"Alright, how about we stop insulting each other," said Gudleik, interposing himself between Ruvark and the two older men of his party. "I apologize for Randulf's behaviour, Ruvark. As it happens, you are correct: he's a recently freed bondsman. The rest of us, well, you're just insulting our clothing." Gudleik looked down at his own tunic, which had seen the better side of a hundred washings. The red dye had faded to a light pink.

Ruvark stroked his prodigiously large black beard and considered the lanky young man before him. "Fair enough," said the dwarf. "Now, as I was saying, I need your aid! My cart has just fallen broken and my ass has escaped. I am in need of a good woodworker and blacksmith. Perhaps you could make a trip to Mimir's Rest for me and call on their services?"

Gudleik looked at the dwarf, then at the cart, then back at the dwarf. Then he shook his head. "That cart looks like it's been sitting there for over a year. There's grass poking up through one of the axles. Besides, you're a dwarf. You're wearing a work of art, that I'm sure you smithed yourself. What's the scam?"

"Scam? No scam, kind sir," said Ruvark, visibly sweating under the mild interrogation. "I simply need... alright, look. The blacksmith is my friend Ivaldi. I need to speak to him, but if I go to the gates they'll nab me. I don't have any fucking papers." Ruvark paused. "You happy?"

"Not particularly," said Gudleik, considering the carnage of the past few days.

"Yeah, well that makes two of us," agreed the dwarf.

"Look, let's just leave the ankle-biter to his own devices, yeah?" said Randulf.

"Father, I didn't know you were such a virulent fucking racist," Porsi accused. "For the love of Odin, he doesn't seem all that bad."

"Aye, they don't seem all that bad - not until they're at you with one of their axes, taking swings at your nut sack because that's all they can reach."

"Fought in the wars, did you?" asked Ruvark. "What Clan were you with? One of the mercenaries? Or a blue whale?"

"I was a merc. Bear, of course," said Randulf, indignant. "Red bear. Before my bondsman days, I spent two summers up north, keeping you bastards from coming down that mountain. I'm a fucking true Freyr's Land patriot, dwarf."

"You fought well," replied Ruvark in measured tones. "Better than most. If you red bears hadn't been in the mix, I'm not sure you humans would have won. Lost my little brother Tugert to one of your swords."

Randulf looked at the dwarf, feeling the sting of shame creep in at the edges of his face. "Erm, yes, well. I lost my father to one of your axes. Never really had an easy time letting it go."

Silence reigned for a while.

"I expect you tried telling passing travelers the truth and were laughed off, were you?" Jogrim asked, breaking the silence. "It's only been a score of years since the wars ended. There's still quite a bit of bad blood."

Ruvark nodded. "Look, I'm just trying to get word to Ivaldi that his mother has passed. He's got to come home to the Eddas to see her buried." Ruvark looked down at his breastplate. "I can't take credit for this - it was his work. He's our best, you know. The best blacksmith in all of the Edda Mountains, which means he's the best blacksmith in Midgard.

Hell, not just smithing - he can craft anything and do the damndest job of it. It's the reason he got his papers and why I'm out here, looking for strangers to pass a message on to my friend."

"How'd he end up here, then?" asked Randulf. "If he's really so good, then why's he not at home with the rest of your kind?"

Ruvark sneered at Randulf for a moment before composing himself. "Family trouble," replied the dwarf, shaking his head. "It's hard to be the son of the King."

"This friend of yours is the Prince?" asked Porsi. "Son of King Hreidmar? That means that-"

"Yes," muttered the dwarf. "Queen Branwyn is dead."

Silence again.

"I suppose that means that..."

"Again: yes," replied Ruvark, sighing. "It's just a matter of time before the wars begin anew."

The city of Mimir's Rest was something the like of which neither Porsi nor Gudleik had ever laid eyes on before. It was a sprawl that stretched out from the gates nearly a mile in each direction. It was walled, too, with great parapets made of wood and stone that cut a lip over the top of the dozen-and-a-half foot high walls. The doors were enormous, but they were pushed open when they arrived, given that it was morning. A foursome of guards with round shields on their backs and axes on their hips stood vigilant, watching the bustle of the crowd in motion.

And there was a crowd, a massive throng of sweaty and noisy Norsemen who were filing in and out of the place, casting smells and sights that were disorienting to the young men. What could only be traveling merchants were dragging little carts with their wares, sacks of grain, clay pots filled with milk, sealed horns and dried herbs. There were beasts of burden - asses, oxen, and horses - pulling some of these. A pair of shifty men eying one particular cart and muttering to each other were interrupted by one of the guards and told to move along. Another duo, an older woman and a younger, bearing arms which looked keener than those of the guards, laughed with each other as they exited the city. A family of four here, a pair of bearded old men, a jester bearing a lyre...

Gudleik's hand instinctively flew to his own instrument. It was still there, safe on his back, in the boar's hide case it had come in. Gudleik's lyre was not exactly a masterwork of Norse craftsmanship. He had bought it for a few coppers from a drunken besotted mess of a jester, who was down on his luck and desperate for a bit of mead. Gudleik had earned the money in Jarl Heinrich's employ, a pittance that had rendered unto the lad an instrument that he might learn to play in an effort to reach skaldhood.

How strange his dream seemed now. When it arrived upon him, things were so... so... different. He was a child, he was Loki-cursed, and he assumed that he was going to be killed when his father forced him to accompany him on a summer raid during the coming summer. He put all of his chips on the bet of skaldhood. He spent every waking moment he could, practicing to be a skald. But because of the curse, he simply could not get better. No matter how much time he put in, his notes all sounded off. He simply could not play the damn thing properly. And sing? Best not even to get into his ability to do that.

But now, after what had happened in Jogrim's temple, when the old bastard had given him the mead and the visions came... was that even real life? Had he really had a conversation with a god? Or was it just the mushrooms the

Seer had put into the drink? Gudleik didn't think that he sounded any differently when he tried plucking a few notes on his lyre, but there was a strange aspect to the music now. Something had shifted within his mind. It was almost as if he could sense striations in the air that vibrated with the sounds, a stratification between the notes and how these pieces of the puzzle suddenly fit together. His fingers still did not work properly, that much was clear. But it had given him hope - all of it.

Certainly Jogrim believed in Gudleik. It was an about-face that was just as shocking as the fact that the Seer could actually now... well, see. Gudleik never thought he'd see the day that he was comforted by Jogrim's presence, but here he was, sticking close to Jogrim as his party marched into this wild and wonderful place that was Mimir's Rest. It was almost as if the old man had become... family? After hating him for so long, then losing all of his family... well, nearly all of his family.

Gudleik's interaction with his mother had not gone as well as what had happened with Jogrim – and that would be understating the matter. At least she had not disowned him in front of everyone in the village. At least there was that.

"Gudleik," whispered Porsi hoarsely, drawing the boy back into the present moment. "Look, over there! See that cracked bow that they've placed next to the doorstep of that building? The one with the mallard's head drawn on the sign above? Father says that means it's a brothel! A brothel, brother."

"And I suppose you'd like for me to go with you, be your literal brothel brother, is that it?" Gudleik asked. "Bragi's mead, Porsi, we have not been here more than five minutes, and you want to spend money we don't have on paid sex?" Gudleik laughed at the earnest expression on his friend's face, then considered the curse he had just uttered. He had named

Bragi without even thinking twice about it. Did that perhaps mean that what had happened in the temple was true?

"I'm just saying," Porsi said, his face reddening. "I mean, we're on some hare-brained quest to save the world from Ragnarok. Full of danger and ill portent, and I'm the fucking sidekick. You'd think you'd not think harshly of me for wanting to get my dick sucked at least once before I died."

"Sidekick?" Gudleik asked. "What makes you say that?"

"Oh, come off it, Gudleik," said Porsi. "You're the one who's immune to the effects of the draugr. You're the one who has two gods fighting for control of your mind. You're the one who's got to learn how to play the lyre from my cunt mother. You're the one who's supposed to write the saga to end all sagas."

"Loki's Grin, Porsi," Gudleik replied, "You need to stop listening to Jogrim. I've come to appreciate him but he's been going around half-cocked and prophesying like a fool ever since he got his sight back."

Hmm, ruminated Gudleik. An unplanned reference to Loki in his speech. There was still plenty of reason to be cautious.

"Yes, well," said Porsi. "All I'm saying is that you are the one who's destined to become a star or whatever. All I'm trying to do is survive."

"Look, Porsi," said Gudleik. "This past week has been one of the strangest ones I have ever experienced. I don't even know what to say about it, except that I did not for a moment expect that life would turn out this way. I expected that I would be dead to a barbarian's sword in some foreign land when my father took me on a summer raid. Jogrim might think that I am destined for some great thing, but I do not know. I know that he gave me some mushroom-laced mead and I spoke to some thing that said it was Bragi and I was his chosen. But, for the love of the god of poetry himself, we've had mushrooms before." Gudleik paused. "Remember that time that you thought I had transformed into a bear and I was going to strike you down? No matter what I said to you, you believed that to be true. And it most definitely isn't. Think about that."

Porsi looked at his friend with a frown. "I don't think this is the same thing, Gudleik. And I don't think that you think it is eith-"

"Give me that fucking thing on your back or this dagger and your spleen become friends, boy," breathed a gruff male voice behind Gudleik. "Good friends." He felt a rough hand grab his forearm and the point of something sharp dig into his flank.

"Erm," whispered Gudleik, "that's my lyre."

Gudleik looked around. They were somewhere in the city, perhaps the market square. Strange faces shuffled to and fro, opening sight lines to merchants hawking their wares from stalls and customers fishing mithril from pouches. Neither Jogrim nor Randulf were in sight. The young men were so lost in conversation that they had completely lost track of where they were going and apparently the older ones in the party had not the presence of mind to keep an eye to them. Porsi was looking at Gudleik, his eyes wide with terror as he surveyed what was behind his friend. He held up three fingers with his hand - there were three thieves. Gudleik's heart raced as he started to shrug off the strap to the lyre case.

"Yes, that's it, my little gosling," said the voice. "I'll have that sword of yours as well."

Gudleik looked down at the hilt of his father's sword. He had collected it up from the temple grounds after Gudleik failed to kill his father's undead assailant and the man fell dead from the draugr magic. A silver bear's head was carved into the pommel, a symbol of the Freyr's Land Warrior Clan.

It was all he had left. These despicable muggers could have the fucking lyre, but he was not about to give up the sword. He started to turn, then was roughly slammed back into place.

"Ah, ah, ah," said the man, pressing the dagger in further. "Look over in front of you, to the wall. See that guard standing there? That's Olaf, our friend. We gut you, he does nothing. You hear me? Nothing. You try to fight us and you'll find yourself in Jarl Danski's dungeon quicker than you can blink your fucking eye, you mincing little cock meat." The voice laughed. "That is, if we don't gut you first." Another pause. "You know what? I'm just going to do this."

Gudleik felt a hot mixture of emotions as his sword was removed from its sheath by the thief. He had spent his younger days hating Jogrim, the blind old drunk of a Seer who had stolen away his life. It was a simmering coal of hatred, one that had not winked out until recently, when things changed so drastically. But here, now, the hot fires of murderous rage were kindled in Gudleik's breast. He sensed the dagger strapped to his breast, an artifact from his father's war training. "Always carry an extra blade," Sigbjorn had told him as a boy, and expected him to be wearing one as he went about his daily business. All it would take would be one swift pull, a whirl, and he could bury the thing in the man's neck.

Two things happened then, in Gudleik's mind. The first was a cackle of delight, a maniacal laugh that sounded both familiar and strange to Gudleik. The laughter was comforting to Gudleik, and part of him wanted to serve it, to do what it wanted - and it wanted chaos and death. The idea of the dagger was absolutely wonderful to this part of the young man. Gudleik put a hand to the dagger.

Then, something else filtered down through his senses. It was music, notes played on a lyre. The melody was soft and soothing and offered a taste of peace to the young man. As he listened, the fire in his heart was quenched. He felt his grip on the hilt lessen and he managed to breathe a bit easier.

"Hey, Agnarr," called a different voice behind Gudleik. "I think 'e's got a dagger of 'e's own! Look of 'im!"

Gudleik felt a rushing of air and a thumping before everything went black.

By the Skin of His Jacobs

The wringing of hands is and always will be a cross-species symbol of cowardliness, exceptionally so when there is an untrustworthy aspect to the hand-wringer. Being a cowardly and treacherous goblin, said wringer fit the standard bill and was in the middle of working up some friction heat when he heard a shout that pulled him from his consideration of the scene before him. The goblin was the newly-appointed High Priest of Dagon, the shouter was the Goblin King. The scene before them, well, it was not exactly an idyllic meadow showered in the summer sun, which was exactly the type of goblin-despised imagery that they had left behind in the Slithering Depths. Instead, the sky was grey, the field was the brown which comes after the spring thaw, and upon the field there stood several neophytes of the newly-founded cult, awaiting their initiatory rites.

"Baldrick!" repeated the Goblin King. "If you're not going to do what you're supposed to, I'll sacrifice you to Dagon myself and replace you with another goblin who isn't such a feeble little gobshite. Say your pretty words and make with the blood oaths! And if you're too squeamish for the grand finale, get the new bloods to do it themselves!"

Goblin dress was one of the few things that had not changed since the goblins left the Slithering Depths. They liked their clothing to be threadbare, dyed one of three different shades of shite brown, and the stitching was meant to be coarse and poorly done. In fact, the more one looked like what an aristocratic and less socially-conscious member of Albian society might term a 'filthy vagrant,' the more distinguished the goblin was considered to appear.

Along with many other standard mores of goblin society, the Goblin King had abandoned his dress. He was no longer dressed in his regular browns. Instead, he had begun wearing something that not a single goblin had ever laid eyes on before. It was a type of finery, but the kind of finery that mermaid or merman might have chosen. Sequined with fish scales, layered with chains of seashells and cod heads, the Goblin King was dressed in a bright orange and purple tunic that stank to high heaven of aged chum. In the center of his chest he wore a strangely filigreed bit of gold in the shape of a snake curled into an 'S.' On closer inspection, you could see that it looked more like a double-ended fish hook.

It was a nautical style, to say the least. Aside from the stench of rotten fish guts, it was despised as strange by goblinkind. Everyone who had looked upon the Goblin King since 'The Change,' as his strange new deal with the foreign god had come to be known, felt as much. They would not raise their misgivings with him, though. Instead, they cowered at their leader. Before The Change, the Goblin King was renowned and feared by his own kind. He had trained and trained himself into becoming a rather middling swordsman, which put him head and shoulders above the rest of his militarily useless kin. But now, with the aid of this foreign marine god named Dagon, he had become something different altogether. Hanging from his hip was a strange blade, called a 'cutlass' by the King, said to be a gift from Dagon himself when he swore his blood oath to the jellyfish-like behemoth whose effigies were found everywhere around Pustule Hall. The sword hilt was covered in living barnacles that seemed to shiver and swell whenever the sword was drawn. It made all of the goblins uneasy, but no one was going to say a word to their King.

Not after what had happened the day after the oath was sworn.

Baldrick pushed all of his misgivings to one side and walked up onto the makeshift dais that had been placed in the field outside Pustule Hall. He put one green and warty hand on the cover of the old tome, whose battered leather cover looked as if it had seen better days. By all accounts, it just looked like an old and yellowing book. The moment he touched it, though, a ripple ran across the surface, which traced the outline of a face. One that was bald, hooked-featured, and frozen in a mask of anguish. A shriek resounded in Baldrick's head, a sound to which the goblin knew from experience that only he was privy. It didn't really shock or dismay him much, though - he was used to the foul ministrations of one of the twin goblin deities, Gluttor, Lord of Pain (his counter-point being Gamblor, Lord of Gambling). Former deities, Baldrick should think, if the King gets his way. Baldrick cleared his throat and began to read.

"Dagon, Lord of the Fishies, won't you smack your rubbery lips upon these unworthy ingrates? Won't you spread your Roe of Despair upon the lands [insert name of land for theological conquest here]?"

123

"Albion, you touched sod!" said the Goblin King, cuffing Baldrick. "You're supposed to say 'Albion'!"

"Oh, right," said Baldrick. "Sorry, I forgot!"

"I'll forget you're my High Priest if you don't smarten up, you knob!" The Goblin King made an exaggerated show of looking down at his sword then back up at Baldrick. The High Priest gulped and continued.

"Won't you spread your Roe of despair upon the lands of Albion? Won't you engage in- do I really have to say this?"

"Yes! For the hundredth time, yes!" said the Goblin King. "Do I need to pull my cutlass on you again?

"No, my liege," quailed Baldrick. "I'll be good! Ahem. Won't you engage in aquatic intercourse somehow magically on dry land in a spectacle that will make the unbelievers change their minds?"

"Best show I ever seent," offered one of the neophytes. "Dat enormous jellyfish floatin' in and giving the business to da Goblin Queen! She looked like it were da best ride o' her life! Can't wait to swear me fealty to dat beast - 'e knows 'ow ta fuck!"

"Silence, knave!" shouted the King. "That's my wife you're talking about!"

Dagon had made the request for vestal virgins from the Goblin King - that was the god's particular kink. Which was indeed quite deity-esque, when it came to requests. But, given that goblins tended to have sexual intercourse when they were very young, the King found himself fresh out of unsexed green skins. Seeing an opportunity to defy the King, the Goblin Queen, long bored with her husband's ugliness and unexciting ministrations, offered her services to Dagon and the jellyfish god quickly acquiesced. When the King tried to deny his new god his desire, Dagon responded by bellowing a long and drawn out diatribe about being Dagon, Lord of the

Fishies, owed sex by all living things, how for a near-sessile gelatinous type he could produce an erection harder than diamond. There were also several promises of a hellish ride through an eternity of damnation if the Goblin King tried to interfere with the sex show.

"It's how I introduce myself to all my new worshipers," had said Dagon with finality. "They's gotsta know - Dagon fucks. I can promise them all of the riches in the world, but as soon as they seen my jelly cock hard up and penetrate my next lady love, they know - Dagon's crew is the place to be." Dagon paused. "Plus I'll make y'all really good with swords and shite so you can kill those humans or whatever. Yo, Queenie, honey, let's see dem tittays!"

Unfortunately for the Goblin King's pride, his wife was all too keen on showing her misshapen and hairy breasts to the undulating and amorphous mass that was Dagon.

"Nice," said Dagon. "You goblin bitches might be ugly to dem humans, but I ain't judgin'. Hell, y'all look good to me - I'll couple with a rock, as long as there's a bit of heat in that hole, know'm sayin'?"

"I don't even know where your eyes are," the Goblin Queen tittered.

"I ain't need 'em," said Dagon, whose voice reverberated throughout the throne room of Pustule Hall. "I'm a god, baby, I'm omniscient, omnipresent, an' my jelly cock gonna make you sing!"

The Goblin King shrugged off his memory. He also shrugged off the memory that came after that one, where he went through his shantytown kingdom, pulling his cutlass and randomly slaying his subjects out of pure, frustrated ire, solidifying his reputation as a tyrant and enlarging their estimation of the marine god's power further. Even worse was the one that came after that one, when he discovered that Dagon had actually...

No, no time to think about that. He had sworn the blood oath to Dagon, which meant he was locked in now. And Dagon needed worshipers the way the Goblin King needed to eat some pork and drink some beer - lots of beer - after the day's labours were complete.

Mercifully, Baldrick had gone around with the dagger while the Goblin King was deep in his ruminations. Each had sliced open his scrotum and placed a barnacle inside. The blood oath was sworn, the King could go. Once the damnable incantation was complete, of course.

"By the Skin of His Jacobs, He whose Immaculate Jelly Ballsack shall never be torn asunder, neither by foe nor by... do I *really* have to read this?"

"Read the fucking passage, you cowardly shite," said the King, drawing his cutlass and pointing it at his High Priest. "My patience is at an end, Baldrick."

"Whose Immaculate Jelly Ballsack shall never be torn asunder, neither by foe nor by jilted bitch lover who couldn't be satisfied with just a taste of what Dagon is packing, I pronounce thee Priests of the Esoteric Order of Dagon. Amen."

"A-fucking-men," breathed the King.

avalon

When Queen Brighid was deciding how to create her Otherworld, the place that came to be known as Avalon in the Blessed Isles, she found herself continually recreating her portion of the Sidhe, her little compartment within the realm of the other gods from the pantheon known as Danu's Children. Her own little slice of the Sidhe, like all of the gods' homes, was a reflection of her spirit. In Brighid's case, that spirit was kind but stern, beautiful and severe, expressive yet taciturn. In the result, her transcendent place was always well-kept, but not sterile. It felt like home, but it also felt like one would get a pretty serious talking to if one made a mess. There were doilies and expensive-looking china in glass cupboards, but there was also a hearth and a big friendly dog named Ox lying upon it. There were portraits of the Queen looking as though she could not pass her daily stool on the wall, and yet she was possessed of a little anachronistic device she had taken from a future realm called a phonograph that played music from what she called the 'big bandera.'

Like her main acolytes within the human realm, Merlyn and Morgan Le Fay, Queen Brighid was quite an advanced fan of flying through the fourth dimension, into the far reaches of time. She might find herself exploring a world where worship to her and her brethren died out, concrete landscapes that spewed poison in the air, an environmental disaster where human beings, like birds with bowel problems, had effectively fouled their own nest. Yet, in spite of the dreariness that surrounded the place at times, these future humans, like people throughout time, were possessed of that divine spark of creation that saw beauty emerge from the depths of their souls. Brighid spent little time in the past, though she did like to drop in on an ancient version of Athens, when the Greek Empire was at its height, from time to time. There she met other gods, ones who seemed like they might have been cousins to Danu's Children, so similar were they in style and purpose for their being.

It was around this point when Brighid began to question the necessity of gods at all. She saw how these ancient gods were involved in the exact same internecine strife that wracked her own familial relations. Brighid's counterpart, a god named Apollo, seemed to be the sole member of his divine tribe to have his eyes open to what was going on. Like Brighid, he was a healer of the soul and of the body. He was the one who inspired poets to channel beauty, he was the one who helped the healers of his world conduct their medical work. He had little concern for the petty squabbles of his brethren - all he wanted to do was to help elevate humans to levels of self-actualization beyond themselves. Brighid fell in love with Apollo (though how that love fell apart that is a story for another day). So similar were they, that perhaps their love never truly had a chance - they had everything in common. Perhaps too much. Beyond healing and poetry, her handsome lover Apollo had an ally named Hermes, just as

Brighid found herself drawn into league with her brother, Lugh. At least, an ally in name only.

Lugh, the smiling knife, the one who had stabbed Brighid in the back after she shared her own vulnerability with him. He had gone straight to Danu with Brighid's misgivings about the direction of the pantheon. Spurred by her encounters with exotic and ancient Apollo, Brighid wondered aloud to her brother whether or not it would behoove Danu's Children to help the people to become more open to foreigners. Perhaps there could be a blending, a melding with the wandering humans who continually spread about the worlds of men, bearing new gods. Instead of going to war with the gods of other civilizations of men, as was the wont of all of the extant gods of Brighid's time, at least in her part of the world, perhaps they might try to broker a peace. It would mean the death of fewer humans, Brighid had intimated. In the world of the future, such ideas as the value of life are treasured. Sectarianism and violence were in many places discarded as ideas of the past - compassion and understanding reigned and life had become so comparatively good for the humans.

During that first conversation with Lugh, when Brighid was still a member of Danu's Children and became all too keenly aware of her isolation in matters of thought, her brother had asked her, "there is still darkness, is there not? In the human realms of the future? I, Lugh, may merely be the Lord of Light and without the same means of time travel as you, dear sister, but there is no doubt in my mind that there are still shadows against which the humans of the coming years are pitted. Why can you not simply be content to simply exist now, during your own time? I expect you did not encounter a version of yourself in this future of yours."

"No, I did not," admitted Brighid. "We lose to the... well, I've already told you who ends up killing us all. No need to go over that again. And yes, there is still darkness. But we are given a chance now, to speed the evolution of the human race. We could whisper our truths about love and compassion to our people, that they might open their arms to-"

"You know who you sound like, don't you?" asked Lugh. "You saw the future and, as you say, you shared it with me. You sound just like those snakes who are going to kill your father. The Dagda's fate is sealed, thanks to the Brothers of Christ. They all will seem so innocent at first, with their brown robes and crucifixes and big books. They will speak of compassion and love and the mercy of their Christ. And then the fucking clubs will come out."

"They are simply misguided," replied Brighid. "They take everything about that story of that carpenter to be literal truth! They think that there was actually this Yeshua character and he literally died and was reborn, that he literally created miracles... and perhaps he did, perhaps he didn't. But rather than looking at the story as evidence that we all might be conduits for miraculous feats and unconditional love, they came up with this ignorant idea that the nature of God's existence is separate from the operation of the human mind."

"Yes, well, that's the nature of humanity, is it not? To at-large misunderstand deities as facts rather than metaphors for the unspeakable transcendent? You would change this aspect of human life? Would you prefer that every human was born with a perfect understanding of what divinity is and what our existence means for humanity? Where's the bloody fun in that?"

Brighid went silent for a while. "I would prefer that we at least tried to create some sort of peace! I am sick of watching human beings die for no good reason."

"You, of all gods, talk of death?" laughed Lugh. "You give our people immortality. Forget Aengus Og's beauty, you are the goddess of poetry. You alone are the reason that the eternal lives in the lives of men. All of this - all of us - we could not be here if not for your intercession with human beings."

"I would give them more, brother," said Brighid. "I would give them the power to create their own destinies. I would give miracles to the masses, without keeping the gate. I would allow them to access the Fundament, the creative energy that underpins everything. Not just certain strange and misunderstood types - I would allow all to access the Fundament. Why must they first cast off their own ignorance before they can achieve the impossible?"

"You're so bound up in ideas of individualism," said Lugh, shaking his head. "You would give power to the ignorant at the peril of the world. You have spent too much time in those future realms, sister. You assume that all human beings *should* have this, that it would be an intelligent thing to offer up power to everyone. The condition precedent for power - true power - must remain a lack of desire to exercise that power. If you change that rule, everything would spin out of control. Power is not something to be aspired to - service should be the goal, power a side-effect. Power should be stumbled upon by one seeking to serve. What that service looks like will be different for all beings, but they must kill their separated selves before they are given miracles. They must see our aspects in themselves before they are given the keys to the kingdom. That is the rule that binds all of us gods together - no matter the pantheon."

131

"You're wrong, brother," assessed Brighid. "You are all wrong. You simply do not trust humans with creation, whereas I wish to see all of humanity shine with the light that we jealously hoard for ourselves."

"You - you're serious, aren't you?" asked Lugh, his eyes wide. "You actually believe in what you're saying. It-it's-it's treason! You speak of treason, sister. Against all of us. Your dream will kill us all. The mystery must remain a mystery. Without the mystery, we return to the void. You're not a human - you remember what the void is. You know what it was like to live a life where all is known. Not even the worst of Clapperleg's horrors comes close to what we escaped, sister."

"I've thought of a failsafe," said the goddess. "One that will keep the humans in line. If they use miracles to go beyond what is possible while maintaining the mystery, they will become impossible themselves. They will transform into this type of creature, a faery. They will be able to live in a grand world of my devising, a place called Avalon. There they shall be allowed to live out their lives in a realm of pure imagination, where they will not interfere with the realm of the physical. No one who fails to learn the fundamental lesson of creation shall die, they shall simply transform into something... less dangerous."

"Life as a magical construct - that sounds much better than death," scoffed Lugh. Then he softened. "Why, Brighid? Why do you want to do this so badly? You know that you have my support in all that you do, but you will be opposed by the others. None of us are irreplaceable - you court your own death. And you are a goddess, Brighid, not a human. You are not immortal through rebirth. If you die, there is no coming back from it. You do understand that, don't you?"

"Is that a threat?"

"It's a request that you consider what you are proposing before you make any rash decisions," said Lugh. "I say this only because I care for you."

Yes, he cared for me, Brighid decided, after the divine hit squad had shown up in her portion of the Sidhe, bearing their silvered weapons and trying to strike her as she slept. But Brighid had planned for that eventuality, catching the ear of a human as a child and making sure that the boy survived the goddess' *Forgetting* to spread Brighid's particular brand of revelation to others. She was weakened, of course, because Belenus had exercised his fatal power. He sapped the memory of her worshipers before the attack. But still, once that single boy bent the ear of her old worshipers, the ones whose minds had been interfered with by Belenus, these others fell right back into line and Brighid was restored. She bound them to her, asked for their sacrifice, and created her first faeries and their homeland, Avalon. Receiving worship from non-human sources was unheard of in the Blessed Isles - all over creation, even (although some ancient and daemoniac gods had mastered the trick millennia before Danu and her children gained their status). But the faeries managed it easily enough. Which meant that Brighid had become immortal. Not even Danu herself was as powerful as Brighid had become.

Still, though, in spite of all that, Brighid did actually want to make things better for the humans. That was her sole aim. So she created her own brand of miracles out of the Fundament. She called it magic, and gave it to her acolytes once they swore their blood oaths to their new goddess. She wanted to have a more human title, though one that carried her grandeur (like all gods, humility was hardly her strong suit) so she told her worshipers to call her Queen Brighid. These humans were all given the rules of creation during their initiatory rites. If they stepped out of line, they would become faeries. Their physical bodies would die and they would transcend to Avalon, where they would be fated to live until their true death took them (which only could occur from physical violence). It did mean that they would be pulled out of the human cycle of death and rebirth, which meant death for faeries would become truly final, just like a god's.

In truth, Brighid knew that she could not actually break the rules of creation. She could only bend them. Which is why she had to make a mechanism like transformation into a faery as a consequence for flying too close to the sun. For every action, there had to be a balancing reaction. She tried to communicate this to her followers, but many did not listen, except for a few wise holdouts like Merlyn and Morgan. Now, Brighid was stewarding an Avalon full-to-bursting with faeries and she could barely remember why she had done what she had done in the first place.

"I've made a huge mistake," she remarked to no one in particular, standing at her balcony overlooking the greenery of the world. Avalon was indeed beautiful, full of game and lush greenery and ponds and lakes and beauty. Faeries were flitting about everywhere, fornicating and teasing each other. It was truly idyllic. At least, this particular picture of the place. In another part of the world, she knew, the place where the true depths of her mistake were known, she knew that the fallen faeries were trudging about, wingless and ugly and causing each other pain. Out of this misery, they had forgotten Brighid and created new gods, ones of pain and... gambling, of all things. The goblins had even taken to calling Avalon – pure and beautiful Avalon – the Slithering Depths! All of Brighid's calculations had been for naught, because of her hubris. Avalon was, to some extent, a microcosm of the human world. And for all of her beauty and joy, pain and suffering needed to balance it out in equal measure.

"I should have listened to Lugh," Brighid said, again to her empty chamber. At least, she thought it was empty. "I should have known that I could not create a world without pain and suffering, that balance would be kept. Instead, the fucking *Fundament* created these damned goblins and they seek to spread discord across Blessed Isles. And now they are in league with one of the Great Old Ones... Danu on a fucking cracker."

"Erm, my Lady?" asked Donk. "Da goblins were your creation?"

"What?" said Queen Brighid, whirling. "Oh, Donk. And Enyd. And... a human? In Avalon?"

"Umm, Rosmerta O'Ceallaigh, at your service." Rosmerta did a small curtsy and wiped a bit of soot from her forehead. "Umm..."

"Queen Brighid."

"The Queen Brighid?" Rosmerta asked, eyes wide.

The Queen simply smiled and nodded.

"We just portaled in, my Lady," said Enyd. "Didn't have time to pick where we landed. We were in a bit of a bind back at Rosie's house. Sorry we disturbed you."

"No, not at all, not at all," said Queen Brighid, crossing to a small circular table she kept in her bedchamber. It was made of carved white wood, but its surface gleamed like the moon. The patterning on the grain was strange, all curved and twisted. It almost looked as if it were made of wicker, except that upon closer inspection Rosmerta saw that it was indeed solid wood. Carved wood, but solid wood. Solid wood that emanated heat. Brighid pulled a chair out for Rosmerta and said, "Please, sit down." The two faeries sailed over to the bed and had a seat next to each other. Rosmerta began to sit down, then realized she had her lute thrown over her shoulder. And that she was butt naked.

135

"Erm, I appear to have left all of my clothes," said Rosmerta. "Mother always told me I shouldn't sleep naked, that perhaps a shift would be in order, but I always liked-"

Queen Brighid put a finger to Rosmerta's lips and touched her shoulder. From the shoulder a strange clinging dress unwound along her flesh, wrapping around each limb and her trunk before becoming something similar, though a separate garment, on her legs. It was a leotard and tights, just as Enyd wore. On it, a strange orange and circular pattern was visible, much different than the black one Enyd wore. At least, what she normally wore - both Enyd and Donk were as naked as Rosmerta, something which Queen Brighid pointed out by clearing her throat. Brighid smiled and tapped her two faeries on the shoulders. Similar leotards emerged on Enyd and Donk. On their legs, each of the three sprouted black tubular cloth coverings that bunched around the mid-calf.

"Bad-ass leopard print, yes?" the Queen offered cryptically to Rosmerta, pointing at the leotards. "And the leg warmers are a nice touch, I thought. From my favourite decade in the twentieth century - the *ey-tees*. I've no problem with nakedness," she added, sitting down. "I'm certainly no Christian. But you'll all catch a draft if I didn't put something on you. Avalon is modeled after your homeland, after all. And it's not the warmest season, spring." The Queen turned to Rosmerta, black hair dropping into her eye as she did so. She brushed it away. "Now, dearest, won't you tell me what happened? What brings you to Avalon - do you wish to swear the oath?"

"Erm," said Rosmerta, suddenly feeling very small. She looked to Enyd, who was beaming at the idea. Her face dropped when she spoke next. "No, Queen Brighid. That is not why I am here. I was asleep, then suddenly I woke up with those two banging on my window and smoke pouring into my chamber from the main part of my cottage. There was no way out, so they conjured the portal, and, well, here we are. I have no idea what happened."

"It were a Christian monk," offered Donk. "Could tell by he's habit and all."

"Yes," said Enyd, shaking her head. "Thank you, Donk, fer dat wonderful illumination. My Lady, it were dat Brother Winfridus again. After what 'appened wit' Cernunnos and da angel Cassiel, I expect da angel were looking for revenge."

"From her?" asked Queen Brighid. "You tell me that Rosmerta has yet to swear her oath to Cernunnos. That is the case, is it not?" The Queen turned to Rosmerta once more. "You are still finding your way, are you not? Trying to make a decision about which god you might support?"

"Uh, yes, my, uh, Lady," said Rosmerta.

"Tell me, please, Rosie - do you mind if I call you Rosie?"

"No, my Lady," blushed Rosmerta.

"Call me Brighid," said Queen Brighid. "So please, tell me: what do you desire most in life?"

"I... I... Well, that is..." Rosmerta's quavering was accompanied by a rush of her own mind, a streaking through which was guided by an anxiety about what she might say to the figure seated with her, the Queen of the Faeries! What would she tell her? That Rosmerta dreamed of becoming a master bard, that the lute she had just laid down was the key to her dreams, that she wanted to do nothing more than to write great ballads about the epic heroism of Camelot and its knights? That she wished to become a courtier in Arthur's court?

"My father says that I should become a druid," Rosmerta replied weakly.

"Pardon my French, but I do not give a fuck what your father says," Queen Brighid stated flatly. She looked at

Rosmerta, smiled patiently, then waved her hand in the air. A puff of pink smoke emerged from the goddess' palm with a small snapping sound, and suddenly a small set of strangely painted vessels arranged neatly on a silvern tray appeared betwixt them. "Tea," said the Queen. "From the Orient... or, I should say, Asia. That's probably more politically correct... wait, which comes first? The Orient or Asia? Don't want to be racist here, in front of the guest..."

"My Lady?" asked Rosmerta.

"She talks to 'erself a lot about strange stuff nayn o' us can parse," assessed Donk. "Like, a lot."

"Thank you, Donk," said Queen Brighid. "Call it an artifact of time travel, Rosie. I get confused quite a bit. Flitting between bits of social evolution all the while." The Queen smiled. "Please, drink the tea."

Rosmerta complied. As she did, it was as if a warm blanket had been thrown over her shoulders. All of the tightness that normally had her chest squeezed into a ball began to slacken.

"There," said the Queen. "Poppy tea. Isn't that better?"

"Poppy tea?" asked Enyd. "You druggin' my Rosie, my Lady?"

"What? Oh, right. Yes, well, there is going to be a period in the future where casual drug use will be alright, and then it will be said to be bad, and people will get killed over it and make lots of money - er, mithril - from it. Then rationality will return and things will simply become controlled and regulated. But, in the meantime, we are in the fucking Dark Ages, so if I want to give my guests poppy tea when they clearly have a significant amount of hysteria... no wait, that will be an antiquated term... a significant amount of 'anxiety,' well, I am going to just give them the tea." Queen Brighid paused to look at Enyd. "Look, I'm not going tell her how to make the stuff. I'm not going to purify it and give her opium. I'm not going to give her heroin! This is a one time thing!"

"Is this tea evil, my Lady?" asked Rosmerta, putting her cup down in horror.

"Morality doesn't come into it, no matter how much people will end up saying that it does," muttered Brighid. "It's a very low dose, something to make you feel a little less frightened at the fact that you are in a magical otherworld for the... first time?"

Rosmerta nodded. The Queen put a hand across the table on Rosmerta's. She took a sip herself as she looked her in the eye. "It must be scary for you. Never you mind that, my sweet. It's not my style to hurt human beings - all I want is what's best for you."

"B-b-but, Enyd said she couldn't guarantee my safety if I didn't bring my lute!" cried Rosmerta. "Everyone knows that you... you... kill people who cross you. You're Queen Brighid, not to be trusted!"

The Queen laughed shrilly, yet mirthfully. "Oh my, looks like the tea has loosened your tongue. Now, Enyd, did you tell this girl that she would be unsafe if she didn't bring her lute?"

Rosmerta could see in the light from the window that the faery was blushing. "Erm, maybe," said Enyd. "And maybe that weren't entirely true."

"'Not entirely true,'" said Brighid, shaking her head. "You know I care about humans more than anything else! I would never strike them down because they didn't have... what, a wooden instrument?"

The Queen looked over at the lyre case that Rosmerta had placed against the wall. "I will bet that the lyre has something to do with your dream."

Rosmerta looked up. The poppy tea had indeed had the desired effect on the girl. All of her anxiety related to the past few months of her life - the impending Beltane ceremony, her father's distance since her mother's death, her mother's death itself - all of that was washed away on a cloud of opiate delight. All that was left for Rosmerta to realize was her own truth, a truth that she had been pushing down for so long.

"Aye," said Rosmerta. "Aye, I love the lute. I love music and I love song, but I cannot make my hands and voice work together. Nor do any of the songs that I've written make any sense at all. I would like to know how to play, how to sing, how to play and sing together, and how to write beautiful music. Music that will move all of the lords and ladies of Camelot! I want to be a bard - I want to be a star!" The pupils of Rosemerta's eyes had narrowed into pinpricks, and a glassy look had descended upon them, but it was clear to everyone in the room that what had been uttered was a scrap of truth that the young woman scarcely allowed herself to entertain.

Queen Brighid smiled sadly at the girl. It was not the first time someone had come to the Queen of Faeries seeking such a boon. It would not be the last - the way that humans were enamoured with fame was a theme throughout all of human history. In her dourer moments, Brighid had referred to this propensity as some ill-used part of the human spirit, an element of vanity enlarged. But like most human desires, there was a seed of something divine, something egoless within. In future years, humans who studied the body would call it some kind of evolutionary drive towards social acceptance, cutting the soul out of it and calling it scientific truth. In truth, it was the propensity towards service. Fame sought as an end was perhaps as the scientists would say, some kind of desire for security and comfort in the arms of others. But fame as a byproduct of the quest for service...

Well, it was not up to Brighid to tell the girl this. It was up to her to offer the pact and see if the girl survived the game of life long enough for her to gain self-realization. The Queen thought back to her conversation with Lugh, what he had said about the requirement that human beings self-realize before power be granted them. He had told Brighid that she was crazy for trying to change the rules of the game, to give the power to just anyone. That it would destroy creation. To be so bold as to think that anything could destroy creation, or change its very makeup - all Brighid had done was change the paint job. The rules were still the same. Brighid chuckled to herself, watching a wide-eyed Rosmerta stare up at her. In the corner of her eye, Brighid spied Donk not-so-surreptitiously make a grab for Enyd's breast.

"This isn't Valhalla - no fucking booby-honking!"

"Val-what?" said Enyd, brushing Donk's hand away. Donk smiled sheepishly and put his hand on the tumescence that was straining against the skin-tight body suit the Queen had conjured for him.

"Another pantheon - never mind." Brighid turned back to Rosmerta. "So you want to be a star? I can give you what you want, child. I can give you the talent you desire. I can make you sing like a nightingale and play like Bon Jovi... no wait, Eddie Van Halen... hmm, maybe James Hetfield?"

"Umm..." said Rosmerta.

"Like I says," Donk intoned sagely, "she's always goin' off. These bloody 'ey-tees' of hers, I'll warrant."

"Shut it Donk, or I'll send you to live with the goblins," muttered Brighid. "Look, I will make you a fantastic singer and lutenist and you will write songs the like of which the realm has never heard. I cannot grant you fame, but I will give you the means to achieve it. Sound good?"

Good? What the Queen was offering Rosmerta was a dream come true. The poppy haze was enough - just enough - to wear down her defences. She knew what her father said, all of the warnings that Keandre had offered her over her years of friendship with Enyd, ever since the little faery had come hanging about one summer when the girl was six. Now that Rosmerta thought back on it, it was around that time that the girl had first heard the foreign woman Brigantia, the import to Erybos from far off Gloucester, play her own lute and enchant the girl with some bawdy ditty about Aengus Og. In fact, if Rosmerta was being straight with herself, it was that very day that Rosmerta first met Enyd. Were the girl of a sounder mind, she might have questioned the link, brought some sort of probing question about the nature of the relationship between when her desire to become a bard was born, Enyd's appearance, and this very moment of truth with the dangerous goddess of the faeries.

Instead, the young woman simply nodded and listened as Brighid explained the Avalonian blood pact, an unbreakable soul contract that Rosmerta had every intention of signing, as soon as bloody (quite literally) well possible.

My Little Gosling

"The thing about raping little cock meats like this is that a man needs a reason to do it," came a strangely familiar voice to Gudleik through the dim haze of wherever he woke up. Placing his hands on the cold dirt beneath him, the young man pushed himself up. "I ain't got the taste for it - I prefer to get my pole stroked by one of Gustav's lads over at the Devious Mallard. Or slip on over to the Horny Hen and enjoy the company of the opposite sex - not my first choice, but I do enjoy a bit of variety from time to time. But, like I said, I'll need a reason if you want me to rape these boys. I work cheap for ya, boss, but I don't work that cheap."

Gudleik's eyes went wide and he blinked in the dim light. He gasped and scrambled backwards, crab-like, away from the source of the voice, as his eyes adjusted to the lack of light.

"Heheheh, nice one! Look of 'im go! 'E t'inks 'e's gettin' raped!"

"If there were any justice in the world, he certainly would be, Orvar, my buddy. Sexy little bugger, that one."

Gudleik could make out the shape of two men, standing next to a small table with four chairs. On it, a candle burned in a small dish. It had once been a tall thing, Gudleik could tell by the mess of wax from which the wick emerged. Now it was just a distended glob, casting barely enough flickering light to allow Gudleik to see the faces of his captors.

"Don't you worry, my little gosling, it was all a jest," continued the first speaker. "Well, not the robbery - that was real. I was talking about just now, when I said you were going to be raped. So, some of it was a jest. The first bit in the market - that was serious." The man paused. "I could tell you were stirring and wanted to have some fun. Our boss isn't here and we are under strict orders: you are our guest. Free to leave, arsehole unploughed. Free to do so, that is, after the boss is done with you."

Gudleik observed his captors. One of the men: tall, clean clothes, seemingly much too handsome to be a thief. The second one was everything the first was not - short, ugly, impish, stains on his tunics. The tall man who had spoken first, the one whose voice Gudleik recalled from the market square as he dug the blade of the dagger into his back. The hot breath, the strong fecal smell of the thief's clothing, the fear Gudleik felt for his own life - all of it came rushing back. What had the other one, the squat and ugly one, called him - Agnarr?

"Why do da boss want 'im, Agnarr? She ain't gonna rape 'im, is she?"

"What, you think because she's the leader of the underworld in Mimir's Rest, master of the literal cloak and dagger shite around these parts, that there's going to be rape? Just because we're outlaws there isn't invariably rape. You listen to too much of that dirtbag jester Maurice's work, Orvar. He peddles cheap laughs appropriate for a barbarian society like ours that goes around... umm, raping and pillaging other lands. Though we have better personal

144

hygiene than most - ever heard of Albion or Camelot? They bathe once a year, smear shite on their badly-made clothing and call it fashion."

"What, like out o' dere privies?"

"No, not human shite, Orvar, you touched git! They'd be asking for pestilential trouble, I'd warrant. Lamb, goat, cow - mostly ruminants, I hear."

"Rumimants?"

"Ugh, what a lot, to be doubly-cursed by a functioning brain and a sidekick whose own can barely parse the value of a sack of grain." Agnarr took a seat at the table and motioned for Gudleik to do the same. "You hungry, boy?"

"I'm not a boy," replied Gudleik. "I've seen nineteen summers."

"A regular fucking greybeard then," replied Agnarr. "Would you prefer I go back to calling you 'cockmeat,' my little gosling? Come - have something to eat."

"Where's Porsi?" asked Gudleik, not moving from his crouch. "What have you done with him?"

"Who? Oh, the other one who came in with you."

"Boss is speakin' wit' 'im now," blurted Orvar. "She's taken some shine to 'im. Prolly because 'e's 'er-"

"Favourite type of... young man," interrupted Agnarr, shooting Orvar an impatient glare. "Come now, boy, we've, appropriately enough, a freshly slaughtered and roasted goose. A few turnips, too, if that's your fancy."

"I loves termips," added Orvar sagely, sitting down at the table.

"Orvar, aren't you forgetting something?"

"Whuzzat?"

"The bleedin' food - go and fetch it from the kitchen!"

Orvar nodded excitedly, stood, and disappeared through a doorway leading out from the dingy little windowless room.

145

Gudleik then noticed that the walls were lined with large and cylindrical kegs, pewter tankards, wooden bowls and spoons, linen cloth, and various other bits and bobs.

"You must be wondering where you are," said Agnarr. A silence hung then... one which continued apace for some time. After a while, Gudleik spoke.

"And that is? Where am I?"

"Oh, I was just observing a fact. It wasn't me preparing to lead in to the offering of information. You want information, you've got to speak with the boss. You looked like a man wondering where he was - I was just trying to make conversation, is all."

"That's not how you make conversation," said Gudleik, shaking his head. "Usually a question is asked or something more than an inane statement like that without follow up is offered." The young man stood up, satisfied that all danger had passed, and took a seat at the table.

"Hmm, well, perhaps I've spent too much time in Orvar's company. Making conversation with him is like talking to a wall, if you haven't noticed."

"Who is Porsi to your boss?" Gudleik asked, ignoring Agnarr's bait to pile on the criticism of the man not in the room. "Orvar was going to say something, but you cut him off."

"Listen, boy," said Agnarr, spreading well-groomed hands before him, "Like I told you - you'll not get any information from me. Anything you want can be got from the boss herself - we're just your standard lackeys. Side-characters, bit part players. It would be... improper to be offering information that moves the plot along - erm, I mean, helps you with your quest. No, wait, I should say... no more on the topic." Agnarr paused. "You'll get some roast goose from us though - fill your belly. Great consolation prize. In fact..." Agnarr stood, grabbed a mallet and a small conical object from one of the shelves. Then he approached a keg and went to work tapping it in. Moments later, mugs were filled with mead and placed before each of the men.

"Knute Kustaason's finest - best mead this side of Valhalla." Agnarr offered his clay vessel for a clank with Gudleik.

Gudleik felt a strange compulsion come over him. It moved jelly-like through his body, making the young man hot with rage. Here was an indecent type who had robbed him at dagger point, pretended like he was going to rape him, and refused to give him any information about where he was or the identity of his captor. The feeling swelled and washed up into his head. At the last moment before he spoke, Gudleik could hear the tinkling of the lyre once more, as had happened in the market when he was calmed down from freeing his dagger from its scabbard. This time, though, it was too little, too late. Some presence rose up within Gudleik and it was as if the young man lost control of his voice and movements.

"You know you smell of shite yourself," said Gudleik, knocking back the mead in one go. "You speak of elevated Norseman hygiene, but you stink like you soiled your own clothes. Not with cow shite, neither. Full on human waste, somewhere about you. I can sense your stench from over here."

Agnarr opened his mouth, his eyes wide with shock, then he closed it and frowned. Gudleik could sense that something had broken within the man before he opened up his mouth to speak.

"Oh, aye," Agnarr began, a silent tear rolling down a cheek.. "It comes from me pores. I asked the Seer for help, he said it was a curse from some foreign privy goddess, Cloacina or some such. I wash myself every day and still I cannot get the smell of shite off of me. This arsehole goddess also gave me some strange blessing as well, the ability to break the fourth wall. But it's rarely much help, since I see so few heroes on quests with narrators hanging about in the ether of imagination, whatever that means." Agnarr paused to shudder, as if he was trying to keep a lid on something that would not stop flowing. "Odin's big beautiful balls, I barely know what I'm talking about sometimes. Mostly though, I just smell of rank shite and criticize others for their lack of hygiene to hide my own shame, like the bleedin' foreigners in the Blessed Isles. Some goddess-given talent, that shite-smellery. It's why I frequent the brothels so much and cannot find work anywhere but here, at Eyja's place - she's a soft spot for... oh, I've said way too bloody much."

Gudleik was shocked at what had occurred - the way that he had twisted an unseen knife with his words and struck directly upon some vital point in Agnarr's guts, which immediately caused their spill. The man looked broken and sheepish, a shadow of the way Gudleik interpreted his presence when he had a dagger pressed into his back in the market, or when he had threatened rape as a joke just minutes before. With a few words chosen, he had unmanned Agnarr... well, not really chosen. It was as if he had been possessed. But it was not by Bragi - no, this would have been the other god. The one who had cursed him since he was a boy. The deity of trickery and chaos. Though now Loki seemed to be content to offer him power, rather than ill-fortune. Gudleik smiled, though he could hear some strange off-key lyre notes burst out in his mind - a warning from Bragi, perhaps? Gudleik shrugged it off. The boy had been completely impotent his whole life and now, finally... this was real power.

"Eyja, you say," Gudleik said, standing and filling his mug from the tap once more. "That is lucky - I have come to this city seeking one by that very name. She would not happen to be an accomplished lyrist, would she?"

"Erm, no information from me, boy," said Agnarr, staring down at the table. "It's against the rules of narrative. It wouldn't be proper. And please, don't tell anyone about the curse."

"It's Gudleik." Gudleik's smile had become wolfish. He placed a hand on the man's slumped shoulder. Agnarr sobbed. Gudleik made a gentle 'shh'ing noise. "My name is Gudleik, my little gosling. My little shite-stinking gosling."

Hel in a Handbasket

"Christ on a cracker, Ramses," said Arthur, looking up from the ritual table he had set up on the ground before the fireplace in his room. The hexstone with strange runes had been placed there, some fragrant herbs were burning in a clay dish, a trio of taper candles burned half down stood erect in the centre, before him lay a scroll that Arthur had obtained from the local druid, Brindel. Beside the ritual table lay a small basket - the handle of Arthur's scabbarded dagger poked out. "You look like a sack of shite. Where were you all day? I waited and waited and waited for you to come along so we could begin the ceremony. I could wait no longer. I've already spoken the words of the incantation."

"I... was... asleep," admitted Ramses.

"Are you still wearing what you had on yesterday?" inquired Arthur. "That gaudy yellow thing? And what's that around the collar, dried blood?"

"You must stop what you are doing, Arthur," said Ramses, the whites of his eyes flush red. "You cannot summon that creature here, my master won't allow it."

"Your master?" asked Arthur, standing and furrowing his brow. "Just who exactly are you-"

"Arthur of Camelot," boomed a voice. What looked to be a teenage girl had appeared in the circle the King had drawn on the floor next to the ritual table. She was quite beautiful, with long black hair, and a dress speckled with white points, somewhat similar to a moonless night's sky. Her eyes were a deep shade of amethyst. "I have long been awaiting this encounter. We shall make beautiful- who's this now? He stinks of... well, death. That's *my* scent, knave! Where did you get it!?"

Ramses laughed. "You're just a little girl! Here my master built you up as this great and terrible goddess from a distant land, and you're naught but a child. Dispatching you shall be easy." Ramses approached the circle. When he got within a few feet, it was as if a wall had been put up. He tried several times to get through before pounding his fists on air.

"This is Midgard-consecrated land now," tittered the young girl. "You cannot come through. Who is it that you serve? That black rattish thing who has invaded my homeland with his blood drinkers? Clapperleg, was it? Well, I suppose he's in for a bit of his own medicine."

"Ramses, what is going on?" asked Arthur. He had blanched. "I thought we were going to try to stop the Christians with the help of this goddess. Who is this to whom you have sworn an oath to now?"

"Clapperleg doesn't ask permission, Arthur," said Ramses, wheeling on his king. "He alone can take souls without our consent. Which is what makes him the most magnificent of all of the deities."

"Pfft," said the teenage goddess. "It's not just him. All gods of death have that power. And besides, the way you speak about permission and consent - you still don't understand what gods are, you little vampire baby."

"Silence, bitch," roared Ramses. "You may be safe there in your circle, but judging by the pristine condition of that blade, Arthur has yet to swear his oath to you. I can still turn him back to Danu's Children and banish your presence from Albion."

"Hahaha," giggled the goddess. "I'm sure Arthur would be happy for that. Though doesn't strike me as the cock-hungry type. You, on the other hand, with that nice yellow jerkin and your well-maintained wardrobe - I expect you've had your eye on your liege for some time now, have you? Let me get a taste." The goddess closed her purple eyes and smiled. "Ah, I can feel you now - stealing off to brothels for a little secret mincery. Do the Christians know you've been laying with men, Ramses Thornbush? You've still your head, so-"

"That's enough!" roared Ramses. "The vampire blessing may only be spread by venereal fashion, but I don't need his consent for that." Ramses paused and considered his old friend again. "Although, Arthur, I would prefer to do this the old-fashioned way... wait, the old-fashioned way might be rape. I imagine our forebears were much less civilized. Perhaps the new-fashioned way? You know, where you acquiesce to it?" Ramses began to advance on Arthur.

"Early humans were like ducks," said the goddess sagely. "All rape, no consent. It's a miracle your women never evolved funky twisted vaginas and you men never got corkscrew dicks in the mix."

"Do you really want a goddess like her-"

"Stay back, fiend!" interrupted Arthur, who had pulled the ritual dagger from the basket and held it before him. "I always knew you were a bugger but I never judged you for it, Ramses. You were friend to me and I loved you as such. Now, though - I hardly recognize you. Of course, I'll not let you fuck me - I may have a shagger's soul, but another man? It's not my taste."

"Come now, Arthur - your mission was to cast out the Christians and their bloodthirsty God. Who better to serve than one of Danu's Children? Clapperleg grew up in these lands. This bitch - this Hel - she comes from a place where they eat babies for breakfast and piss on their wives for sport."

"Both of those claims are lies," said Hel flatly.

"Regardless," said Ramses, turning back to Arthur. "They're different. They're strange, these Midgardians. If you invite this goddess into Albion, there is no telling what might happen. We shall become enemies, Arthur. Mortal ones."

"You're not mortal," advised Hel. "Not anymore. Judging by the crimson shade of your eyes, you've already fed. Which means the deal is sealed - there's your consent to Clapperleg's contract. Now your death needs the whole stake through the heart, sunlight, perhaps even one of those Christian crucifixes, for some odd reason. You're going to live forever. Sounds like quite the deal, doesn't it?" Hel laughed a laugh that made it clear that she did not actually feel that it was a good deal.

"My master is going to kill you, bitch," said Ramses. Then he turned to Arthur and put a hand up. "I love you Arthur Pendragon, more than you can ever know. But if you do not acquiesce to my request, I will take what I need. I cannot risk letting you ally with this foreign cunt."

"I'm ready to go, Arthur," interjected Hel. "You know what you need to do."

"Aye," said Arthur.

In one quick motion, he held his free hand above the basket, placed the dagger against it, and sliced off the first

153

finger of his hand. Ramses sprinted forward to try to stop the ritual but he was too late. The finger dropped in and a tinkling echo could be heard through the entirety of the castle, rousing some of the knights and ladies from their slumber. In Arthur's chamber, the fire, which had been roaring, lowed to embers. Frost spider-webbed out from the basket, reached Arthur's foot, and began freezing its way up his body. Ramses was pushed back bodily from his former master, pressed up against the wall near the door by sheer unseen force. The vampire watched as the frost emerged from his Arthur's skin near the cuff of his injured hand. The icy matrix crept and crept and crept until it reached the stump of his finger, which had been steadily flowing blood. The wound was staunched immediately when the cold devoured it. The frost then emerged from his collar and climbed his neck, forming little icicles on the ends of his ivory beard. Eventually the magical frost made it to his eyes, which shifted from a watery blue to a deep purple, just like Hel's. Arthur's crown became rimed with frost and his hair took on the same icy affect as his beard.

"Looks like you're too late, Ramses," said Hel, tittering once more. "Give Clapperleg my regards." With that, she flicked her wrist and Ramses went flying through the air. He smashed into the window and soared out into the night air, eventually landing on an empty merchant's cart, one that a farmer used to hawk his vegetables during the market days. The thing shattered into splinters with the force of Ramses' landing. The vampire groaned and rolled over. His sole witness was a drunken vagrant lolling in an alley off the main thoroughfare. The mendicant rubbed his eyes and looked down at the clay jug filled with *uisge*.

"I've gotta stop drinking," he said to no one in particular, before putting the bottle up to his lips and having another swallow.

"Not me," said Ramses, standing with more than a little difficulty. His yellow jerkin, once bright and beautiful and pristine, was now a dirty and torn mess. "I need to start."

The vagrant shrugged and offered Ramses the bottle.

"How quaint," said Ramses, staggering over towards the man. It became evident to both man and vampire that Ramses had broken his leg in the fall, owing to how the fibula poked out through shredded pants.

"Y-y-yer leg," said the bum. "You'll need to get it set!"

"Oh, I'll get it set, alright," said Ramses, revealing dagger teeth and falling on the man, who gurgled helplessly as the vampire took everything from him.

land ho!

"I want to tell you the story of my wife's death."

Cernunnos turned from his ministrations, put down the etching tool, and raised an eyebrow.

"I'm an omniscient being, Keandre," said the god. "I know how she died."

"Yes, well, perhaps you would simply humour me? We've been on this... you-forsaken boat for two weeks now. We've discussed every last detail of creation, from the explosion at the beginning of time, or the end of time, or whatever - I'm still not sure I understand what you meant. Anyways, you told me about that, you told me about the creation of the gods, about the birth of Danu, of the birth of you and your siblings, about the first druids... and then you got into the mechanics of sex in a level of detail I never thought I would ever learn. And why you love drinking ram seed so much - though I definitely did not need to hear about that."

"It's like a fine wine! A cup running over with life-"

"Eurgh, please, enough." Keandre put a hand over his mouth and urged as he recollected visions of manually procuring the stuff for his god over the years. Part of the deal

156

with summoning Cernunnos into the Blessed Isles meant that he had to be placated with a 'sacrifice' of ram seed. The only sacrifice, as far as Keandre saw it, was the druid's appetite when he furtively approached the farmer's field and prayed that no one would come upon him as he went to town on one of the horned beasts with a (mercifully gloved) hand.

"*That* is the sacrifice, don't you see? Your own disgust, your decision to proceed regardless: that is what makes the delicious vital fluid so valuable to a creature like me!"

"Get out of my head, damn you!" muttered Keandre.

"Sacrifice isn't about anything but doing what you know is right in spite of discomfort and inconvenience. That's the kind of shite that gives both of us power. But please, I assume, based on your statement and diatribe that you are tired of metaphysical discussions. Tell me about your wife's death."

Keandre fumed quietly as he gathered his thoughts. Cernunnos was one hell of an enervating creature, even if he was Keandre's patron deity. For all his talk of fertility and life, the damn goatish bastard drained his vitality at times. Being cooped up in the boat with him had been pure torture.

"Look," said Cernunnos. "I don't like this any more than you do. If I had my druthers, I would be at home in my apartment in the Sidhe, cooking up schemes that would see beasts and women impregnated by express desire and seeming chance, bringing new life into the Blessed Isles and joyfully going about my shagging business. Not to mention shoring up my investments in bread dildos, orgies, and surreptitious slap and tickle liaisons with my darling... hmm, well, you don't need to know about her." Cernunnos began to pick at his enormous fingers with the etching tool, pulling black soil from beneath the nails. "Instead of my preference, I am stuck in the hold of a... me-damned boat with a bellyaching bloodsworn of mine who is unimpressed with learning the secrets of the universe. We are going to a frozen shithole of an alien land, to deal with a renowned trickster cock of a god. Loki is forever a needle in the side of good and decent deities - at least, from what I know of him. It's not going to be an easy thing, convincing him to cease his attempts to encroach upon the Blessed Isles."

Keandre took stock of Cernunnos yet again. He was an enormous black-skinned man-thing with ram horns emerging from his forehead and goat legs on bottom, along with an enormous flaccid member hanging between his legs. There were glowing green spiraling patterns everywhere on his skin, like fluorescent tattoos, speaking in the strange symbolic language of the pantheon made up of Danu's Children. Some days he appeared to his druids with stag antlers, but Cernunnos had admitted to Keandre on their voyage that he didn't like them very much. They were a bit less imposing than ram horns and they were always getting caught in branches. How stags managed to navigate forests were a mystery to Cernunnos, in spite of the fact that he was patron deity to the beasts. Worse still were goat horns, which did symbolize virility appropriately, but they were small, straight, and thin. Not like the twisted and girthy ram horn - that sent the right message. According to Cernunnos, that was.

Normally, the god could be found thundering around the countryside, flipping from pure gregarious and smiling affect to thunderous rage at the drop of a cap. Usually, such rages were incited by those who sought to interfere with sex or procreation. The Christians, with their chastity and self-flagellation for 'impure' thoughts, were particularly incensing to Cernunnos. But they were a known quantity and they had already taken hold in the souls of many of the inhabitants of the Blessed Isles. Especially on Albion, the land of Camelot.

Loki, though, he was something new. A fresh bud on the tree of god worship on the Blessed Isles. One that could be nipped if the appropriate measures were taken. At least, that is what Cernunnos told Keandre after they discovered the skull etched with unfamiliar runes beneath the house of Calder the cuckolded hunter. Here was a man who had sold himself over to the foreign god and found himself castrated by Cernunnos for attempting to interfere with Aiden, the ealdorman of Erybos, lover of Calder's wife Romana.

"Why get involved?" Keandre had asked Cernunnos before they left the Isle of Valentia, Keandre's home island. "Why not just let Loki do what he does? Why force me to come with you to... negotiate with him?"

"Why?" had roared Cernunnos. "You're asking me, a being of unimaginable power, why? I could crush you like an insect, knave."

"You could have just said, 'it's none of your business,'" had replied Keandre. "Didn't know it was such a touchy subject."

"We live and die on worship, Keandre," had said Cernunnos. "Without worship, we wither and disappear. Just look at what happened to The Dagda. He was once the greatest of us, pure divine masculinity, a whole father who seemed unstoppable. Unkillable, even. Then the Christians invaded Albion, slaughtered his druids, and one of their angels murdered The Dagda. And gods - we gods do not come back from death. Once we're dead, we are dead. Not like you humans, with your rebirth and eternal life." More than a hint of jealousy had invaded Cernunnos' tone. "You don't know what it's like, to have no existence within the physical realms. Why, without you humans, we would be..."

"Nothing at all?"

Cernunnos smirked then. "Well, to be fair, without us, you would be nothing, either. You all worship us, in one form or another. Every time a boy seeks to become a man, he serves a god. Every time a mother births a child, she serves a god. Every time an idea takes manifestation in this world, it is the work of a god. Every time a human being seeks to become greater than themselves, they pay their dues to their god. It's only when you become conscious of this link that you ever take hold of your destinies and become what you desire. You all imagine yourselves to be simple folk, when in fact you are truly beings like us. But that is too much for you, so you continue to tell yourselves your lies - that you are subject *to* the world, rather than the subject of the world itself."

"I hate it when you get so fucking cryptic," had replied Keandre. "Can't you just speak plainly? I mean, you're a god, I'm a mere mortal. We couldn't be more different."

"Have it your way," had said Cernunnos. "At least, in that respect. We're going to Midgard and we are going to stop Loki's invasion of the Blessed Isles. Pack your shite, mere mortal."

It had been weeks since that conversation. Weeks of more unparsable admonitions and mystical exhortations. It all flew over Keandre's head, though. Keandre had always considered himself to be a 'good' druid. He did what he was told by his father, followed the lineage, got into the family business, started baking the bread dildos and making the village poultices. He used Cernunnos' magic as he was supposed to, acted in a druidic fashion, if such a thing existed. He was a support pillar for the community. Aside from his misgivings about the thrice-baked bread olisbos, magical crusty dildos that addicted the women and men who used them in a serious manner and fell apart after short periods of use (and necessitated a fresh purchase in the result, lining Keandre's pockets with mithril and maintaining his status as a valued member of the community), Keandre didn't question a damn thing. So when offered answers that would have made any spiritual seeker worth their salt squeal with delight, the aging man balked and wished he were somewhere else.

Most of all, it made him miss his wife, Romana. His daughter, Rosmerta, was a sweet girl, but Keandre had a hard time understanding her. Rosmerta wanted to be something other than a druid. She railed against it, dreamed strange dreams of lute and lyric, alienated herself from the community, and communed with gods-fucked faeries, of all things. She was a total enigma to Keandre, a creature whose motivations were as opaque as those of his own god, Cernunnos. Why would anyone want to escape from the safety and security of a comfortable life at home with his... wife?

Tears flowed as Keandre felt the loss of his beloved sting him once more. No one had understood him as Romana had - no one. They had met at the Samhain Festival in Danu's homeland, freezing their arses off as they danced through the cairns and the bonfires lit up the Caledonian mists. They were so young and vivacious then, rubbing shoulders with hundreds of druids from across the Blessed Isles. There was plenty of *uisge* mixed with rye grain blistering with psychotropic fungus. If ever Keandre came close to understanding any of the shite that Cernunnos related to him during their sea voyage, it would have been around the time of that first Samhain Festival where he had met his one true love. Romana and he wrapped their hands the very next Beltane. The following year, they were married and Rosmerta was on her way into the world.

"Now *that* is a memory," Cernunnos said softly. "Do you understand why I love what I do so much, Keandre? Do you understand why you are *my* chosen? I do not want to hear anything about her death - I'm no Clapperleg. I want to hear about how you met, how you felt when you slipped into rapturous union with that woman. Let those be the memories we share - not some story about wolves and blood and tears. Honour her death, keep that awen pendant close to your skin," Cernunnos pointed to the pendant that had slipped out of Keandre's robe. Keandre and Romana had exchanged an identical one when they married. Rosmerta now wore her mother's pendant, the one that Keandre had given her. The druid himself still wore his wife's gift.

"Celebrate these memories of her," Cernunnos nodded. "These should be the ones on which you dwell. Let me help you with that, brother. You have been in the cold for two long years."

"You- you did this," said Keandre, putting the pendant back into his robe and taking in his god once more. "You orchestrated all of this - you played with my memory, with my mind."

"You damned fool," said Cernunnos, shaking his head. "I *am* your mind."

The god turned from Keandre, back to the workbench. He picked up the hammer, put it to the end of the engraving tool, and began striking at the metal of the bracer once more. "Here, almost finished." Cernunnos gently tapped a handful more times, then set the hammer and tool down on the workbench. The cylindrical tool rolled as the boat caught a swell. Keandre caught it before it reached the floor. When he looked up, Cernunnos was smiling at him. His green eyes were rippling with emerald energy, energy that was flowing off the god's body in electric rushes, through his fingers and into the polished silver of the bracer. It was traced with similar markings to the ones tattooed into the god's skin. Some incantation in the language of Danu's Children glowed green within the bracer.

"What is this thing for?" asked Keandre.

"You're not a fighter," said Cernunnos. "Neither am I. Well, I can hold my own in a battle where sexuality is involved, but that's about it. However, there is someone very close to me - very close to me, indeed - who knows a thing or two about war." Cernunnos put a meaty paw on Keandre's shoulder. "We are not going to a peaceful place, Keandre. You're going to need to know how to defend yourself if one of these barbarians gets handsy... wait, no, there I go, bringing sex into it again. You're going to need to know how to defend yourself in case someone tries to slit your throat or drive a spear into your chest. Yes, that's much more on the money."

Keandre blanched. "W-w-what? I thought we were going to negotiate with Loki!"

"You touched git," laughed Cernunnos mirthlessly. "We are going to kill him."

Cernunnos clapped the bracer on Keandre's wrist. It covered the majority of his forearm. Leather sprouted from the inside and wrapped itself around the druid's flesh. Flashes of fire burst in Keandre's vision. The sound of steel clanging on steel and cries of anguish rang in his ears. The reek of burning flesh and the thick iron scent of blood exploded within his mind. The druid's fists closed and opened as great sinewy thews exploded out of nowhere from beneath his flesh. Determination blew out every other thought from Keandre's mind.

"Courtesy of my sweet baby, The Morrigan, triple goddess of fate and war," grinned Cernunnos. "These impotent Norsemen aren't going to know what hit them."

"I am just one man," roared Keandre, picking up the workbench and launching it at the wall, where it exploded into splinters. "But I will do what is necessary to kill this pretender fuck Loki!"

"Alright, let's just dial it back a notch," said Cernunnos tearing off the bracer and picking up the tools again. The leather nearly broke Keandre's wrist before giving way as the god ripped it from him. "I want you fierce, but not homicidal psychopath fierce."

Keandre crumpled to the ground as the blessing flowed out of him and his muscles regained their normal size and tone. "What... did... you... do... to... me?"

"I'm just fucking with the threads of fate here," said Cernunnos, mouth upturned like a hyena as he tapped away with the tool and hammer. He looked at Keandre, wide eyes, perfect white teeth, and full insanity in bloom on his face. "I have no idea what I'm doing!" Cernunnos slapped the thing back on Keandre's wrist, threw his head back, and cackled monstrously. "A fucking belly laugh - all the wisdom you need!"

This time, when Keandre rose, he was not quite the overmuscled freak he had been for the first go-round. But something had changed in his countenance. No longer the bent creature he had been most of his life, his chest was out, proud, and he had a cold grit as he gazed upon his patron deity.

"I understand," he said quietly. "I finally understand."

"Fucking and fornication and making babies is one half of the equation," said Cernunnos, pulling a scabbarded sword wrapped with a leather cord up from an unseen space behind a pillar in the room. "Death, especially if it's the death of that which you love most - your wife, perhaps, or perhaps just the death of that which you thought you were - that is the road to awe." Cernunnos threw the sword to his druid. Keandre drew the sword and began a blade dance throughout the below decks, bobbing and weaving through a magnificent battle with his shadow as if he had been a swordsman his whole life. Suitably impressed, Cernunnos eventually tore his gaze from his chosen and peered out one of the portholes in the vessel.

"Oh, would you look at that! Land ho!"

Frog-Cocked Bastard

Merlyn leaped from lily-pad to lily-pad, trying to increase his odds of catching dinner in the warming ponds on the Caledonian border near his tower. At least, he thought it was near the Caledonian border - it had been weeks since Brighid had transformed him and he was losing track of time and space. At night, which was fast approaching, the polymorphed wizard watched the stars and prayed that he was still in command of some of his human faculties. It was getting difficult to hold on to them, though, as if the passages of his mind had been greased and he was slipping out of traditional human mental soil and into the amphibious terroir of his new frog body. Nonetheless, Merlyn knew that Beltane was fast approaching - in fact, if his calculations were correct, it was this very night. Which meant the first day of summer - at least, for the people who still payed homage to Danu's Children.

For the Albians, though, and those people of the Blessed Isles who had adopted their new deity and calendar in the mix, Beltane was just another day. The Christians did not even think summer started until the midsummer solstice struck. They even separated the year into four seasons, incorporating things called 'spring' and 'autumn' into their version of the Wheel of the Year. For all his addiction to time travel and the trappings of the future, like a smartphone that allowed him to access the kind of pornography that would turn a decent person's hair white, Merlyn was a traditionalist when it came to the seasons. He preferred the old ways of doing things - summer starting on Beltane and giving way to winter on Samhain. Two seasons, though plenty of festivals like the Lughnasdh, when harvest began, and Imbolc's celebration of coming growth in the dead of winter peppered throughout.

Still, there was magic in Beltane, of a similar but different sort as that of Samhain. Lovers performed handfastings, whether to celebrate another year of marital bliss or as the kick off of a trial year for nuptials. If these would-be married folk survived the year to do a second handfasting, such a ritual was usually accompanied by marriage proceedings. If they didn't, they could untie their knots and go on to find different partners.

Merlyn himself had had little success with women over the years. He had been (and still was, if the wizard was being honest with himself) in love with Arthur's half-sister, Morgan Le Fay. She had never had even the slightest reciprocity for his feelings, in spite of the fact that both Merlyn and Morgan were two of the few people who had successfully navigated faery contracts and maintained their human shape and sensibilities. The two had seen too much, too many of their friends had been forced into faeryhood by breaking some divine law - at least, that is what Merlyn told himself when he pondered the whys of the lack of a relationship between himself and Morgan. He also told himself that she had let herself be seduced by a devil, a magical creature who had more than a little in common with Merlyn's father, Balor the Tumescent.

Thoughts of Balor sent the wizard spinning. His own progenitor had cursed him with some spell cast by the Goblin King, an enchantment that was rotting his frog-penis away at the very moment. The thing was flaking skin and the tips of his froggy fingers were changing to a strange shade of purple black, exactly as his father had said would happen. The Goblin King had admonished Merlyn to kill Arthur - the curse was meant to ensure compliance. Merlyn had broken more than a few curses over his time as advisor to Arthur - the guy was like a magnet for that kind of shite. He did not think it would be much more than a minor inconvenience that required the intervention of his rebel goddess Brighid. As had happened before, he would ask for help, she would give it, and Bob would have been Merlyn's uncle (a sore spot for the wizard, since the only uncles he knew of were brothers to his incubus father, self-interested lechs all - and not a one of them named Bob). All he should have done was ask Brighid for her help with the curse and sent her on her way.

Instead, though, he had found himself exasperated with a sentient tower breeding fucking demons in its belly, preparing to unleash some fresh hell upon Albion while just playing the part of an innocent, fatherly type of edifice, if such a thing existed. That tower - Gary - he was clearly some kind of magical beast from a hell-dimension. As usual, Merlyn was the only thing that stood between it and rampant chaos and destruction throughout the realm of Albion. And he could say goodbye to his cock and fingernails if he did not get a handle on the curse laid upon him by the Goblin King. What was that expression the future folk used? A dilly of a fucking pickle, indeed.

168

Merlyn looked up. The sky was a dim pink and the stars were exposed through a thin layer of shifting cloud. Yes, definitely Beltane. Which meant that the barrier between the Otherworlds and the human realms were at their thinnest. If there was to be a night he would escape from froghood, this would be it. Apprentices became druids on Beltane - oaths were sworn, rituals performed. How would he escape though? Perhaps, he could find a princess to kiss him - without a doubt that would do the trick. A princess kissing a frog - a curse-breaker if there ever was one. Merlyn scanned the pond - nary a princess around. But what was that, up on the hill? Why, it looked like a castle!

That meant - hmm, Caledonia. The belly of the beast - Caledonia was Danu's land. Merlyn, as emblematic adept of Brighid, was despised as an apostate who had corrupted the King of Albion. If his identity were discovered, he would likely find himself at odds with the chosen of Danu herself. By all accounts, she was a cold, miserable bitch, as unforgiving as the misty and frigid lands of Caledonia where she was worshiped. It was understood that she considered her daughter Brighid to be her greatest failure. Danu's chosen, Lairds of the Caledonian clans, had become zealots to the cause of exterminating Brighid. When last Merlyn had advised Arthur, spies in the northern territory had intimated to the King that the Lairds had ceased their internecine feuding over ancient wrongs and were banding together to invade Albion, to crush Arthur and to put an end to Brighid-worship. They would destroy Camelot, Avalon, the faeries - hell, they would even run out the miserable self-flagellating Christians while they were at it (Merlyn was sympathetic to that part of the plan). Their lightning rod, their leader who was to command their armies, was a drunkard of a Laird named Fearghas, who made up for his adoration of the bottle with no end of wit and calculation.

Here was a chosen of Danu, it was said, a man who embodied the goddess in everything he did. The spy had told Arthur that the laird was putting the finishing touches on the invasion plan - and this had been weeks before. With Merlyn's luck, the invasion would have already started. And here he was, waiting for that big bastard of a bottlefly to come down just close enough to...

Merlyn's frog-tongue lashed out, struck the fly, and pulled the fat-bodied insect back into his open maw. It happened in an instant. An instant later, a shadow, barely visible to the shape-shifted magician in the dark light of the gloaming, dropped over the frog. Merlyn tried to jump away but felt a hand close around him, a thin and dainty thing... perhaps, might it be a princess? Merlyn deflated internally as he realized that this were just a boy, perhaps twelve years old or so. In the gloom, Merlyn could see that he had curly dark hair and a smile on his face, though his eyes betrayed a vacancy of thought that was incontrovertible. If the boy were not dressed in such finery, Merlyn would have assessed him as the the commoner son of some incestuous pairing, perhaps bumpkin siblings who could not help themselves as puberty hit. As it stood, the boy was probably the result of some noble incestuous pairing, perhaps silver-spooned siblings who could not help themselves as puberty hit. Or, more likely, given the nobility, some fool-headed desire for 'pure blood' that resulted in genetic abnormalities as the gene pool became as stagnant as the pond from which he had been plucked (Merlyn sometimes had a hard time reconciling his knowledge which came from his incursions into the future and the idiocy that ruled the day of his own timeline). Based on the shape of the boy's jaw and the thin covering of hair, puberty had indeed struck once more in his line and the boy's world was in full change.

Hopefully he didn't have a sister of the same vintage.

"Hi dere," said the boy, smiling at Merlyn. "My name is Robbie. What's yours?"

"Ribbit," offered Merlyn.

"Ribbit, is it?" replied Robbie. "Not much of a clever name, though. Let's pick somet'ing diff'rent. How about I call you 'Dirty Wee Shite-Cock.' Dat's what Mallory called me when she found me feeling good with the ewes. She told me dat she loved me, but I was a 'gedenterate sheep-shagger wit' warmed-over 'aggis fer brains.'"

'Degenerate,' said Merlyn, correcting his diction. At least, that's what he wanted to say to the boy - all that came out though was another, "Ribbit."

"I like you, Dirty Wee Shite-Cock," said the boy, putting Merlyn in the breast pocket of his frock-coat, making sure to have it so that Merlyn could see out from his position. "But let's just call you 'Shite-Cock,' for short. Don't go jumping out, now. We're going back to the castle to play for a while." Robbie leaned in conspiratorially. "Don't worry, I won't let Cooky take you and eat you like 'e did with my last frog, Perverse Abobimation."

'Abomination,' Merlyn attempted. All that came out was, 'Ribbit.'

"Glad you likes me plan, Shite-Cock," said Robbie, skipping out from his position next to the pond, traipsing back towards the road that led to the castle. "We're going to be the bestest of friends, Shite-Cock - I knows it already!"

ꝓroꝓaꞡanꝺa

"Would you look at that, twelve perfect reproductions of the face of evil." Cassiel moved to the next easel, inspecting the work with a smile, then the next, then the next. After he was finished, he crossed the room to Brother Winfridus, put out his hand, and said, "I'll have the ring, please."

Brother Winfridus looked down at his hand. On the right ring finger, a large red ruby set into a golden band sparkled in the daylight streaming in through the open window. The thought of giving up the item, which was imbued with such power, made the Brother angry. Why should he give it up? It allowed him to paint pictures of unbelievable quality in record time. Still, the shiny armour on the angel and the sword on his hip made the monk think twice. And, in spite of himself, Brother Winfridus was certainly a coward. Perhaps he could simply return the ring and fetch the scourge.

"Yes, yes," sighed the angel. "Ring now, self-flagellation later." Brother Winifridus removed the ring and dropped it into the angel's palm "But you must accept my praise, Brother - you did so well. I mean, look! *That* is the devil! That is how we will sway these bumpkins to the lap of the One True God

- we will show them their Cernunnos, red-skinned, adorned in flame and full of fire and hatred. Believe you me, we will convince them that he has never had their best interests in mind. By the time Keandre returns to Erybos, none of them will believe that Cernunnos ever did anything but hurt them. With Rosmerta out of the way, there is nothing to stand in our way."

"You know, her body was never found," said Brother Winfridus, stifling a tear. He had killed the girl. He might have had incessant lustful thoughts about her, a cacophony of fuck-admonitions that led him invariably towards the scourge that ripped flesh from his back the way wheat berries fell to the blows of the threshing rods every harvest, but still Brother Winfridus felt sorrow at her loss. She was simply a kind young woman born to the wrong family, one whose ways were on the way out. Brother Winfridus was enough of a zealot to believe that the procession of the One True God towards a position of ultimate power in the Blessed Isles was an inevitability, but still he wished there could be a more merciful way of bringing change.

"You yellow-bellied whoreson," breathed Cassiel. "I know your mind, knave. You think that Yeshua would have gotten anywhere without sacrifice? He was willing to sacrifice everything for his beliefs, including his body."

"Yes, but that was *his* body, wasn't it?" asked Brother Winfridus, some strange strength suddenly taking hold of him. "You had me kill the girl so that you could make your little power-play. Well, you've made it. Cernunnos and his druids are out of the way for a while. All it took was a poor woman burned to ash."

"Oh, that 'poor woman,'" sneered Cassiel. "A slutty Jezebel if I ever smelled one. Rotten fish and dissolution, that is all that cunny would have provided to one Brother Winfridus, if you could even have wooed her. You think you could have, you little fucking lap dog? Your type – elderly weakling - disgusts women, it always has. Consider it a blessing, given the way that women corrupt men as sure as night follows day. Eve was just the start of it." Cassiel paused. "Besides, you said the body wasn't found. Perhaps she escaped into the night with her little fucking devilkin. God-damned faeries - tools of Satan worse than Cernunnos himself, I'll warrant."

"You don't seem too worried about that, if she did escape," said Brother Winfridus. "What if she comes back? What if she comes back and offers the people of Erybos those damned bread dildos and cock poultices again? How will we compete with that?"

"You forget," said Cassiel, holding up one of the paintings, "fear is a much stronger motivator than bouncing on a fucking bread dildo."

"They're highly addictive," countered Brother Winfridus. "You should see the way the women of the village talk about them. I swear, if ever the fiend of Satan has been made plain to me, it is through the eyes of a woman whose bread dildo has just fallen apart."

"Your lack of faith is disturbing," muttered the angel, putting the painting down and producing the bloody flesh-encrusted scourge from its resting place near the monk's prayer bench. "Time to go to work on that, knave. Tear the weakness from your flesh and I will tell you exactly how we are going to take control of this island."

That Bitch Eyja Randulfsson

"The biggest collection of wild animals this side of some desert shithole a world away to the south. Tell me you're impressed, Randy, sweetie - I know you are."

"Impressed? Sure. Looks good - though looks like a bad case of mange ripped through that wolf pack. And what did you call this one again, Eyja? The orange one with the black lines in his fur?"

"A tiger," replied Eyja, turning from her estranged husband to the massive beast circling in one of the great cages made of wrought iron bars. "And it's a 'her.' This here is my sweetie, Freya."

"Eh," said Randulf, "you think that's wise? Naming an animal after the goddess of beauty and fertility? I mean, you're probably inviting all kinds of divine wrath here."

Eyja made an exasperated sound, turned from Randulf, and made her way over to a low couch against the wall of her 'office,' which is where the woman conducted her business. Business, as it turned out, of the lowest kind. Randulf's missing wife had been busy in the days he had been indentured to Jarl Heinrich. Aside from politics, Norse society did not have too many sex-based barriers to advancement within the sub-realms of their world. Shieldmaidens went to war with the warriors, they could work most jobs, they could become businesswomen of great power and renown. The only real door closed to a Norsewoman was political - they could not become a Jarl and Queens of Midgard did not last long if their husbands died without a male heir. They were either assassinated or forced into marriage with an upstart who had bested his competition in single combat. That particular ceiling, which was most definitely made of stone or some kind of metal, did not bother Eyja - she was a trumped-up madam, gregarious tavernkeeper, master of a stable of thieves, and purveyor of all kinds of black-market products, and that was the height of her ambition. She liked it that way.

At least, she frequently told herself she did.

The only black market that existed in Norse society had to do with religious admonitions. Seers, using edicts handed down from their chiefs in the Great Temple at Upsalla, made it clear that only certain crops could be grown in certain years, that plundering certain coasts was illegal one year to the next, and, of course, that trade in magical creatures was always forbidden. Even the dwarves, who had warred against the humans for decades - they were not to be taken as slaves. Kill them, yes, but definitely no using them for any other purpose.

At least, not without papers from the Great Temple.

And there were so many purposes for magical creatures... well, they were mostly sentient and had wills of their own, but many a Norseman had kink for the magic flowing through their veins. Eyja saw an opportunity and took it - she hired paperless dwarves, gnomes, and elves as prostitutes and she had come to be known for it. Mimir's Rest was such a den of iniquity, so renowned for its depravity, that she had been left pretty much to her own devices by the Seers and King Hrokr, earthly master of all the human lands of Midgard. Everyone was paid in cold, chunky, mithril - Jarl Danski (the local leader), the guards, the prostitutes, the staff. The money that was left over was voluminous - enough to see Eyja bedecked in finery, jewels, and enough makeup that would make one of her own working girls blush. Randulf assumed that she thought that this gaudiness was a good look, or something. Instead of its desired effect on her husband, it made him sick to see her so drunk on power and mithril.

In spite of all of her ministrations with makeup, she still appeared as homely. At least, to the masses. Eyja's appearance was precisely beautiful to one Randulf Randulfsson. Her hair, a blonde which had greyed slightly, was woven into a thick braid the fell over her shoulder. Rings studded with sapphires kept the thing from coming apart. On her body, she wore a long flowing yellow robe, split down the centre and with finely-detailed spring flowers embroidered into the rectangular border that hugged the edges of the dress. She had gained some weight during this period of excess, though not an enormous amount. She still looked good to the former bondsman, but when she smiled, which had been rarely when he knew her before and now which seemingly occurred constantly, the recently freed man saw some of the same emotion that he had sometimes caught in his own eyes in the looking glass at Jarl Heinrich's place in Ygglheim.

It was the quiet desperation of someone enslaved.

"This really is quite a lot of... stuff, Eyja," attempted Randulf. "You must be happy... but what happened to the lyre? When I saw you last, you were planning on staying on in Mimir's Rest and making your fortune as a skald. I used to love listening to you sing the tales of Thor and Loki, of Freya and Odin, of Ragnarok and the coming fall of the gods. Have you given it up?"

"Oh, that," said Eyja wistfully. "Yes, I gave it up. Turns out not too many people are appreciative of women skalds in this town. They'll pay good money for elf cunny, though, so a woman's got to do what a woman's got to do."

"Do the beasts make you happy?" asked Randulf, pointing at the cages. Aside from the tiger and the wolves, there were a pair of bird cages with enormous feathered things within, two smaller but still sizable wildcats, foxes, badgers, and... a gnome? "You're keeping a gnome in a cage?"

"Yeah, this is fucked up, ain't it?" said the gnome, putting his hands on the bars of his cage. "Like, what the hell? Somebody call a Seer, amirite?"

"Oh, you give that shite a rest, Joe," said Eyja. "It's not forever. You just have to work off your debt to me."

"Debt?" asked the gnome named Joe. "What debt? I have no idea what she's talking about, buddy. I was just going about my gnomey business, crawling over logs and toadstools and shite in the forest, roasting squirrels and manufacturing magical devices of great worth, when this bitch's animal catchers throw a net over me, knock me out, and then I wake up here, Bob's your uncle."

"Ah, you know uncle Bob?" asked Randulf, lighting up for a moment, before furrowing his brow. "He's been dead for two decades - how old are you?"

"Are you serious with this guy, Eyja?" said Joe, turning back to his jailor. "You were married to him?"

"Don't try to change the subject, Joe," said Eyja, shaking her head with a smile. "You neglected to mention the part where you blew into my tavern, made a bet on a pit fight, and skipped town without paying when your man lost. Besides, it's not like you've got to do much to work your debt off - I'm starting to think you like being cooped up in my cage." Eyja bared her leg. "Maybe you like to see it when my thighs slip out from my dress."

"As if, bitch," said Joe. "Gay as three ounces of mithril: that's me. Can't seem to help attracting straight human men, though. In fact, it kind of gets me off. I like to bamboozle them with my stable of gyrocopters and specially-brewed gnomish mead before I marry them. That mead will make a cock as hard as a rock and let you fuck for hours. Sure as shite will rot the teeth out of a man's skull though - I nicknamed my first husband Snaggletooth, cause he's only got the one left. Still, makes for a great blowjob, I tell you what."

"Not doing much fucking from there, though, are you Joe?" Eyja said. "Look, it's not that hard to make me a mechanical bird - I've been offered a half-dozen of them through my contacts in the black market over the years. Now, not a one is available and I want one - no, I *need* one. I mean, they're just so *cute*! I know you can do it, but you are refusing on some strange principle."

"Refusing?!" roared Joe. "I don't have the proper fucking materials! I've told you that a million times. You want your bird, you have got to get me the sound of a cat's footsteps and the cold of a glacier. Not the ice. The cold." Joe paused. "You would have been better off just buying one of the damn birds."

"How the fuck does one procure those?" said Eyja, standing from her chair. "They're abstract ideas without physical form."

"Ask the bloody gods, they use shite like that all the time in their smithing," replied Joe. "All I know is, you get them for me, and I can make you your damned mechanical bird. But it won't be enough. It never fucking is with you humans. Even when the teeth start falling out of my husbands' mouths, they

180

still want me to pour the mead in my belly button so they can drink it like we're at a fucking fertility festival. Still though, like my pappy used to say, the road of excess leads to the palace of wisdom."

"Your pappy sounds like an erudite man," said Randulf, crossing his arms.

"Erudite? Oooh, my, I think I had you all wrong," said Joe, batting his eyelashes. "Sounds like you're not such a moron, after all." Joe paused, getting close to the side of the cage. "Say, what say you help her get these things, I'll make the bird, you and I go out to the forest, we go for a little ride in my gyrocopter, I give you some of my special mead, and then we get down for a little dark and dirty."

"I'm straight!" said Randulf. "That's my wife, right there."

"OK, well tell me this then," attempted Joe. "You know codpieces - you ever catch yourself admiring them? You know, like, 'damn, that's a pretty good codpiece? Wish I had the gumption to put on a piece of clothing whose sole purpose is the expansion of one's ego in a social setting?'"

"Erm, maybe once or twice," admitted Randulf.

Joe smiled and nodded, raising his eyebrows. "Them codpieces you've been eying - do you prefer the big ones or the little ones?"

"Big ones," said Randulf. "I mean, the purpose is inflating the perceived size of a man's genitals as a show of power, so bigger is indeed better in these circumstances."

Joe pushed back from the bars and crossed his own arms, mirroring Joe. "Well, I guess you're not all that straight, then."

"Can't argue with that logic," said Eyja flatly. "Tell me, Joe - does that work?"

"All the time," said Joe earnestly. "Though I usually have the gyrocopters and sex mead handy," he added. "A little difficult to get the full bamboozlement on the go without my stuff, you know?"

With that, the door blew open. Agnarr stood at the threshold. "Eyja, you've got to come quick: one of the boys we scooped up in the market. Not his son," he added, pointing at Randulf, "the other one. You need to come because he is... saying really mean and cutting things. I mean, I just cried my eyes out into my roast goose. Lad didn't even touch me but fucked me up on an emotional level beyond anything I've ever felt. Nearly cut my own throat out of despair-"

"How many times have I told you - no coming into my office, Agnarr!" said Eyja, glowering at her lackey. "I cannot abide your stink."

"B-b-but, you've a full stable of wild animals pissing and shiteing in their cages constantly. I mean, this place is like a dozen privies rolled into one."

"You smell worse," assessed Eyja. "Whoever this Cloacina goddess is, she has it out for you bad, Aggie, my love."

"You've taken a page out of this Gudleik's book with your nastiness," said Agnarr. "But, I'll be honest, when he says stuff like that, it's much worse. It's almost as if his words have a power of their own, a way of worming into your skull and making you feel terrible."

"And... you came to me... because he says mean things?" said Eyja. "You just burst in here like you had big news, like you just tracked down the sound of cat's footsteps for me. Instead, your big news is that our guest is good at insulting you?"

"Naw, you don't understand, my lady," said Agnarr, casting his eyes down to avoid stoking her wrath further. "This is magic, I think. And I think you could probably use it to your advantage. In negotiations and the like. Hire the boy - I swear it will be worth your while."

"Erm," said Randulf. "Gudleik has some kind of grand destiny. The Seer we came with, Jogrim-"

"You brought a Seer here!?" screamed Eyja, turning to her husband.

"Yeah, the other fellow I was with - sprightly old man. Was blind for decades - probably why he's off ogling your girls right now. He's the Seer of Ygglheim."

Eyja pulled a blanket from some unseen alcove and threw it over Joe's cage. "Agnarr, go speak with Danatiel and the rest of the elves. And the dwarves without papers. Tell them they need to hide - *now*."

"Erm," said Randulf. "I'm not sure if that's necessary. This Jogrim... he's not your average Seer, I don't think. He's really caught up in this quest with Gudleik. You know, they are planning to stop Ragnarok. It's begun... at least, that's what Jogrim says."

"The mentor figure who helps the hero on his path to self-discovery," nodded Agnarr wisely. Then he shook his head and curved it up at the ceiling of the room. "Damn it, Cloacina, you fourth wall breaking whore, get out of my head!"

"I don't care if he's on a mission from Odin himself," exclaimed Eyja, fetching a small club from beneath her desk. "A Seer is a Seer. I can never trust the wretches to accept being paid off or to stay paid off. Some will take the mithril and be on their way, others are true believers." Eyja slapped the palm of her hand with the club. "And others - well, others are just greedy."

"Pot kettle black," called a muffled voice from beneath the blanket of Joe's cage.

Eyja crossed to the covered cage and smacked the bars through the blanket. A gonging sound resonated mutely throughout the room.

"Look," said Randulf. "We came here for lyre lessons. If you're not prepared to give them, then we will just have to be on our way. Please don't crack our guide's skull."

"You forget, Randy, sweetie," Eyja said, her voice pure husky sultriness. "Just like before, *I* make the rules." She turned to her stinky lackey. "Agnarr, take Randy to fetch the Seer. We will meet you downstairs. It's time that I met this Gudleik Sigbjornsson."

⸀Inter(e)mission

"You know, I feel like I paid too steep a price. It wasn't worth it, Dagon's power."

"Oh, is that so," said the goblin prostitute. By human standards, she was absolutely hideous - hairy moles everywhere, assymetrical, misshapen skull and body, one tusk minuscule compared to the other, yellow teeth, rank stench about her. To the Goblin King and the rest of goblinkind, this woman was a specimen of untold beauty. She did a great job at hiding her disgust for the Goblin King's own features, which would have given him at least an 8 or 9 out of 10 rank within the superficial human system of beauty judgment (if one was so inclined to diminish a person's worth by using such a system - but the Goblin King isn't a human being and he does it all the time with fellow goblins so fuck it). "Tell me more about this... Dagon."

"I know you don't give a fuck and are just doing your job," said the Goblin King. "But I appreciate it nonetheless."

"All I do is give fucks... well, sell them," replied the goblin prostitute. "Speaking of which, are we going to do it or is this going to be one of those weird listening jobs where you start crying about daddy ignoring you and mommy not giving you enough love? Cause I have a nine o'clock. You're the King and all, so I can push it back, but I need to know."

"How about a little half and half?"

"Half and half... like a blowjob and a fuck?"

"No! Half and half, like a listen and a fuck."

"Ooh," said the goblin prostitute. "Um, sure. Why not. I know you've got the mithril for it."

"If I had known I'd be reduced to this..." said the Goblin King. "It all started when Dagon went to town with his jelly cock on my wife, in front of my subjects. I mean, I knew that power required a certain amount of mystique and a perception of faultless strength, that letting my wife get ploughed by a jellyfish god as an exhibition might be a bad idea politically, but I thought, 'you know what? I'm about to receive untold arcane power from an ancient god. I can deal with the fallout.' When he gave me the sword," the Goblin King gestured to the barnacled cutlass resting against the wall of the prostitute's room, "I was sure that all was well. I even got a chance to lord over the swearing-in of all of the new acolytes to Dagon's religion. Who would have thought that this being of unimaginable evil was just using me to gain a worship foothold in Albion, that he would toss me aside like a used piece of garbage after he got what he wanted?"

"What's a 'used piece of garbage?' Wouldn't that just be a 'piece of garbage?' Isn't 'used' implied in the very word?"

"What's that?" said the Goblin King. "Oh, a wise gobliness, are you? Whatever, I'm used to being questioned and not taken seriously. I mean, I was married to the Goblin Queen for decades. Now, though, it looks like she's got a new master to give her tongue lashings to."

"The way I heard it," said the prostitute. "It's Dagon who's been doing the tongue lashing. The way she came at that first fuck ceremony... made me jealous when I heard the story."

"Listen, you want me to pay extra to get you to shut the fuck up?" asked the Goblin King.

"No, I like interjecting," said the prostitute. "Let's keep going like this."

"I get no respect. No respect at all," said the Goblin King, bugging his eyes out and shaking his jowls. "Say, can we get something to eat around here? I'm in the mood for pork. Long, if you've got it."

"Of course," said the goblin prostitute. "The Warty Rump is a high-class... erm, low-class, goblin brothel. We've got no running water, no one bathes, period - even when we're on our periods - and we sacrifice a goblin child to make a pot of stew every week. You want I should get you a bowl?"

"No vegetables?"

"Of course not! We are as far from Tuskless as it gets. None of these foul human customs - we do as goblins are meant to do. Be base humanoid creatures so vicious and savage that we provide a counterpoint to humanity's more evolved aspects."

"That's what I'm always saying!" said the Goblin King. "This whole, 'let's become more human' thing makes me sick to my guts. You know some of my subjects are marrying humans? I've outlawed it, of course, but I know it's still happening."

"I thought you were dethroned," said the goblin prostitute, standing from the bed and going to call for soup from the door. The way she hobbled from her uneven skeletal structure caused the Goblin King to stiffen. "You know, you don't have any subjects any more. You're just a lowly Mr.

Goblin, like the rest of us. You're going to have to give up the title. What's your real name?"

"Scratch My Nuts," said the Goblin King. "I don't like it very much, so I would prefer to keep the name 'the Goblin King,' if you don't mind." The Goblin King looked at the goblin prostitute, who had her mouth open as if she were about to speak. "Before you ask, my father broke his legs when we were still living in the Slit. Though he had no problem reaching his own testicles with his hands, he still demanded that I help with the scratching. He was a real piece of shite - a bloodsworn of Gamblor. He used me in a bet when I was nine. I ended up having to go work at a pig farm for a decade when I was a child. Don't get me wrong - it was great work, being around those animals and cleaning up pig shite. And the smells - oh my, the wonderful smells... say, I don't know your real name. You know mine, so maybe we could-"

"Nawp," said the goblin prostitute. "It's 'you' or 'her' or 'goblin prostitute,' if you're not into the whole brevity thing. Not sure why I need to say 'goblin prostitute,' and not just 'prostitute,' seeing as how we're both goblins living in a xenophobic goblin culture, but I guess I'll just leave that one alone."

"I get no respect!" repeated the Goblin King, doing another jowl shake and eye pop.

"What do you expect - you're the comic relief within the pages of a comedy. If anyone's not going to be taken even the slightest bit seriously, it's you."

"I have no idea what you're talking about, goblin prostitute," said the Goblin King. "So I'm going to proceed as if you said nothing at all. Getting back to the expository spilling of my guts, Dagon has seized power and deposed me. He's calling himself the Jelly Cock King, and my wife is now his wife. Before I left, I asked him whether he could just call himself the 'Jelly King' or perhaps 'Jellyfish King.' I knew what his answer was going to be before he even said it."

"Oh?"

"The people need to know that Dagon fucks," said the Goblin King.

"Ahh," said the goblin prostitute. "Can't fault him for that. I mean, that's important information."

"Now I've got an ancient fell god of untold demoniac power sitting in my throne in Pustule Hall, fucking *my* wife, raising *my* kids, plotting *my* invasion of Camelot." The Goblin King took the bowl of hot soup that was offered to him. "And here *I* am, spending an hour with a prostitute - a *goblin* prostitute - and eating Cannibal's Chowder... wait, this isn't so bad. I mean, this isn't so good, which means that it's my delighted preference as a true green masochistic goblin. In fact, what the hell do I need to do? Certainly not seize my power back. Who needs it!?"

"Plus you've got that hideous nautical-themed sword," said the goblin prostitute, pointing to the barnacled cutlass. "But what are you going to do for mithril? You were the King, so I assume you still have plenty, but certainly you don't have an inexhaustible supply of it. You're going to have to work eventually."

"Oh, that," said the Goblin King. "I have no plan. Besides, it's a much more pressing issue than that! I already bet my hoard and lost all of it on the touched donkey races."

"What?" said the goblin prostitute. "How do you intend to pay me?"

"I don't," said the Goblin King. "I mean, I am the Goblin King, after all."

"You're the Goblin fucking Bum!"

"Well, not yet," said the Goblin King, motioning to the erection poking up against the blanket of the bed. "I mean, I haven't fucked any bum yet. Please Gluttor - let that have been an offer."

"Get out," said the goblin prostitute, knocking the Goblin King to the floor of her room. The bowl of Cannibal's Chowder smashed and sprayed everywhere, chunks of long pork squishing between the goblin prostitute's toes. "Get out - get the fuck out of here you degenerate and ugly piece of shite!"

"Oh, perhaps you could whisper such sweet nothings in my ear," grinned the Goblin King, rolling his naked body towards his clothes and cutlass, deftly avoiding the wasted soup.

"You know that you're the fifth john who's tried to rip me off this week?" said the goblin prostitute. "Granted, we're goblins - it's the cost of doing business. Part of the thrill of the job is to try to guess whether or not the next goblin who tries to stick me with his green cock actually has the mithril to pay. I usually figure out the scam long before now. You wanted my respect?" asked the goblin prostitute. "You've got it." The goblin prostitute paused to bat her eyelashes at the Goblin King. "It's Dirtaphine, by the way."

"What's that?" asked the Goblin King, pulling on his pants.

"My name - it's Dirtaphine. Come try to trick me into free sex any time." With that, Dirtaphine kicked the Goblin King over again, this time directly into the mess of rank broth and boiled goblin child flesh.

Both of the goblins tittered.

a treatise on magic

Rosmerta looked out across the fields of Avalon. They were verdant, full of life, speckled with brightly-coloured bushes and flowers, strange mushrooms, and a multitude of little homes that looked like these mushrooms. Little windows showed domestic scenes, small crooked chimneys spurted white smoke into the air, faery children zipped around, faery parents shouted colourful yet loving obscenities at the kids about coming in for supper and ceasing with tomfoolery.

In spite of having known Enyd for years, Rosmerta never truly *knew* her. She never knew what her home was like, what her Queen was like, what the politics were like. She had simply assumed that the faery lived in some kind of strange limbo where anything was possible, if she ever did turn her mind to it at all. Usually, though, Rosmerta was far too self-interested in whatever was happening in her own life to ponder the fate of her friend.

Avalon was overpopulated. That was as clear to Rosmerta as the magical sky above her was a two-tone shade of pink and purple. Brighid had told Rosmerta that Avalon was her own creation, that it was some kind of rebellion against her mother for what she saw as an undue alienation of humanity's right to self-define and self-direct without the influence of gods. Rosmerta had thought to bring up the fact that Brighid herself was a goddess, that there still had to be a deity in the equation for her little project to work, but Rosmerta always thought better of it. It was not her business - not really. Perhaps later that evening, after the Beltane ceremony was complete and she had sworn her oath to Brighid, perhaps then she would speak more candidly with the goddess of Avalon.

Beltane. Tonight. The day always had a particular significance to Rosmerta and the people of the Blessed Isles, given that it was the first day of summer. It marked the start of a period of intense growth and change, and it was one of the points when the barriers between the Otherworlds of the gods and the lands of human beings were at their thinnest. There was a reason that blood oaths were sworn on Beltane. Certainly, an oath could be sworn at any point in the year, but there was an auspiciousness and level of connection that was simply incomparable. Good things came to those who waited, and with blood oaths, it was always worth waiting.

How would Father feel about Rosmerta's decision? He would be incensed, fume, perhaps even disown the girl. But those considerations, which had led Rosmerta by the nose throughout her entire life, had lost much of their appeal. Hell, without the visit to Macha's home in the Valar Mountains, Rosmerta would probably never have agreed to Brighid's offer. Brigantia, the widow from Glastonbury who was living her last days in Erybos, had been right. There was a bit of trickery involved in Enyd the faery's plot to get her to bring Cernunnos' fertility magic to the goddess of war, Macha. But the trickery had nothing to do with pulling wool over Rosmerta's eyes. It had everything to do with removing it.

After Brighid had plied Rosmerta with poppy tea and told her about the blood oath contract, the goddess had pointed to a bed and told the girl to sleep her intoxication off. The next morning, Brighid was nowhere to be found. Enyd, though (without her paramour Donk) - she was waiting for her. The little faery conjured a portal into Macha's homeland in the Valar Mountains. There was no question that a goddess of war lived in the place - it was rough, barren, and the people were unfriendly. But the Christians had not yet arrived, and all Rosmerta had to do was flash her mother's awen pendant at one of the grumbling mountain people. Within moments, she was brought to a female druid named Cox.

"Just Cox," had said the druidess. She was dressed differently than Rosmerta's father Keandre normally did. Keandre's garb was all verdant green, adorned with oak leaves and with a thick foxtail running around the collar of his robe. Cox, on the other hand, had a brown and rumpled tunic that disguised her breasts. She wore a dagger plain to see on her hip, and her face was lined with a criss-cross of pink scars. One eye had a milky cast, and she leaned on a staff for support. In the hut behind Cox, Rosmerta could see a bent and decrepit elderly man slowly going about cleaning up dishes from a recently-eaten meal.

"That's my Dicks," said the druidess, not turning as she spoke to Rosmerta. "He's the only other druid in the Mountains."

"Let me guess, it's 'just Dicks?'"

"What? No," said Cox. "His name is Walter. To you, anyway. To me, he'll always be Dicks." Cox sighed and put a wrinkled hand to her chest. "We consider family names to be pet names. Consider it an artifact of our military-themed goddess of worship. They wouldn't call him Walter if he were in the army, would they?"

"Is he your husband?" inquired Rosmerta.

"Eh, sort of," muttered Cox. "We handfasted at a Beltane ceremony forty years ago. We never did do it the second time. Nor did we break the handfasting. Forever betrothed, I suppose you could say." Cox paused. "But I'm sure you never came here to discuss the forever pushed back Dicks-Cox union."

"Eh," said Enyd, doing a backflip as she fluttered. "Already seen one o' dem. Hell, I sees 'em at every faery orgy I attends - and dere's a lot. Not much excitement in one, I must say. I much prefer the dicks-cunts union."

"Aside from a heteronormative faery, what have you brought me, Rosmerta O'Ceallaigh?" intoned Cox. "I understand that you bring the blessing of great fertility magic from our Macha's brother Cernunnos."

"Yeah, I can make you a poultice to help your goddess perform in bed, if that's your preference," said Rosmerta. "I mean, that's what Enyd told me was necessary. Why she brought me here. And, as I understand it, Macha wants to keep this on the down-low?"

"Aye," said Cox.

Rosmerta waited. "Care to elaborate as to why?" she asked finally.

"Not really."

"Maybe tell me why you had to contact a faery, an emissary of hated Brighid, the sister who betrayed all of Danu's Children by going her own way - care to tell me literally anything about what I'm doing here?" Rosmerta fumed. "You want my help, you've got to throw me a bone."

"You've fire in you," said Cox, laughing the wheezy laugh of the elderly magus-type. A little puff of azure smoke emerged from her mouth. "You remind me of myself, when I was your age. Young, sprightly, not needing poultices to fuck your husband."

"Wait," said Rosmerta. "The magical smoke - you're Macha."

Cox inclined her head. "Aye."

"But you're so old and feeble! How can someone like you be the goddess of war?"

Cox used her head to motion to Dicks, who had finished cleaning the dishes up and had taken a seat at the table again. He had produced a pipe and was smoking it.

"He's my last druid," said Macha. "I'm in dire straits, girl. Once he dies, I die. Lose Dicks, and Cox will go, too, sure as night follows day." Macha paused. "I won't be gone - not totally. I'm still part of The Morrigan, the triple goddess of fate and war. But I don't get to be myself as The Morrigan. I have to share power with my sisters. It's not exactly fun."

"So what do you plan to do? Certainly a woman of your... advanced age... cannot bear children."

Cox chuckled. "No, dearie, I certainly cannot. Nor do I need your fertility poultice - the story about needing that was just a scheme to get you here. Truth be told, I believe in what Brighid is doing. I think my brothers and sisters do, too - at least, some of them. But they're all so shite-scared of our mother, Danu, that they all toe the line. Me, I'm on the way out, so I have the luxury of being able to tell the truth without fear of repercussion."

"Why?" asked Rosmerta. "And why me?"

"Because I need to show you something, girl," said Cox.

With that, Cox had touched Rosmerta's head. She had seen, alright. Seen plenty more than she would have been happy to see, too. Of course, the goddess of war would have a special line on the coming clash of the gods. Except that this was to be unlike anything seen before. When Rosmerta returned to Avalon and asked Brighid about her visions, the faery goddess simply smiled at her. Some rot about the purpose of divination not being to tell the future, that looking at the future from the present moment's only purpose is to bring one back to the present moment.

"But you've seen the future," had said Rosmerta to Brighid. "You know what it holds! How do you live each day, knowing what is going to happen?"

"Anyone who claims that they know what is going to happen, even with command of all of the magic in the world, is only deluding themselves. Sometimes that delusion is necessary, so that they take the correct action in each moment as it arrives. The purpose of an oracle is to ensure that one walks the path correctly, that they give over totally into faith." Brighid paused. "I am a goddess, so I do know the future, all of the branching paths of decision that will take us to all kinds of different places. But I cannot communicate it to you. I can give you guidance, certainly. But the point of life is to live it, not to live in fear or excitement of the future. Certainly, you can feel those emotions and it is good to do so. But do not fall into the trap that so many of your species do."

"What's that?" asked Rosmerta.

"That things will get better at some point in the future. They are already perfect, right here and now. The point of time is to bring you back to this realization. And when you do come to this realization, things do get better as time rolls along."

"That's a... a... pada... pada-"

"A paradox," agreed Brighid. "Just think of what that word implies, Rosmerta. A paradox is something where the duality sits completely whole. Things are both one way and another way. If you take it literally, the whole thing crumbles. But try to look at it symbolically, to see the deeper metaphor beneath the surface."

Rosmerta frowned. "I don't really get what you mean."

Brighid smiled and sat back languidly in her seat. "You will, girl. Believe me, you will."

"But why? Why do you say that? Why all of this fuss over me? I'm just a-"

"Just a what?" asked Brighid. "Just a girl? Just a lowly daughter of a druid? Just a nobody? I thought you wanted to be a star? A great bard in service to kings? One whose genius eclipses even that of kings?"

"Erm, I do," said Rosmerta.

"Tell me, Rosmerta," attempted Brighid. "Say you 'succeed,' as it were. What are you going to do with that success? Towards what end are you going to direct that power? Have you even thought about it? Why do you want this so damn badly?"

"I-I-I... I don't know," admitted Rosmerta. "I just... just do."

"Pssh," said Brighid. "You can do better than that."

"I want to make people like me," offered Rosmerta.

"Oh, puh-lease, girl," said Brighid, shaking her head. "People do like you. You don't need to be a fucking bard to be well-liked. If ever there was a terrible, awful, rank horseshite reason to seek after this kind of thing, it's that one. And it happens all of the time. And other people, similarly fucked up about the direction of up and down - they feed into it. That whole vanity scene is diseased beyond measure, Rosmerta. It's got its purpose and place - there is nothing excessive or missing in this world, but that is not your path, child. You're going to try again."

Rosmerta thought about it for a while. Her mind went reeling back to the moments when she practiced with her lute and when she learned how to sing. She could do each of the things without problem on their own, it was putting them together that forever eluded her. But when she did play and learn, when the music that she made or sang was pleasing to her ears, something occurred within. A great river of bliss flowed out from the core of her being into every part of her. With each consonant note plucked on the string, with every word sung in perfect melody, all of her cares and worries were lifted away.

"Now," said Brighid softly. "Don't you want to share that with the world? Don't you want to let others experience that?"

Rosmerta smiled at the goddess, the calming influence of the memories drawing up similar feelings in the present.

"That is the reason - that is the only reason - to make and share art. If you cleave to that, if you do not let anything interfere with that, you will certainly find what you seek. Success is a side-effect, not a goal, of doing that. And success is not measured in mithril and fame. It's measured in laughter and tears of joy." Brighid paused. "But I would implore you, Rosmerta, do not seek success as an end in itself. Remember, living your life in the future is a recipe for tears. Whether you are sweating it out, writing terrible page of music after terrible page of music, struggling to make your lute hand take a rhythm of its own, or you are in command of the magic that I am going to grant you, you must learn to appreciate each and every step on the path. Because that is the point of this whole thing. A wise man from the future once likened life itself to music - that the point is to surrender to it as it's happening. If we truly treated life as a journey, where the purpose was to make it to the end, then the best lives would be the ones which were over the quickest. Or, using the music metaphor: one great cymbal crash and that would be it."

"There is a reason that you are a musician, Rosmerta," continued Brighid. "A reason that you have a musician's soul. You have a job - it's a job that is just as important as a baker's or a stonemason's or an ealdorman's (or ealdorwoman's). Your job is to remind people. The reason that music exists - the reason that it endures throughout every human culture and endeavour - is because it is a microcosm of life itself. No, Rosmerta, you are not special. And you are also the most special person who ever lived. Take the two opposing poles, drive them together in the center of your being, and let it all out. You want a treatise on magic? There it is."

The goddess' words had confused Rosmerta beyond measure. Rosmerta spent days wandering Avalon, meeting faeries and learning about their lives. They were like humans - just like them, in fact. Except that they were free. They bore none of the baggage that humans did, none of the malaise and soul-destroying unhappiness that humans did. They were always happy, always content, always rutting. Brighid caught Rosmerta as she was passing into a willow grove in one of the forests, the mists having descended upon the magical Otherworld.

"I thought I would make something perfect with the faeries," said Brighid. "I thought that I could create a world without pain, without sadness, without disease. You humans all think that those who swear blood oaths to me are bamboozled, tricked by me. But I never trick anyone - it's against my nature. Those who come to live in Avalon forever do so out of choice. They look on the world of human beings, see the darkness and shadow, and choose to remain in the light. They willingly become faeries." Brighid shook her head. "They are misguided. They think they are abandoning hell for heaven, but it truly is the opposite that is occurring. Your world, with all of its sadness and misery to go along with the joy and beauty - it is absolute perfection. This place - it's a false illusion. One which is coming apart at the seams." Brighid paused. "I want to show you something."

Brighid had led Rosmerta out from the willow grove, through the fields, well beyond where Rosmerta had explored. Past the last faery settlement, they disappeared into the forest for what seemed like hours. And then, finally, the pair emerged into another clearing. What struck Rosmerta first was the stench. It was overpowering - a mixture of feces, urine, and roasting flesh. Before them, a shanty town of poorly-constructed tents and buildings stood - just barely. Green-fleshed creatures milled about, grumbling and smacking each other from time to time. In one corner, pack beasts with obvious deformities were running a course as a sea of goblins cheered and shouted obscenities. A large farm in the middle of the settlement was nearly overflowing with pigs, beasts squat in so tightly they could barely move. Nearby, a full pig was turning on a spit over a bonfire. On a second spit, what was clearly a humanoid body was charring from the heat.

"Goblins," said Brighid, smiling. "At first I was disgusted by them. I mean, seriously? Gambling, pain, and cannibalism? They don't treat their animals very well, either. But then I realized what they were. When faeries make their way through that forest we just crossed, they become goblins. They know full well the life that awaits them for leaving the beauty and safety of Avalon, but still they cross. They want to become goblins. At least, perhaps, they want to escape the perfection of Avalon. A short and strange life as these ugliness-worshiping misanthropes is preferable to total perfection in the faery-realms."

"You will be approached by this idea in many forms," said Brighid, turning to face Rosmerta. "Many people get caught in the idea that enlightenment is some kind of positivity game, that the person who imagines themselves to be totally perfect is the one who is best or gets to leave this plane of existence. These Christians have made a whole religion around the idea, deifying a human being and calling him King. In lands far to the East, where you will never visit, they do it with fellow human beings all of the time. Do not get taken," said Brighid. She pointed to a handful of goblins gathered around a semi-well-dressed goblin (it was not a high bar). This slick goblin (who had a pencil-thin mustache, no less) had three dirty sea-shells in front of him. He put a bead between thumb and forefinger, showed it to the crowd, then put it beneath one of the shells and began moving it around. After a while, one of the other goblins pointed to a shell. When it was lifted, there was no bead beneath. Violence erupted, knives were pulled. When it was over, three goblins lay dead, including the master of the game.

"It's all a shell game," said Brighid. "All of it. Don't get caught. Find your own truth - that's the real wager. How much can you learn to trust yourself over everything that's coming in from the outside." Brighid paused. "It will require courage - bucket loads. More than you thought possible. But that just gives the game a bit of spiciness. Makes it palatable to the tongue. Remember, if it were all easy - if we were all faeries - we'd have to create goblins."

Rosmerta shook herself from her recollection. It still didn't make sense to the girl, not really. Gods were gods and humans were humans, never the twain shall meet. Goblins were despicable creatures, faeries strange, and she was caught in the middle of it. Still, though, Brighid had promised her skill with the lute and song, if only she would give up a drop of her own blood on Beltane. She could not turn away from such a promise, not now. Especially not after what Macha had shown her of the coming war. Gods from all over the human realms were about to clash and her job was... to sing about it? It didn't make sense, but the visions were quite clear as to what would occur if no one with a poetic blessing intervened.

The hellfire and destruction of literalism would be the end of it. The end times. A heavy burden rested on Rosmerta's shoulders, one that she would be able to bear only with the goddess' blessing. Her entire life, everyone had told her the same thing: faeries were evil creatures and their contracts were rife with deceit and destruction. But the destruction that would befall the world without the transformative power of poetic metaphor... well, it did not bear thinking about.

"Why me?" Rosmerta had asked Macha as the woman lay dying in her bed, the last gasps of life going from the goddess of war.

"Ha," coughed the elderly deity. She hacked up half a lung before she made full answer to the girl. "Same question, over and over again. Doesn't matter who it is - you humans are so damned predictable. A better question - why *not* you?"

With that, Macha's life fled from her body. Dicks had already died at that point - Macha used the last of her life force helping Rosmerta to bury her last druid.

The sun had set on Beltane Eve. The fires were lit. The faeries were arranging themselves in a circle around the cairns. Brighid touched Rosmerta lightly on the arm.

"It's time, Rosmerta," said the goddess. "Time to meet your destiny."

Ψιth Our Powεrs Combinεd

"Dad, we've got to get him out of there."

Randulf Randulfsson, ignoring his son's words, drank deep from his drinking horn and watched the men throwing axes against a stump through the window outside. It was a cool spring morning, but the early sun and rising temperatures in the day was good evidence that the summer was approaching. Randulf reflected on the one good part of his indentured servitude with Jarl Heinrich - he had never been expected to participate in the summer raids. Not that Jarl Heinrich would have anything like that on his mind at the moment, given how Ygglheim was decimated by the draugr. The men outside - Jarl Danski's subjects - would not be spared the social expectation of voyage to foreign lands for murder and plunder. One that was enforced with axes as keen as the ones they were launching against a stump that had taken so many blows that it looked like it were liable to fall apart at any moment. Randulf had to get out of the place before he was scooped up and pressed into military service. Rumour was that the Jarls of Thor's Land did not force its people on the raids.

"He's not our problem, boy," replied Randulf after a while. "Besides, your mother is still the selfish cunt she always was. She says she's given up drinking, and that may be so, but she's replaced that addiction with base vanity and greed. She commands many loyal men and she has claimed Gudleik to be her own. You were there - she gave Gudleik a choice to either serve her and learn what she knows about the lyre or leave without any knowledge. Gudleik chose to serve."

"You know I'm not talking about Gudleik," said Porsi, spitting on the ground. "That turncoat is fucking dead to me. It's Jogrim - she's got him caged up with that gnome of hers. She tortures both of them daily." Porsi paused. "He swore a blood oath to Freya, Dad. Aren't you the least bit worried about the wrath of the gods?"

"The gods?" roared Randulf, turning to face his son. Faces seated at other chairs looked over at the commotion. "Where were the gods when your mother abandoned us? Where were the gods when we were eating shite in Jarl Heinrich's stables? Where are the gods now that your mother has become a tyrant in this city?" Randulf realized he was being watched and lowered his voice. "I've never seen any evidence of the gods in my life, son. They either don't exist or are content to leave me alone. I may pray to them from time to time but I cannot worry about something which is clearly the figment of my imagination and that of the world's at large."

"And what of Gudleik's power, eh?" asked Porsi. "You heard him, the way he spoke to that man. There was something magnetic about his speech. When he told him that he was lower than a gull's shite, I felt the sting of the words. Gudleik has command of some kind of magic, that must be clear to you. And you were in Ygglheim - you saw the draugr and the corpses that they left! You have seen plenty of evidence of magic. If magic exists, how far of a leap is it to say that the gods do, too?"

"The boy has simply become a good orator, like his father, and his father's father behind him," stated Randulf flatly. "You know that Gudleik's father, Sigbjorn, commanded men in battle his whole life. So did Gulbrand. Those kinds of things get passed down in the blood, Porsi."

"Oh, for the love of - Dad, he used to be Loki-cursed, unable to do something as simple as go fishing without causing a massive disaster, and now he can command men to shite their keks with mere suggestion." Porsi paused. "You know," he continued, "Gudleik told me that Jogrim gave him some drugged mead while they were in the temple in Ygglheim. He said he had a conversation with the gods - his gods. Loki and Bragi. Both have blessed him. Perhaps this is what it means to be blessed, rather than cursed, by the trickster god." Porsi slumped his shoulders. "Happily transformed into an arsehole - sounds like Loki's work."

"Hmmph," said Randulf, shrugging. "Draugr, magic, the gods - real or not, it matters not a whit, anyway. We're leaving for Thor's Land tomorrow. We'll get a nice quiet job at the Nyxheim Mines and forget all about this chapter of our lives."

"Chapter?" said Porsi, incredulous. "Dad, this *is* our lives. What if Ragnarok is coming? Gudleik has made his choice to side with that bitch Eyja - she's no mother to me. But we need to get Jogrim out of there. He has unmistakedly received intercession from the gods - he was literally blind and now he can literally see - none of that metaphorical shite associated with ignorance of reality and revelation."

"You know what?" said Randulf, downing what was left in his horn of ale. "You do what you want. I'm going to Thor's Land tomorrow morning. You can either join me or you can rot in this shitehole. I spent two decades indentured, doing what I didn't want to do. Whatever life I have left I am spending it far, far away from your mother and Mimir's Rest."

"Gudleik," said Jogrim, "is that you?"

Gudleik didn't answer, not at first. Eyja had sent him to her office to fetch up an old sheaf of parchment, buried for years at the bottom of a chest near the cages of the menagerie. The young man had started rummaging when the Seer called his name. How did he know it was Gudleik in the office, and not Eyja or Agnarr or one of the others?

"Gudleik," said Jogrim, "I know it's you. I can sense your presence." Jogrim paused. "Do you think you could take the blanket off of my cage and we could speak? I'm not going to try to convince you to let me out again. I just would like to speak face to face."

"Why?" asked Gudleik after a while. "I don't need you, old man. Not anymore. I don't need anyone."

"Yes," said Jogrim. "You've made that abundantly clear. One taste of power from Loki and you are as corrupt as a Jarl from one of the old stories." Jogrim did not speak again for a while. "I am not judging you, Gudleik. I hope you understand that. I can appreciate why Loki's blessing would feel good to put to use. I mean, you can command men to follow your tongue just by words alone. It is not a trifling thing."

"Hell, if I had your power," came another voice from Jogrim's cage, "I wouldn't even need gyrocopters and magical sex mead. Or bamboozlement, even. I'd just say the word and I'd have all the straight guys I wanted, lining up to kiss my pecker."

"Thank you for your input, Joe," sighed Jogrim. "Necessary and illuminating as ever."

Gudleik looked at the cage. It was covered with a blanket, the way Eyja liked to keep it. He had spent nearly a decade hating Jogrim while the old blind drunk ignored him and told the rest of Ygglheim to do so as well, but ever since the draugr rose and he regained his sight, the Seer had nothing but Gudleik's best intentions in mind. Perhaps he should pull the blanket off and listen to him.

As the thought crossed Gudleik's mind, a faint melody plucked by a lyre came chiming up from the depths. It was quickly squashed by a discordant mashing of noise, one that bore with it disgust and anger at the Seer for past wrongs. To forgive him for his past transgressions? Who would ever be so weak? Certainly not Gudleik. Never again would he be caught by vipers like Jogrim.

"I don't care what you have to say," Gudleik muttered. "I hope that pervert gnome buggers you while you sleep."

"Hey," said Joe. "I ain't a rapist! I resemble that remark."

"'Resent,'" laughed Gudleik harshly. "You resent that remark, you stupid little magical fuck. You should seriously consider killing yourself. Maybe kill that Seer while you're at it."

Gudleik felt the familiar pulling sensation as reality bent and tumbled in response to his words. Loki's blessing was indeed powerful. Even now, the gnome's mind would be doing battle with Gudleik's magic, to see if he was strong-willed enough to fight off an overwhelming desire to comply with Gudleik's command.

"You might be immune to my words, Seer," said Gudleik, continuing his nasty chuckle. "But, is he?"

207

"No, let it sound out for just a little while longer before you mute. Don't slam the strings, press them. Like this. Y-no, not like that. Ymir's frozen cock, Gudleik, are you listening to me at all? Maybe you should ask that god of yours if he might help make your fingers work properly."

Eyja threw her lyre on the blanketed chair next to her and slumped back, shaking her head. "You're never going to get any better, which means you'll always be working for me. I should be happy - in barely more than a few weeks you've made me far richer than I ever thought possible. But I feel personally attacked by the fact that you cannot learn from me!"

Gudleik put his lyre on his chair, pushing down a growing rage. This was supposed to be the next step, but on what journey? He remembered drinking the mead at the temple in Ygglheim, but the memories of his time with the gods was fading fast. To be fair, even when it was fresh the recollection was dim. He knew that Ragnarok was on its way, that he needed to learn how to play the lyre and it would somehow put a stop to the coming end times, but beyond that, his mind was empty. Instead of staying empty, though, it had been filling with anger and red-hot emotion. With every person Gudleik had influenced with his magic, it was as if the container for his ire was growing. As if the lure of destruction was growing. He was having a hard time staying discerning when it came to targets.

Even now, as the young man looked on Eyja Randulfsson, his lyre instructor and boss, he felt his fists clench up. He could probably get her to fuck a goat in the market square or something equally perverse. It would tank her reputation as a fierce woman not to be trifled with. There would be an internal power struggle in her business outfit, people would be killed, chaos would flow like unctuously sweet mead.

"Maybe we should take a break for the day," said Eyja, one eyebrow raised at Gudleik. 'I don't like the way you're looking at me,' she did not add. "Here, why don't you go buy yourself something nice - on me. You do good work Gudleik - maybe consider thinking about hanging up the lyre? You can just keep working for me and I will make you rich."

"I won't," said Gudleik, taking the offered bag of mithril. "I have to play. And you had better hurry up and teach me, or there will be consequences."

Eyja took the young man in again. Yes, he was a serious liability. Not worth the risk. Perhaps, when he was sleeping, Eyja could get Agnarr to take him out of the picture. Dagger to the throat - something quick and painless. He had been, after all, a great boon to her business. Couldn't let such loyalty go unrewarded.

But Gudleik Sigbjornsson *did* have to die.

After the lyre lesson, Gudleik found himself wandering the forest outside of Mimir's Rest. He had not followed Eyja's advice. He didn't want to buy anything, though. He just wanted to... wanted to... wanted to... sow destruction. It felt so good to give into that voice in his mind. Every time he humiliated a man by forcing him into exposing himself in a crowd, or to self-mutilate with an axe, or even to kill himself, the feeling of pure, unadulterated strength built within him. But if he were being honest with himself, it was unsatisfying. He wanted more, more, more! If it were up to Gudleik, he would see all of Mimir's Rest end in fire and blood. Mother turned on daughter, father on son, brother on sister - it made Gudleik want to howl at the noon-day sun.

"There you are!"

Gudleik looked down. He found himself staring at the wide-eyes of Ruvark the Magnificent, the dwarf that he and his party had left outside of Mimir's Rest with a promise to speak to his cousin, Ivaldi. As far as Gudleik knew, the message had not been delivered. They had been otherwise occupied, and the plight of the strange dwarf had simply never come up.

"I've been out here for I don't know how long, sleeping rough like a fucking second-class citizen. Which helps, because I am!" Ruvark paused. "Where's your honour, boy? No one - and I mean no one - will listen to me and I need to get a message to Ivaldi. Fuck, I'm sure I'm going to be picked up by the Jarl's men any day now, and then it's goodbye Ruvark. No longer will Midgard be graced with the presence of the great skald of King Hreidmar's court!"

"Watch your tone, knave - wait, you're a skald?"

"Best skald in all of the Edda Mountains!" Ruvark paused. "Well, I like to say so anyway. In truth, there is many a fine dwarven skald. I am but a humble servant of the King. Except, not so humble, because you kind of got to stick out like a sore thumb to get noticed in this business. I mean, my full title is 'Ruvark the Magnificent,' so it certainly seems like I'm full of myself. But 'the Magnificent' is kind of like an honorific for skalds – I'm surprised you never caught on earlier. I don't really care about much but making my audience happy. And through that, this shite all happened." Ruvark pointed down at his body. Gone was the armour that he had been previously wearing. In its stead, he wore a flowing long green robe with runes and animals stitched upon it. It was a skald's style of dress. "I don't know, I don't really question it."

"Do you - do you think you can teach me?"

"Teach you?" said Ruvark, incredulously. "You've left me hanging for a month and a half out here, and now you want me to do *you* a favour? You're like all of your kind - out of your bloody mind."

Gudleik considered the dwarf for a moment. He had insulted the man, which sent his mind galloping further down the road of rage and destruction. But there was something about the dwarf, some kind of strange recognition. He knew he had seen Ruvark before, but there was something about his eyes. The sound of the lyre, which had been getting dimmer every time Gudleik manipulated someone else's mind, barely made itself known above the din of fury. Gudleik began to tell the dwarf to kill himself, then stopped.

"How about I go and fetch Ivaldi for you?" said Gudleik, feeling a strange sensation ripple down his body as he chose to spare the dwarf. "Then you give me some lyre lessons."

"Ha!" said Ruvark. "You'll not pay me off so cheaply. There is probably a war in my homeland because of your failure to act. After the Queen died, I know her brothers were sniffing around at King Hreidmar's position. They have no doubt formed a coalition to oppose the King. Ivaldi, son of the Queen, would have had a chance to put out the fire, but you and your friends dragged your fucking heels. I would bet every ounce of mithril I own, which isn't much, that dwarven blood is being spilled in the Edda Mountains right now."

Gudleik considered Ruvark again, then asked, "How would you like more? Much more! You are speaking to a rich man. I can make you rich."

"Oh," asked Ruvark, his eyes sparkling. Then he shook his head. "You have no idea what it's like, to fight against your nature. I am a dwarf, which makes me as greedy as a fucking dragon. Every time mithril is brought up in conversation, my mind focuses like a well-launched arrow. I have to consciously put the thoughts aside. It has become easier over the years, but still, my nature is my nature and I am a dwarf."

Ruvark paused. "I will teach you, man, if you get my cousin. But we will not be staying here. You will have to journey with us to the Edda Mountains. To King Hreimar's court. It will be a long trip and dangerous. But I will not accept mithril from you." With that, Ruvark seemed to become more at ease. An internal battle had been waged, and the dwarf seemed happy with the outcome.

"Could you teach me that, as well?" asked Gudleik.

"What?"

"How to fight your own nature?"

Ruvark took Gudleik in again. "Oh, I see." He chuckled. "Yes, you are most definitely destined to be a skald - what was your name again?"

"Gudleik. Gudleik Sigbjornsson."

"Alright, Gudleik Sigbjornsson. It's a deal. Get my Ivaldi out here, and I will teach you everything I know." He paused. "Who knows, you could be Gudleik the Magnificent before I'm through with you."

Ruvark extended a hand. Gudleik looked at it, at the dwarf's smiling face, then grasped it. Concordant notes on a lyre exploded deep within his mind. It was only then that Gudleik realized how much tension he had been holding in his shoulders. He let them fall, and was happy for the brief moment of peace.

The Cloaca Revelation

"Robbie, for the love of Danu, boy, would you give it a rest with the frogs? Ye've seen thirteen summers - certainly your interests must be changing." Laird Fearghas took a swig from his mug of *uisge*. "I mean, ye've shagged enough sheep, at least that's the way Cooky tells it. Don't ye 'ave no interest in women?"

Robbie looked down at the breast pocket of his frock coat. Merlyn's head was poking out and the frog was breathing quickly, as frogs are wont to do. Robbie liked that about froggies - it was like they were in a rush to get air into their bodies. It was a fascinating trait, one that consumed the boy's mind whenever he looked at the beasts. Why did it have to be so quickly? Why didn't they breathe slowly, like Robbie's dad did after a night on the bottle... so, after any given night of the week.

"Dis is Shite-Cock, Faither," said Robbie, pointing at the frog. "He's my new friend."

Laird Fearghas shook his head and took another drink. "Clan Fearghas is in trouble," he observed. "I'm going to need to stay alive as long as I can. If your mother weren't so old, I'd try to get another heir and disinherit you." Laird Fearghas paused. "No offence, boy," he added. "You're just a bit touched, is all. 'The price of pure blood,' that wily bastard of a druid Wilcox called it." Laird Fearghas peered at his boy with glassy and blood-shot eyes. "I didn't bairn up your mother because I gave a shite about pure blood, boy. I did it because she makes my pecker stand on end with that beautiful face and juggies and arse of hers. I'm the Laird of Clan Fearghas - I take what I want. So I took your mother. And I've been given a monster by Danu for my weakness."

Robbie shrunk over and looked around. "M-m-monster? Where, father? Fetch out your longsword!" The boy ran to his father's side. "Kill it!"

"Ah," said Laird Fearghas, looking down at his boy. The stench of alcohol, normally quite strong from the Laird on most days, was overpowering that night. It was Beltane Eve, which meant that the ceremony would have to be attended to in a matter of hours. Fearghas, who found himself besotted every night of the year, got especially lit up on Beltane. As the Laird stared at his flesh and blood, the boy's words resounded in his head. Perhaps it would be better just to kill him. So Clan Fearghas ended with his own death. It's not as though it had much to recommend it - a bunch of drunk men and exhausted women who had grown inured to the insult of being married to them for the majority of their natural lives.

Robbie, who appeared to have grown peaceful as the suspected monster attack did not come, removed Merlyn from his pocket. "I think 'e might be sick, Faither," said the boy, showing Merlyn's underbelly, then his fingers to the laird. "Look - 'e's weiner is all flakin' skin and the tips of his fingers turnt black. Perverse Abobimation, me last frog, never had neither. Pecker nor black fingers."

Laird Fearghas blearily scanned what his boy was showing him. It took a while to get his eyes to co-operate and focus on the image. After a moment, said unruly eyes widened, then his brow furrowed and he set his jaw.

"Do me a favour, lad," said Laird Fearghas. "Give that frog a kiss, would you?"

Robbie looked up at his father. "Kiss 'im?" he asked. "But I can't feel good with Shite-Cock - he's too small."

"I'm not asking you to fuck him, you daft little bugger, I'm asking you to kiss him!" Laird Fearghas fumed. He steadied himself by grabbing the side of his desk. He put the mug down and drew his blade from the scabbard on his hip. "Just humour me, Robbie," added the Laird. "Kiss that frog, full on the lips."

Robbie looked up at his father, shrugged his shoulders, and kissed the frog. At first, nothing happened. Then a crackle resounded through Laird Fearghas' chamber. A strong stench of ozone erupted from the frog and it became too hot for Robbie to hold. He dropped it to the floor and a man-sized explosion of pink smoke erupted from the skin of the frog. A moment later, it cleared. In its place lay a naked old man. One bearing a shocked expression on his face. He made to stand, but Laird Fearghas was on him with the sword, pressing it into Merlyn's chest.

"Who are you?" muttered Laird Fearghas.

"You broke the spell," remarked Merlyn, shocked. "But... where's the druid who instructed you in how to break the enchantment? Where's the princess?" Merlyn turned over on his side and hacked for a few moments. A little mess of black mush came up from his throat to land on the polished oak of the floor. Merlyn urged when he saw what was there. "Fucking bottleflies," he added, pointing to a pair of translucent wings sticking out from the side of the pile.

"Shite-Cock! You're a man!" Robbie paused. "I guess that means we won't be able to go play with Cooky."

"I asked ye once, knave," said Laird Fearghas, swaying as he pushed the blade of his sword against Merlyn's chest. "Who are you?"

Merlyn shrugged, pushed the blade off, stood up, and said, "Merlyn of Camelot, at your service." He gave a low bow. "I suppose you're going to want to hang me now."

"Look of he's pecker, father," said Robbie pointing at Merlyn's crotch. "Flat and black and crusty - it looks like the worms I likes to bake on rocks in the summertime! An' his finger tips - all black. Just like when he was a froggie!"

"I knew it," said Laird Fearghas, smiling at his own abilities. "From the moment I saw that cock on ye, I knew ye were enchanted by those fuckin' faeries."

"Brighid herself, actually," said Merlyn. "But how did you know? And how did you associate that with faeries?"

Laird Fearghas swept his free arm at the walls, which were mostly bookshelves set into the wood. "These aren't just for show, enchanter. I do like to read up. Some of them is bestiaries and treatises on beasts. And every fucking naturalist who has ever written about frogs is clear - they ain't got nae cocks. They've got little holes whence they oozes shite and piss and jism."

"Cloacas," agreed Merlyn, wincing at the point of the sword jammed in his sternum.

"'Cloacae,' what with it being Latin and all."

"Yes, Brighid and her kin, for all of their magical talent, are quite ignorant when it comes to biology." Merlyn paused. "Or maybe they just like the idea of frogs with massive peckers. Why - I could not say." Merlyn considered the man before him. "I assume you knew how to break the enchantment, as well? From your own studies?" The Laird replied with a nod. "You're clearly a man of above-average erudition," Merlyn said. "So how did..." Merlyn looked at Robbie.

"I bairned up me sister," replied the Laird. "Married her and all. It weren't advisable, but neither is drinking myself to death with *uisge*. Yet, here we stand." The Laird used his free hand to scoop up the mug and drain the rest of its contents. "An' before you ask again, it were him." Laird Fearghas pointed at Robbie. "He kissed you and broke the spell."

"But," said Merlyn, "he's a prince, not a princess. The enchantment needs the kiss of a princess to break the spell."

"Eh, when the lad was born, he was blessed with the best of both worlds. Wilcox told us that his lady parts weren't so developed, but his pecker were. He could continue the line if he grew up as a man. So we made the choice - Robbie was to be Robert, and no Roberta."

"Huh?" asked Robbie, furrowing his brow. "You mean dat slit I 'as is a cunny? An I'm a girl?"

"Hermaphrodite," said Laird Fearghas.

"Intersex," retorted Merlyn. "That's what the folk in the future call it. A little more politically correct." Merlyn turned from the Laird to the boy. "Nothing to be ashamed of, Robbie. And they will be plenty kind about sex and gender in the future - you can be whatever you want to be. Don't even have to choose between man and woman. Some people will be dicks about it, try to oppress you if that's your choice, but no accounting for being human and all."

"I likes bein' a lad," said Robbie.

"That's OK, too," Merlyn said, smiling at the boy. "You choose your path, and don't let anyone tell you any different."

Robbie smiled at that, happy to be acknowledged as a person, rather than a touched git, for the first time in a long time.

"Say," said Laird Fearghas, "ye don't strike me as a bad sort. Danu had ye painted up as some kind of villain... ye knows the one..."

"Twirls a mustache and says, 'ha ha!' a lot?" Merlyn paused. "No, wait, you wouldn't get that reference."

"I meant ta say one that exchanges his own soul for worldly power," replied the Laird.

"Oh, like a Judas," Merlyn said. "No, wait, you wouldn't get that reference, either - the Christians aren't here yet." Merlyn nodded at the Laird. "Yes, I do know the concept of which you speak. But I'm not looking to fuck anything up. Just the opposite - I'm trying to save the world from destruction." Merlyn shook his head. "It's a never-ending battle. With Arthur around, I've got my hands full."

"Pendragon," said Fearghas, gritting his teeth. "A traitor of the highest sort. He and those Christians - they killed The Dagda. He was his mother's favourite, you know that?"

"How could you not like The Dagda?" replied Merlyn. "He was happy and warm and gentle, with a proud chest and kind word for everyone he met. I may have been a chosen of Brighid, but I always admired The Dagda." Merlyn slumped his shoulders. "I tried - Brighid help me, how I tried. To steer Arthur in the right direction. To get him to see sense when he would not. I knew that uniting the kingdoms of Albion was a smart play, but the rest of it - his capers and quests - I was always tasked with keeping it all from bursting apart at the seams."

Laird Fearghas nodded at the naked wizard. "So," he asked, "what's with the cock and fingernails? It looks like yer pecker is made of charred paper. Like if ye touched it, it would fall apart."

Merlyn sighed. "It just might," he agreed. "I've been cursed by the Goblin King. I won't be able to lift the curse unless..."

The wizard observed the man before him. Dressed in ornate finery, completed with a tartan kilt, he certainly looked the part: like the strange blend of noble and barbarian who ruled Caledonia. Fearghas might have been drunk, but there was something about this Laird that engendered trust within the wizard. He could not explain it - Fearghas still had a blade to his chest. But Brighid had betrayed Merlyn at the drop of a hat, just because some sentient tower had deceived her with his 'family tower' act. He felt no loyalty towards his Queen, given how quickly she had turned on him. And Arthur, well... perhaps the 'Once and Future King' was not quite the saviour he had been made out to be.

"Look," said Merlyn, "maybe we can make a deal. Brighid did this to me. I must admit, I'm lucky she didn't turn me into a faery, given the way that she does that to subjects who displease her with the way they conduct themselves. But, like it or not, my own goddess has abandoned me. Arthur is a tithead of the highest order - and I am sick of cleaning up his messes. All I really care about is keeping the world safe. Well, that and a working pecker." Merlyn looked down at the mummy cock. "If I kill Arthur, this goes back to being a regular bit of tackle." Merlyn frowned. "I don't even know how I'm going to put clothes on without tearing the damn thing off." The enchanter turned back to Fearghas. "So, what do you say? You let me live, I'll go kill Arthur. I know you want it - you've been... what's that word you Caledonians use? Ah, yes. 'Ganting.' You've been 'ganting' on it since he became King of Camelot."

The Laird felt the familiar Danu-anger come coursing up through the center of his being as Merlyn spoke of Arthur. A hated bastard was he. Thoughts of his death sent joy showering down from the heavens into every part of the Laird's body.

"Say I agree," said the Laird with a hiccup. "How do I make sure you keep your word?"

Merlyn looked out the window, at the fires being lit on the hills around the castle. "It'll be Beltane in a few hours. Everybody knows that whatever your wish, it will come true on Beltane. I'll swear an oath to you - one that will *kill* me if I fail in my task. Kill Arthur by Samhain or I die myself. Sound fair?"

The Laird felt a shudder of ecstasy course through his being as his goddess sent word of her approval. He sheathed his sword, walked to his cabinet, and fetched out a mug. He stopped for a moment, looked at his boy, then pulled a second mug. A few moments later and the three of them - Fearghas in his kilt, Robbie in his frock coat, and Merlyn, naked as a jay bird - held *uisge*-filled mugs in their hands.

"To the death of Arthur," said Laird Fearghas. "The Once and Future King," he added, spitting on the floor.

"To treasonous murder plots struck on Beltane Eve," agreed Merlyn. "And farewell to mummy cocks."

"To feeling good with the ewes when the farmer ain't lookin'," added Robbie.

With that, they all broke into laughter. After several seconds of side-splitting hilarity, Robbie paused, a pained look on his face, and glanced up at his father.

"I think I shite me keks."

Lichery

Sir Galahad scanned the beaches around the side of the lake before removing his trousers. Satisfied that there were no witnesses, the man disrobed and began flicking the end of his knob with his middle finger. After a few moments, the erection he was seeking appeared and he started to masturbate. As the man was furiously pumping away at himself, he mused (not for the first time) that having a girlfriend who happened to be a magical being who could only be summoned by jacking off into a lake was a bit of an ask. It was even worse now, since the Moors had killed her and she had to be resurrected by Galahad's love. As soon as the knight brought her into Albion from the Otherworld called the Sidhe (the one occupied by Danu's Children and their magical associates), the Lady of the Lake was going to gush and fawn over Galahad for his steadfastness and loyalty.

Probably a bit ironic, given that what had brought him to the lake was treason.

Before too long, the man spasmed and sent his seed spraying into the perfectly still waters. It was a beautiful May Day morning, which is what the Christians in Arthur's court insisted on calling Beltane. Because the Christians wanted it, everyone had to follow it. At least, that was the way it had been. Now though, with Arthur... transformed... the way that he was, and how the Christians were soundly excised from the court ever since said transformation, the knight could call it Beltane if he wanted to. So he did.

"Beltane," Galahad muttered.

"And a gorgeous one at that, Gally honey," called a voice before him. The Lady of the Lake appeared to be a well-kept and beautiful woman... at least insofar as her torso and upper body were concerned. Her bottom half was an ungraceful combination of toad and human, slimy skin, webbed toes, lack of dexterity. Galahad did his best to keep his eyes up when he was giving her the business, but every once in a while they wandered down and he felt a strange revulsion. Given enough ale, that revulsion turned into curiosity. A couple of drunken nights he had engaged in cunnilingus with the Lady of the Lake, and he felt strangely empowered and excited by his act, which is part of why the knight had not broken up with the rusalka.

The Lady of the Lake was a pond nymph. Maligned in stories as being evil creatures who tempted men to their deaths in the lakes and ponds of Albion and the Blessed Isles (and further out into the greater world), rusalkas were actually quite benign. They interfered in the affairs of men, but only to help build them up. They asked for little in return, but there is one thing that the stories had right: they have one hell of a sexual appetite. Maybe that's why the knight had to shoot his seed into the lake, though Galahad was not so sure. It seemed like all the gods were obsessed with semen, blood, and other bodily fluids - barely a ritual around that didn't involve cutting one's self or whacking it for no discernible reason. Still, though: Galahad made sure he was well-rested before every encounter with the Lady of the Lake.

"You know," said the rusalka, all sultry and sexy (except for the part where she was waddling on her froggy legs), "they say that all wishes truly made on Beltane will come true. What do you wish for, Galahad, my love?" The Lady of the Lake slipped her arms around Galahad.

'An extended reprieve from the insanity of this place,' the knight did not say. Instead, he smiled and caressed one of the Lady of the Lake's perfectly pert breasts. "I wish for... for your help. With Arthur. Well, maybe after we can talk about that."

The Lady of the Lake shook her head. "Oh, for the love of The Dagda - not again. He hasn't fucked things up again."

"Aye," said Galahad. He glanced down at the rusalka's monstrous frog legs in spite of himself. And he began to tumesce. Shrugging it off, he tried to keep his mind on the plan. "This one seems worse than the last time."

"You mean when I had to feed him Cernunnos jizz and suck his cock to prevent him from ending the world with those fucking Holy Grails? Oh yes, I'm sure it could have gotten worse than that."

"He's made a pact, with some foreign goddess."

"What?!" asked the Lady of the Lake. "How? He already swore a blood oath to Brighid! A mortal is only permitted one blood oath per lifetime! Those are the rules."

"Well, rules that can be broken, apparently, because he's... well, you should see him. He does not look right. Purple eyes, frost trailing his steps. Even sitting near him makes you shiver. And does he ever have that... that..."

"Unspeakably evil and ominous aura usually associated with fell creatures?"

"Exactly," said Galahad. "Still the same old Arthur in many ways, though. All hare-brained schemes and no real plans to do anything of note. Ever since the men returned from the Questing Beast... Quest... he's been on us about going to war with the Christians. The Christians that Arthur invited to Albion. The ones who killed The Dagda and taught our people shame and self-hatred and judgment."

"What about forgiveness and sacrifice and compassion?" said the Lady of the Lake. "You know, like the things Yeshua actually stood for?"

"Oh, right, that," said Galahad. "Well, it's probably buried under it all but let's just say that part of the whole mythology is not exactly well-represented in the Christians in Albion. It's like they're caricatures of perverse renunciates, ones who get off on self-flagellation and generally shiteing the celebration. For some, it's shame for latent homosexuality and old-fashioned buggery-thirst, too, I'll warrant. Probably why they go to town on themselves with the flagrum the way they do."

"You mean party-pooping," said the Lady of the Lake.

"Huh?"

"'Shiteing the celebration,' - you mean party-pooping."

"Sure, whatever," retorted Galahad. "You always know better than me."

"Oh, don't be like that, Gally honey," said the Lady of the Lake, trying to bring him in close. He pushed her away.

"Look," said Galahad, "I do love you, but you always do that. Make me feel like an idiot then tell me not to worry about it. It's really not very... nice."

"Not very nice," said the Lady of the Lake. "Duly noted. I will try to be better."

Galahad looked at the rusalka and shook his head. "You always do that, too. Try to placate me. You're going to try to change the subject now. How many times have we done this dance?"

The Lady of the Lake opened her mouth to speak, closed it, then said, "OK, let's continue on this awkward subject. What else do you have to say? Because I don't have anything, except that I'm sorry and you know I love you, too."

Galahad felt bad then, as if he had pushed too far. "I-I'm sorry, my love. It has just... well, it's been a trying couple of weeks. Arthur has been completely irrational and off his rocker, as per usual, but he accidentally killed a chamberlain just by standing close to him. Froze him to death, just like that. Plus he's trying to convert people in Camelot to worshiping this new goddess of his, Hel. It's bad enough that everyone pretends to be Christian but secretly goes to pray with the druids in the cairns whenever no one is looking. Now he's trying to put in a third option. If I had it my way, it would be one god for everyone."

"It is," said the rusalka, cocking her head at Galahad. "It all is one God, it's just that the expression is different, but that's just for show. There is literally no true difference between any of them."

"What do you mean?"

"What do you think a god is, Gally my sweet?"

"Omniscient, omnipresent being that can do sweet shite like create the world and all of life. Limitless power and grace - you know, a *god!*"

"Why do you humans need that?" asked the Lady of the Lake. "I mean, the world exists, doesn't it? Why not just live in it and enjoy it and not worry about how it came about? Why do you need to question existence?"

"Because, well... just because."

"Do you believe this god of yours caused reality to exist?"

"Well, damn," said Galahad. "I suppose *one* of them did. Maybe it was this Yahweh, maybe it was Danu, maybe it was some strange foreign thing that we don't know of."

"So this being, in its magnificence, also created a human being that desired to question its own lot. I mean, if you go in for that. If you're one of these types that thinks God was just some dickhead gambler who started things off and then pushed back and went on Her merry way, then you're not much different than an atheist."

"What's your point?" asked the knight. "So we question where we come from in spite of the fact that living is going to happen regardless of whether we do it or not. What does it matter to the existence of God, or gods, or whatever?"

"How do you imagine that magic is done, Galahad?" asked the rusalka. "You know, when Merlyn the enchanter or I use a spell to make a portal to another dimension or create the best damned sword ever forged."

"I don't know," admitted Galahad. "I mean, I don't even know that it exists."

"What?"

"Magic."

"You just bloody jizzed in a lake to summon your rusalka girlfriend and you're not sure magic exists?"

"Fair point," said the knight.

"Look, picture a world where there were no overt examples of magic, like what we have here in this faery-infested den of insanity called Albion. You know, just the natural world, phenomena easily classifiable as such, no goblins, no wizards - none of it."

"Ha!" said Galahad. "Keep dreaming - that kind of world is impossible."

"Says who?" asked the Lady of the Lake. "You?"

"Gods and magic definitely exist - you're telling me that a world without them is possible?"

"No," said the rusalka. "I'm telling you that a world that seems that way is possible." She paused. "If you had no evidence of gods or magic - if I wasn't here, feeling your boner press up against the mishmash of seaweed and other pond vegetation that is my bush - would you believe in us?"

"Not a chance," said the knight after a pause. "I would be a complete idiot to do so. To believe in something without evidence - you'd have to be a knuckle-dragging moron."

"Sure," said the rusalka. "But what if you did have evidence? Personal evidence. Evidence that could not be transmitted to another person, not perfectly, not through any normal means of transmission - spoken word, written word, music - would you believe then?"

"I suppose I would," said Galahad. "But it would depend on the circumstances. Would there be much evidence? Like would I be able to command lightning to shoot out of my fingertips and smite my enemies?"

"I just told you - there would be no overt examples of magic. That would be one such thing." The rusalka paused. "I should modify what I said - overt examples *might* exist, but they would be only there for specific people, appearing at specific times, and most attempts to communicate these things would be laughed off as superstition or insanity. Mostly though, the magic would be private. Just for you - a secret world of irrational wonder and awe."

"Sounds pretty sweet to me," nodded Galahad. "So, what does this have to do with the existence of God or gods or whatever?"

"Look," said the Lady of the Lake. "If most examples of this kind of magic are private to an individual, how would they communicate what they have learned?"

"Why would they want to?" said Galahad. "Couldn't they just bottle it up and not share it?"

The rusalka frowned. "Pretty shady behaviour, if you ask me. We're talking about magic here - the stuff of dreams, destiny, absolute bliss and joy - and you would want to keep it to yourself?" The rusalka paused. "Besides, people like that - selfish ones - would never be given access to the stuff. You think someone like Arthur would be given magic in that kind of a world? A man who treasures worldly things and thinks himself to be someone better than his subjects? If he had magic, he would make a fucking mess of the place, wouldn't he? Better to give it to someone who had dropped all attachments to earthly things, who has gone all the way in their desire to sacrifice and surrender their own sense of self." The rusalka paused. "Perhaps like Yeshua."

"But he was special!" said Galahad. "I mean, he made the fishes and the bread and he sacrificed himself for the sins of the world and came back from the dead. I mean, totally exceptional human being. Not like us mere mortals at all. I might not agree with the self-flagellation and taking exception to buggery, but if there is one thing the monks got right, it's that Yeshua needs to be worshiped as a special thing."

"This is coming from the same religion that prohibits idolatry," said the rusalka, shaking her head. "Like I said, if you try to communicate this shite by regular means, it gets fucked up. Those monks are just one example of a sick and twisted interpretation of a bunch of words on paper. The only real poison in this world is literalism. And literalism can only be implied in one sense - if there's a world out there and a world in here." The rusalka tapped the side of her head. "The phrase 'objective reality' is the most corrosive idea to the human spirit. As long as you think it exists, magic cannot."

"You think the whole world is about you? But that's insane! Totally batshite!"

"A wise old owl said that the psychopath drowns in the waters in which the mystic swims with delight."

"Wait a minute!" Galahad exclaimed. "You mean that magic and God are the same thing?"

"What the thing is doesn't have a name," said the rusalka. "We use this word 'God' to talk about it, but it doesn't bend to the world of form. The only person who can truly know its existence is each one of us. And it is in everything. It is everything. Everything and nothing, all in one nice mind-manifesting package. I suppose we could call it consciousness itself, couldn't we?"

"And the world just tries to trick us into disbelief," agreed the knight. "But why? Why would - in this imaginary world of sterile unmagicality, of course - why would we ever subject ourselves to it?"

"Ah, 'subject,'" said the Lady of the Lake. "We certainly do 'subject' ourselves to it." She paused. "You've seen children play, haven't you? What's the first game they play? Don't even need to teach it to them?"

Galahad pondered for a moment. "Peek-a-boo."

"There you go," said the Lady of the Lake. "A recipe for magic." She paused. "Now do you understand why we wouldn't want to make the truth easily communicable? As in, 'here you go, here's why you're here and who you are?' Where would be the bloody fun in that? Imagine - an infinite being, playing a game whose stakes seem so high because it has tricked itself so thoroughly, who learns that the stakes were as low as they could possibly be, all while inhabiting the world it created."

"So, you said it couldn't be communicated by regular means," said Galahad. "How would one communicate such revelations?"

"Well, you give it to them straight and they'll dismiss you as nuts - or they'll crucify you for it. Works wonders for spreading the word, mind you, but not very sly is it? I mean, wouldn't you want to *play* the game? Dress it up in funny clothes... ah, there's one for you. Comedy. The most transcendent means of expression there is. Comedy is truth - the very best kind. You want to talk about microcosm of reality... how would you react if you thought you were mortal for years and years, built up all kinds of fears about death and disease and scarcity, then discovered that you were immortal, abundance everywhere, that the whole thing was a game and not to be taken seriously?"

"I supposed I'd laugh, wouldn't I?" asked Galahad.

"You're damned straight," said the Lady of the Lake. "Now, it's about time a cock gets sucked."

"Sounds like he's become a lich," said the Lady of the Lake, propping herself up on her elbow. She and Galahad were laying on on the grass, post-coitus. "Too bad you're not Merlyn - he usually has cigarettes from the future for me."

"Um, real romantic, honey," said Galahad. "I know you're an oversexed magical being, but do you think you could wait until we're dressed before you start talking about your other lovers?"

"Aww, are you jealous, my sweet?" asked the Lady of the Lake, not unsympathetically. "You know I love you, but my soul is a bit strange. It doesn't really pair off with any others. Which is why I can't be exclusive with you. It wouldn't be right."

"Yeah, yeah, blame it on some mystical poppycock," Galahad paused. "Sorry," he added. "It doesn't really bother me, not if I'm being honest. I'm grateful for the time we get to spend together."

"You'll find her," said the Lady of the Lake. "There is a woman coming for you. Who knows when, who knows how, but she's coming." The Lady of the Lake smiled sadly at her lover. "One of the downsides of being a *magical* oversexed being. I can see a few things into the future myself. As long as it's not too specific, it'll usually be accurate in its own way. I'm happy that prescience works that way, though - keeps things interesting when you don't know the *how*."

"I'll always love you," said Galahad. "No matter what."

"I know that." The rusalka kissed her lover. "Now, given that Arthur has become a lich, I expect he will discover his own powers soon enough." She paused. "You remember how I said it would be bad for Arthur to have power while retaining his ignorance? Well, buckle up, because this is the world we live in - morons in charge who can really make a mess of things. I'm sure that in our little made up seemingly unmagical word that wouldn't be the case. If people were mostly ruled by objective logic, it would make no sense that they would have selfish jerks running the place."

"But, if God is present everywhere, wouldn't even the totally ass-hattery of the kings and emperors be perfectly divine as well, just as necessary as the sacrifices and lessons of people like Yeshua? In fact, from a bird's eye view, wouldn't there be absolutely no qualitative difference between a murderous despot and a self-realized prophet?"

"Shh, keep it down," said the rusalka. "You're ruining the bloody game!" She composed herself. "OK, so, we need to stop Arthur. We'll need a half-baked zany plan that has very little chance of success but will be extremely colourful and contain plenty of flash and pomp."

"You thinking what I'm thinking?" asked Galahad.

"An army of unicorns conjured from the Sidhe?"

"Eh, sure, let's go with that."

"What, what did you want to do?"

"I was going to suggest we do something to his cock - shrivel it up or something. You know, so he'd see the error of his ways."

"What is it with you Albians and the damned mummy cocks? I swear, you say us gods are bad for the crotch obsession, but you humans have it way worse." She paused. "Still, it would be kind of funny. How about the mummy cock *and* the unicorn army?"

"Now you're talking my language." Galahad smiled.

"Oh, wait, let me…" The Lady of the Lake reached out and plucked something from Galahad's teeth. She held it up for him to see. "A bit of my seaweed bush. Worse than eating a bunch of cilantro. You sure you don't want me to shave it for you?"

"What so you can look like a little girl version of a half-woman, half-frog? No thanks. I'm a bushwhacker, born and bred."

"I'll show you bushwhacker," said the Lady of the Lake, pushing Galahad over and mounting him.

Hiden Goseke

"You know, this story is far from over."

Bragi looked up at his adopted brother, Loki. Both of the gods were sitting in the back room of the Thirsty Troll, one of the less reputable whorehouses in Asgard, the home of the gods of Midgard. Between Loki and Bragi was a little round table upon which rested a velvet blue covering and a battered leather bag filled with runes. It was at this place where both Loki and Bragi had thrown the magical bits of carved mithril, breathing life into Gudleik Sigbjornsson, the erstwhile fuck-up of his hometown of Ygglheim. Well, he was an erstwhile fuck-up for a short period after he left Ygglheim, and then became a current fuck-up, once he had realized his own power to use words to glamour other human beings.

"Gudleik is starting to get my message," said Bragi. "What did you expect? That he would simply continue to sow chaos and destruction at your behest? That he would never change course towards redemption?"

Loki kicked back on his chair, balancing on the two back legs, were he stayed for a moment, before slamming back

233

down and sending the bag of runes showering down over his brother. Bragi shook his head and began picking them up.

"You're a sore loser," said Bragi.

"I told you," said Loki, "the story's not over yet. Have a look." Loki waved his hands, which jangled with rings and bits of metal, in front of him. Red smoke puffed out from his palms and a little conjured window into the human realms appeared in the air between the two gods. A bird's eye view of Mimir's Rest could be seen within.

Gudleik was walking through the market, making his way to the blacksmith's to find Ivaldi. Behind the young man, a pair of cutthroats were tailing him, shifting through the sea of bodies as they loped after him. It was quite evident that Gudleik's demise was the purpose of their mission, a point which was confirmed by the sudden appearance of shiny metal in the hands of both of the outlaws.

"That bitch Eyja Randulfsson," muttered Bragi. "She wants him dead."

"And why not?" giggled Loki. "He's like a mad dog gone wild. At least, that is how she views him. The more I needle that little cockmeat into acting out my symphony of discord, the less people are likely to trust him."

"Perhaps," said Bragi, unconvinced. "But you're an Asgardian, Loki. You might be a giant, you might say you wish for Ragnarok, but we both know that's not your true purpose."

"Oh," said Loki. "And what about our wager for Gudleik's soul? Would I really have bet the eternal essence of one of the men I had hooks into like this Gudleik if I really thought that I would lose?"

"Of course, you would!" cried Bragi, throwing the bag of runes back onto the table. "For the love of Odin, it's the same tired old story, brother. You're Gudleik's-"

"Ah, ah, ah," said Loki. "There's a time and a place for certain revelations, wouldn't you agree? Can't go around spurting your muck before you've gotten a pump or two out of the old tallywhacker, eh?"

"Alright, have it your way, brother," laughed Bragi. "I'm the god of fucking poetry, though. If I don't know the motivations of the gods, who the hell does?"

"Quiet, he's about to get shivved like a little bitch," said Loki, pointing to the magical window.

True to Loki's word, Gudleik did not know that his kidney had been pierced by the thief's blade until dark blood came drooling out his side and he found himself lying on his back. The sole living son of Sigbjorn Gulbrandsson lay quietly dying in the gutter of the market square, his mouth attempting to make words as the blinding pain seared his mind. The crowds of Mimir's Rest were more than a little used to such displays of mortality, and so they simply stepped over his body as his life force ebbed. His eyes had dimmed considerably when the first person to give a fuck came across him.

"Gudleik!" shouted Porsi, whose stated hatred for his friend evaporated as soon as he saw him on his way out. "For the love of Freya, Gudleik!" Porsi slapped him a few times, but it was clear that the young man was dying.

"Guess we better save his ass," said Bragi, turning from the window. "Look, try to make it seem serious, alright? You know I'm going to use my magic to heal him at the last second. It's not called *deus ex machina* for nothing."

"What's that mean? Sounds like some southern fop's linguistic breakfast."

"It's Latin," said Bragi, raising an eyebrow at Loki. "It means 'God from the machine,' but that's a bit of a shitty translation of its true original meaning. You know, in stories, when all seems lost and help arrives just in the nick of time?

Divine intervention? Odin's speckled cock, haven't you ever enjoyed a play or a book?"

"Fuck off nerd," said Loki, farting loudly in Bragi's direction. "I enjoy life - leave the horseshite that is artistic expression to geeks like you."

"I provide the conduit for the human experience of the divine," said Bragi, his voice raised. "I am art itself. What do you do? Fuck shite up royally so guys like me can fix your messes."

"Hell, I am an artist of the arsehole, a magnanimous motherfucker when it comes to chaos," retorted Loki. "Without me, you'd have not stories - absolutely none. A story needs conflict. Ergo, you need me."

"One day, this guy will transcend us both," said Bragi. "You know it, I know it. Gudleik's destiny is-"

"Damn it," said Loki. "I told you the story ain't over! You've got to keep it in your pants. I bet you jackrabbit every time you mount a warm body, you premature ejaculation of a god. Go play your harp."

"Yeah, in a minute," said Bragi, turning to face the door. A goddess with long flowing blonde tresses and a face so beautiful Bragi's mouth opened just a little sashayed in to the runecasting room. "Right on time," said the god of poetry when he found his words. "Freya, thank you for coming."

"Someone needs my blessing?" she said. "I bet it's that dashing Porsi Randulfsson. I've been waiting his whole life for this moment. I love to give my chosen their heart's desire." Her face hardened a bit when she looked over at Loki. "Unless *someone* tries to interfere."

"I'll interfere with you," said Loki. "Take you right here, if you want. Bragi can't watch, though. Or, maybe he can, if he gets one of his skalds to sing about the coupling."

"I'd sooner mount a dead branch on Yggdrasil," retorted Freya.

"That's it," said Loki. "Talk dirty to me, baby."

"Right," said Bragi. "Look, why don't you reach down there, give Porsi his healing blessing, and Bob, as they say, is your uncle."

"Wait," said Loki. "Wouldn't it be like, Uncle Hrodebert, given that we're in a fictional version of an ancient Germanic culture's divine pantheon?"

"Have it your way," said Bragi. "Who's the nerd now?"

Freya smiled at the pair of gods, closed her eyes, and a stream of yellow smoke, visible only to the gods, streamed into the top of Porsi's being, enveloping him with highly etheric wisdom... or something like that. Whatever it was, it had the effect of reminding the boy of some lesson he had been given in wound dressing years before, the exact plant needed to staunch the flow of blood, and the recipe for a magical draught that would knit the wound. Well, the magical draught part was something new, given to him by the patron goddess that he didn't know had been waiting for him. In his mind's eye, Porsi saw a beautiful naked woman (as jaybirdesque as Freya preferred to appear to her chosen) reciting the incantation he would need to utter over the potion. Within moments, Porsi had pulled Gudleik to a nearby inn and went to work on his first job as a healer in Midgard.

"There," said Freya. "Thanks," she said, batting her eyes at Bragi.

"Oh," said Bragi, turning red. "No need to thank me, workings of fate and all that."

Freya simply smiled. "Do you want to come with me up to one of the rooms? I mean, we're gods and all and totally unplanned fuck fests are kind of par for the course in our paradise that is Asgard. Also, I figure we could get drunk on the Mead of Poetry and come up with new ways of describing the old in and out during pillow talk." She smiled. "Plus, you know, I'm Vanir and your Aesir so it wouldn't be like it was incest, though that kind of shite has never stopped gods in any pantheon I know of.

"I would love to," said Bragi, rising from his chair and gathering up his harp. "You know, Idunn and I are in a bit of an open relationship."

"Ahem," said Loki. "Aren't we going to finish this? I mean, let's recap: Rosmerta O'Ceallaigh has sworn a blood oath to the Faery Queen, Brighid, in exchange for skill with lute and voice. King Arthur of Camelot is now a lich in service to Hel, who is bringing her army of draugr to the shores of Albion. Merlyn has switched allegiances to Laird Fearghas and his touched lad Robert and has agreed to kill Arthur by Samhain. Also, some weird bullshite with a sentient tower filled with demons and his son – I don't know. Gudleik was supposed to bring Ivaldi to Ruvark the Magnificent and learn how to play properly from him, until he was gutted by ne'er do wells and saved by Porsi." Loki paused. "Did I miss anything?"

"Randulf Randulfsson is running to Thor's Land because he's afraid of that bitch Eyja Randulfsson."

"Do we really need to do that, call her 'that bitch Eyja Randulfsson?'" asked Freya. "I mean, it's sexist and all."

"Yes, Bragi," said Loki, "wouldn't want to transgress any changing social norms, would we?"

"Oh for the love of - I make art, sweetie," said Bragi. "That shite rolls off the tongue, and plus, Eyja Randulfsson is a bitch. I bet were she given half a chance (and if it profited her in mithril), she'd kill Randulf and feed him to her tiger. As it stands, he's a recently freed bondsman without an ounce of the silvery-white to his name, so I doubt she's got murderous intentions for him, but you never know." Bragi paused. "It would probably make for a cracking good story, though."

"Hmmph," said Freya. "Still doesn't change the fact that it's a sexist name."

"Whatever, let's just put her to one side," said Bragi. "Did we miss anyone? Any pertinent threads not rattled off?"

"The Jelly Cock King and El Goblerino," said Bragi.

"No, wait - 'El Goblerino' - that was a plot hole. Or, at least, it was something started and never finished."

"Why'd you even put it in?" asked Loki. "I mean, maybe because Spanish comes from south of this fictional version of Great Britain, and Dagon comes from south of Great Britain, I think Ancient Babylon, and will be reinterpreted by the American Lovecraft? But really, the link between the two is tenuous." Loki paused. "Although, the fact that Dagon was a fertility god has not gone unnoticed."

"Look," said Bragi. "You can't expect perfection out of me. Ever notice how all the best stuff is riddled with imperfections, little tiny details missed that doesn't detract from the overall enjoyment of the oeuvre?" Bragi paused. "That's on purpose. It's a metaphor about the imperfectly perfect nature of nature. I do it to everything."

"Yeah, right," replied Loki. "Seems to me like you're just making excuses for half-assing it." Loki paused. "Not that I would be judging you - I half-ass everything. I don't even know what whole ass looks like." Loki gave Freya a lascivious wink. "Though I'd like to get a look at *your* whole ass."

"In your dreams, you dickwhacker."

"Oh, whisper your sweet nothings to me," said Loki, eyelids aflutter.

"You look like you're having a seizure," Freya added.

"Cernunnos and his druid, Keandre, coming to kill you!" shouted Bragi, slapping his forehead. "And the damned

Brother Winfridus and the sexless bastard angel Cassiel, with their paintings of horned Cernunnos, the devil himself!"

"You really put a lot of fucking characters into this," said Loki. "I mean, couldn't you have simplified it a bit? I mean, even the title doesn't make sense. The Hammer Of The Gods? Where was the hammer? I mean, Thor was mentioned briefly, along with Mjolnir, and he and Dad are off to start a war in the Blessed Isles. But, seriously."

"So I could use this line," replied Bragi, turning to Freya and dropping his trousers, revealing his erect member. "I'm about to drop dis hammer on dat ass."

Freya tittered and grasped the god of poetry by the shaft.

"That's it?" said Loki, uncharacteristically frustrated. "The title of the book, which could be interpreted as a metaphor for the havoc caused by all of the numerous deities running around, is actually a contrived dick joke? One that was only to be revealed in the last sentence of the book? You broke the fourth wall for this bullshite?

"Ah," said Bragi, allowing himself to be led out of the room by the Norse goddess of fertility. "Wrong again, brother of mine. This is actually the last sentence of the book.

"Nailed it!"

So this is how cunts that never shag fuckin' well live. A life ay impotence, resentment, anger and frustration; nae fuckin' exuberance in life, forced tae become an Internet troll or a miserable drunk in a boozer.

A Decent Ride, Irvine Welsh

Afterword

Thank you for reading The Hammer Of The Gods: *So You Want To Be A Star* (Book One of The Druid Trilogy). Try saying that five times fast.

I want to thank Zack Rousseau, my loyal and faithful editor and friend. Also my mother, Lise Rowe, for plugging her nose during the COVID-19 outbreak and reading along and providing notes.

Many thanks to Shaela Creshion for her beautiful cover illustration. Absolutely amazing work, Shaela. I would also like to thank Cynthia Dunphy for her work on the cover and for her graphic design work generally. You are a superstar, Cynthia, and I appreciate you so much.

To all my advance readers: thank you for your help! You are awesome.

Thanks to my friends and family who listen to me prattle on with filth and philosophy and irreverence as I go about my life. This series could not have happened without you – and I am so incredibly grateful that you do what you do.

Like all of my work, this book is Powered by Caritas, which means that a portion of the proceeds will be going to charity. More information can be found at poweredbycaritas.com.

This is enjoyable on its own, but if you have not read it yet, Top Man: The Epic Wager, A Prequel to The Druid Trilogy, is available for free as a gift for joining my mailing list at andrewmarcrowe.com. You'll also get free stories and exclusive deals on my stuff as it comes out, just for being a member!

Next up: Emerald Helm, Tales of Courtly Valour I. This is the first book in the companion short story series that makes up The Avalon Cycle, my bawdy love letter to the world.

Much love,

Andrew

Free e-Books

Want to try out the prequel to this book, Top Man: The Epic Wager (A Prequel to The Druid Trilogy)? How about my other fantasy series, The Clovir Cycle? All you have to do is join my mailing list. In addition to an electronic copy of Top Man, you will get a copy of The Amaril Company, A Prequel to The Yoga Trilogy, my somewhat more serious philosophical fantasy epic. I will be honest - it's a two way street, because building a relationship with my readers is one of the most exciting things for me. I update on a sporadic basis with information about upcoming books, my podcasts, sales, more freebies, and other things I have in the hopper. You can unsubscribe at any time.

Go to andrewmarcrowe.com for more info!

Links

Website: andrewmarcrowe.com
Powered by Caritas: poweredbycaritas.com
Facebook: facebook.com/andrewmarcrowe
Instagram: @loungingjaguar
Twitter: @loungingjaguar

Bibliography

To keep up to date on all of my writing, please join my mailing list by going to andrewmarcrowe.com! You will get free copies of my books, stories, essays, and news!

Fiction

THE CLOVIR CYCLE

Eight books, including a prequel novella, four anthologies of short stories, and three main titles in a trilogy, form Andrew's first fiction series. Fantastical, spiritual, mythological (particularly Hindu and Celtic), darkly humourous – these interconnected stories tell the tale of a world filled with despair. And yet, somehow, might the light prevail?

These books are definitely for readers of a more mature stock, as the themes and language are quite bracing at times. A suggested reading order page can be found at the beginning of all of the volumes, aside from The Yoga of Strength. It is also available at andrewmarcrowe.com/books/

★ ★ ★ ★ ★

THE YOGA OF STRENGTH
A FABLE
(BOOK ONE OF THE YOGA TRILOGY)

A Hero's Journey into the Heart of Reality

The Yoga of Strength is the story of Andrew Cardiff, a long-time squire on the cusp of elevation to Knighthood within the Yellow Order of the Kingdom of Thrairn. There is only one issue: he is an abject coward and slave to his baser instincts. Thrust into a world of magic and treachery, Andrew tumbles along a path that threatens devastation at every turn. This unlikely hero must plumb the depths of his soul in search of the courage and strength that have always eluded him. Around him, the world is crumbling. Will Andrew discover his answers at the center of the mystery before it is too late?

Go to andrewmarcrowe.com/the-yoga-of-strength/ to get your copy today!

★ ★ ★ ★ ★

THE YOGA OF PAIN
A LOVE STORY
(BOOK TWO OF THE YOGA TRILOGY)

Pain Is Both The Key And The Door

Like The Yoga of Strength, The Yoga of Pain is both an adventure story and a parable about life. It delves into the emancipation of the divine feminine and the letting go that we all must do to become content while we are still breathing. The book follows the two wounded heroes, Kathryn and Simon, and asks questions about the nature of pain: why do we feel its sting? Why isn't the world just sunshine and rainbows all the time? What can pain teach us about liberation?

Dropping January 15, 2020

Got to andrewmarcrowe.com/the-yoga-of-pain/ for more information!

* * * * *

THE AMARIL COMPANY
A NOVELLA
(A PREQUEL TO THE YOGA TRILOGY)

Que Sera, Sera

Centuries before the Trimurti of Unity faced off against the Trimurti of Separation in the Kingdom of Thrairn, in its place stood the Heraclytan Empire. Their honourable Emperor dead to treachery, a handful of loyal Warriors fight to save their doomed land as the iron grip of the newly-formed Red Tradition tightens around the smoking husk of what once was. These bloodthirsty Mages have seized control of all of the magic in the realm. Absent divine intervention from a disappeared trickster deity, can these masterless men, with no small measure of help from a tough-as-nails Druidess, find a way to keep hope alive?

248

Free for members of my mailing list!
Go to andrewmarcrowe.com/the-amaril-company/ for more
information!

$$\star \; \star \; \star \; \star \; \star$$

TALES OF SIGHT

The world of The Yoga Trilogy, Clovir, is filled with characters, many with their own stories. They are tales of ups and downs, of wins and losses, of blindness and sight. While they are not necessary reads, they will help flesh out and render colour into this realm of darkness. Tales of Sight will be released in four parts, starting with Clovir: An Overture and finishing with Clovir: A Farewell.

Go to andrewmarcrowe.com/tales-of-sight/ for more
information!

CLOVIR: AN OVERTURE
TALES OF SIGHT - PART I
(A COMPANION TO THE YOGA TRILOGY)

What Darkness Hides Within The Murk Of Cistern Ale?

Rolf the Tavernkeeper is a man with problems. The competition is crushing his business. His sister, a single mother named Karla, has moved into the Green Dragon and the baby is not making things any easier. You don't even want

249

to hear what is going on with his brother, Alfred the Executioner.

When financial desperation, the family ties that bind, and a hefty dose of cowardice see Rolf make selfish choices and dark alliances, he takes a course of action sees him become embroiled in behind-the-scenes plotting with the most powerful group in the Kingdom of Thrairn. Have his fortunes finally changed? Or will his gamble see him dead before dawn?

Go to andrewmarcrowe.com/tales-of-sight/ for more information!

* * * * *

AN ATIKAN INTERLUDE
TALES OF SIGHT - PART II
(A COMPANION TO THE YOGA TRILOGY)

Welcome to the Black Pits

Betrothed to a decrepit King, Lady Petunia Thule, daughter of a country noble, spends her days despairing her lot. Her father, a greedy social climber in charge of the King's penal iron mine under the Crooked Spears, a hopeless place called the Black Pits, is eager to see his daughter married and his family's position secured. Getting her to the Thrain capital of Isha is of utmost importance.

What neither of them expect is the strange intervention of John Tisdale, a man unfairly imprisoned by Lord Thule for his kindliness with his daughter. On the long road from Kalingshire to Isha, it is said that anything at all can happen. John and the Lady are about to find out just how true that old adage speaks.

Dropping October 17, 2019

Go to andrewmarcrowe.com/tales-of-sight/ for more information!

THE LISERIAN CHRONICLE
TALES OF SIGHT - PART III
(A COMPANION TO THE YOGA TRILOGY)

Something's Rotten In The Empire of Liseria

Youngish Monk of the Liserian Repository, a true believer by the name of Naoki, is ready to take his vows to advance in the monastic ranks. His mentor, Tetsu, a Monk feeling the sting of his age, would rather that the younger man slow his pace, to appreciate where he finds himself, rather than submitting to his thirst for power. When disaster strikes at the heart of the Liserian Empire, the two Monks find themselves to be the sole bulwark against encroaching Chaos.
All of Clovir is edging towards disaster. Can these Holy Men of an Empire throttled by tradition find common ground with an ancient enemy before it is too late?

Dropping 2020

The Avalon Cycle

A mash-up of Arthurian legend, Norse mythology, and the Celtic pantheon of heroes and deities, The Avalon Cycle is an engaging and epic story told over eight books with a twist: it is a bawdy tale in the tradition of limerick jokes and books like Fool by Christopher Moore. A palate cleanser after the somewhat serious tone of The Clovir Cycle, The Avalon Cycle is about fun and laughs, though the story is still full of reflections on the human condition. It is particularly focused on the metaphorical births of artists in two warring nations who come together and fall in love and must face a world-destroying threat together. Be advised: the jokes are numerous and sexuality focused. An early reviewer of The Yoga of Strength, Andrew Marc Rowe's debut novel, said that the author had a crotch obsession in reference to the sexual content. Andrew has doubled down on that criticism, albeit in a humorous way.

Top Man
The Epic Wager
[A Prequel to The Druid Trilogy]

Want To Bet?

Gudleik, son of the Skati of the Bear Clan of Freyr's Land in Midgard, dreams of becoming a skald. From a powerful family and surrounded by success, he should have it all – instead he is shunned for being Loki-cursed and knows his doom is coming. Still he plucks his lyre...

On the other side of the known world, Rosmerta, daughter of Keandre, bloodsworn druid of the horned god Cernunnos of the Blessed Isles, is expected to follow in her father's footsteps. But her own dream of following the bardic path seems just as out of reach as Gudleik's. Her lute lies dusty in her cottage...

Cue the music: things go bonkers when the gods get revved up and start wreaking havoc throughout the Celtic and Norse countryside, calling our heroes to adventure. A weary Merlyn of Camelot is sits in the middle of it all, forced into the mix by fate (and a rather inconvenient curse).

A real divine mess, the whole of creation gone sideways. A new beginning or the end of days? The souls of our heroes are on the line – it's time to place your bets!

And get your free copy of the prequel to Andrew Marc Rowe's epic bawdy tale... that, as well.

The Hammer Of The Gods
So You Want To Be A Star
[Book One of The Druid Trilogy]

It's Hammer Time!

Pitted against a perverse pantheon of warring deities, Gudleik Sigbjornsson and Rosmerta O'Ceallaigh are two dreamers living worlds apart, hoping to create a better life for themselves by following their dreams. It won't be easy: Gudleik's soul is the battleground between two gods of Asgard. And Rosmerta is supposed to do as her parents have done: offer her life to the service of an ancient Celtic fertility god. But the gods are only half of it... the biggest foes the two will face are to be found within their own minds.

Can Gudleik overcome the ugly blessing of a trickster god and prevent Ragnarok? Will Rosmerta find the courage to forge a new path? Will there be a whole load of dirty jokes and comments on the human condition?

Yes, yes, there will be... to that one, the third question.

Also, check dis out: there is a bunch about Merlyn and King Arthur of Camelot, a Goblin King, an ancient fell jellyfish god, encroaching Christian zealots, characters whose proclivities are too crude to mention here, because, well, gotta make the advertising copy pop, you know?

An epic fantasy comedy as blue as the cover art, get your copy of The Hammer Of The Gods today!

Iris Ascending

A chef's special of family-friendly humour, magic, mythology, heroes and heroines and mythical beasts, Iris Ascending Andrew Marc Rowe's first foray into children's fiction. Side-splittingly funny (Andrew hopes, anyway), this saga was written to entertain, while dealing with the challenges that children face in an uplifting manner.

$$\ast \; \ast \; \ast \; \ast \; \ast$$

The Unicorn
Volume 1

Iris, twelve-year old girl on a unicorn hunt, is desperate to find one of the creatures before she becomes a woman and the opportunity to take the wizard's fancy robe and hat is closed to her forever. In the forests of Helidonia, her homeland, she is ready to put everything on the line for her dream.

Zeus, King of Olympus, has really let everyone, including himself, down. His son is missing, his wife has abandoned him, and his bosses have shown up, looking for him to right his wrongs.

The fates of a little girl and the big cheese of the heavens above have mysteriously intertwined. Can the pair solve the riddle of their shared destiny before time itself comes to an end?

Dropping 2020

Go to andrewmarcrowe.com/the-pleiades-remixes/ for more information!

Non-fiction

The Avatar Pentology

For those with less of a fiction addiction, Andrew's first five books of philosophy, the Avatar Pentology, are collections of his Reflections about life. Each book has a particular concentration: Sophia, Paradidomi, Estiasi, Kardia, and Phanerosis – Wisdom, Surrender, Focus, Heart, and Manifestation. Written in a conversational style, Andrew's hope is to communicate what elements he can of the ineffable truths he has realized in his own life.

Knight of Sophia
A Book of Reflections

Philosophy a la carte: this is a book of Andrew Marc Rowe's musings about life, stitched together from essays he has written and released over the months since inspiration for The Yoga Trilogy first struck. In a conversational tone, the author offers his thoughts on a life well-lived and the grander questions that have plagued him since he was a wee lad barely out of diapers, startled to find himself adrift on a spinning rock in space.

Released September 2020

Go to andrewmarcrowe.com/reflections/ for more information!

Magus of Paradidomi
A Book of Reflections

The second instalment in Andrew Marc Rowe's philosophy series, this collection focuses on *paradidomi*, which is Greek for surrender. Like most truths in life, the conclusions on surrender that the author has come to are somewhat paradoxical. We can learn to soar through our lives only by surrendering to it in its entirety, rather than white-knuckling the wheel. In the result, you will find Reflections with much soul-baring and self-acceptance. It is his humble hope that readers might find inspiration to let go within the pages of this book.

Coming soon!

Go to andrewmarcrowe.com/reflections/ for more information!

About the Author

The author, Andrew Marc Rowe, moonlights as a wizard when he is not working his desk job as a lawyer. He lives in St. John's, Newfoundland, Canada, with his daughter Iris and a stable of unicorns. He likes long walks on the beach, getting caught in the rain, and betting the farm on insane cannibalism-related wagers with goblins. You can find him at andrewmarcrowe.com (sign up for his mailing list to get free e-books and e-mail lovin').

Want to get in touch? Send him an e-mail at andrew@andrewmarcrowe.com Include references to coprophagia to beat the spam filters (definitely not because he gets off on that shit).

ABOUT SOPHIC PRESS

A small independent press located in St. John's, Newfoundland and Labrador, Canada, Sophic Press was formed to serve as a publishing imprint for the work of Andrew Marc Rowe. The Clovir Cycle, Andrew's first foray into fantasy fiction, featuring The Yoga Trilogy, Tales of Sight, and The Amaril Company, is being published by Sophic Press. One caveat: The Yoga of Strength, the first book in The Yoga Trilogy, was published by Atmosphere Press, a wonderful independent publisher located in Austin, Texas.

Although currently closed to submissions, Sophic Press will one day offer editing and publication services, with a focus on spiritual fiction / conscious media. In the meantime, there is plenty of content from Andrew Marc Rowe on the way.

We hope you enjoy what is coming.

Printed in Great Britain
by Amazon

44856087R00163